MW00330757

JAPANESE TALES
from TIMES PAST

Naoshi Koriyama was born on Kikai Island in Japan's Amami islands in 1926. He studied at the University of New Mexico and the State University of New York at Albany. He taught at Toyo University in Tokyo from 1961–1997 and is professor emeritus. His publications include *Like Underground Water: The Poetry of Mid-Twentieth Century Japan*, co-translated with Edward Lueders (Copper Canyon Press, 1995); Poesie (Forum/Quinta Generazione, Italy, 1990); and numerous other books of verse. A talented dancer, he enjoys demonstrating his Amami dance at international poetry meetings.

Bruce Allen was born and grew up in the Boston area. In 1983 he moved to Tokyo where he has lived ever since. He holds degrees from Amherst College and Sophia University. He is Professor in the Department of English Language and Literature at Seisen University in Tokyo, where he teaches courses in translation and environmental literature. His research interests are in translation, environmental literature, and ecocriticism. He has concentrated particularly on the work of Japanese writer Ishimure Michiko and has translated several of her works, including her novel *Lake of Heaven* (Lexington Books, 2008).

Karen Thornber is Professor of Comparative Literature and of East Asian Languages and Civilizations at Harvard University. Her research and teaching focus on comparative and world literatures, the literatures and cultures of East Asia and the Indian Ocean Rim, translation, and the environmental and medical humanities. Her books include *Empire of Texts in Motion: Chinese, Korean, and Taiwanese Transculturations of Japanese Literature* (Harvard, 2009) and *Ecoambiguity: Environmental Crises and East Asian Literatures* (Michigan, 2012).

JAPANESE TALES
from TIMES PAST

Stories of Fantasy and Folklore from the
Konjaku Monogatari Shu

ew translations from Japan's most famous collection of folk wisdom

Translated by
NAOSHI KORIYAMA and **BRUCE ALLEN**

With a foreword by
KAREN THORNBER

TUTTLE Publishing

Tokyo | Rutland, Vermont | Singapore

ABOUT TUTTLE
"Books to Span the East and West"

Our core mission at Tuttle Publishing is to create books which bring people together one page at a time. Tuttle was founded in 1832 in the small New England town of Rutland, Vermont (USA). Our fundamental values remain as strong today as they were then—to publish best-in-class books informing the English-speaking world about the countries and peoples of Asia. The world has become a smaller place today and Asia's economic, cultural and political influence has expanded, yet the need for meaningful dialogue and information about this diverse region has never been greater. Since 1948, Tuttle has been a leader in publishing books on the cultures, arts, cuisines, languages and literatures of Asia. Our authors and photographers have won numerous awards and Tuttle has published thousands of books on subjects ranging from martial arts to paper crafts. We welcome you to explore the wealth of information available on Asia at **www.tuttlepublishing.com**.

Published by Tuttle Publishing, an imprint of Periplus Editions (HK) Ltd.

www.tuttlepublishing.com

Copyright © 2015 Periplus Editions (HK) Ltd.

LCCN: 2015003755

ISBN: 978-4-8053-1341-1

First edition
24 23 22 21 20   7 6 5 4 3
1912TP

Printed in Singapore

TUTTLE PUBLISHING® is a registered trademark of Tuttle Publishing, a division of Periplus Editions (HK) Ltd.

Distributed by

North America, Latin America & Europe
Tuttle Publishing
364 Innovation Drive, North Clarendon
VT 05759-9436, USA
Tel: 1 (802) 773 8930
Fax: 1 (802) 773 6993
info@tuttlepublishing.com
www.tuttlepublishing.com

Japan
Tuttle Publishing
Yaekari Building 3rd Floor
5-4-12 Osaki Shinagawa-ku
Tokyo 141 0032 Japan
Tel: (81) 3 5437 0171
Fax: (81) 3 5437 0755
sales@tuttle.co.jp
www.tuttle.co.jp

Asia Pacific
Berkeley Books Pte Ltd
3 Kallang Sector #04-01
Singapore 349278
Tel: (65) 6741-2178
Fax: (65) 6741-2179
inquiries@periplus.com.sg
www.periplus.com

Contents

CONTENTS

CONTENTS

Acknowledgments

We would like to acknowledge our appreciation for the assistance we have received from a number of people and institutions. Thanks to Karen Thornber for her support and comments, and for contributing the foreword. Thanks also to Professor Scott Slovic for his comments and support. Discussions with Professors Koichi Kansaku, Akira Suganuma, and David Bialock, and with Mr. Stanley Barkan have helped us deal with questions regarding the historical, religious, and literary background of these tales, and with the publication process. Our thanks also to Cathy Layne, our editor at Tuttle, for her thoughtful advice and guidance. We are also grateful for the generous support we have received from our respective universities: Toyo University and Seisen University.

Our translations are based on the following source: Mabuchi Kazuo et al., eds., *Konjaku monogatari shu* (Tokyo: Shogakukan, 1976).

Naoshi Koriyama and Bruce Allen
Translators

A Note on Place Names

The place names we have used are the historical names used in the original text. Their corresponding modern names or locations are given below.

Historical name	Modern name, or location
Awa	Tokushima Prefecture
Bingo	Eastern part of Hiroshima Prefecture
Chikuzen	Northeastern part of Fukuoka Prefecture
Chinzei	Kyushu
Echigo	A large part of Niigata Prefecture
Etchu	Toyama Prefecture
Higo	Kumamoto Prefecture
Ise	Mie Prefecture
Iyo	Ehime Prefecture
Izumi	Southern part of Osaka Prefecture
Kaga	Southern part of Ishikawa Prefecture
Kamutsuke	Gunma Prefecture
Kawachi	Eastern part of Osaka Prefecture
Kii	Wakayama Prefecture
Michinoku	Aomori Prefecture and part of Iwate Prefecture
Mikawa	Eastern part of Aichi Prefecture
Mino	Southern part of Gifu Prefecture
Musashi	Parts of Tokyo and of Saitama and Kanagawa Prefectures
Ohmi	Shiga Prefecture
Sanuki	Kagawa Prefecture
Settsu	Parts of Osaka and Hyogo Prefectures
Shimotsuke	Tochigi Prefecture

Shimousa	Northern part of Chiba Prefecture and part of Ibaraki Prefecture
Shinano	Nagano Prefecture
Suruga	Central part of Shizuoka Prefecture
Tamba	Parts of Kyoto and Hyogo Prefectures
Tango	Northern part of Kyoto Prefecture
Tosa	Kochi Prefecture
Yamashiro	Southern part of Kyoto Prefecture
Yamato	Nara Prefecture

Foreword

The twelfth-century *Konjaku monogatari shu* (Collection of tales from times now past) is the greatest work of Japanese *setsuwa bungaku* (tale literature), a genre that flourished between the ninth and thirteenth centuries but traces back to Japan's earliest extant text, the eighth-century *Kojiki* (Records of Ancient Matters). Tale literature notably impacted Noh drama and other Japanese art forms and continues to fascinate contemporary Japanese readers and writers. The *Konjaku monogatari shu*, which draws on countless Chinese and Japanese sources and echoes of which are found throughout classical and even modern Japanese literature, is also one of the world's most expansive anthologies of tales, bringing together in thirty-one volumes more than one thousand sacred and secular stories about India (five volumes of Buddhist tales), China (five volumes of Buddhist and Confucian tales), and Japan (ten volumes of Buddhist tales and eleven volumes of secular tales). Partial translations of the *Konjaku* collection flourished outside East Asia beginning in the 1950s, with English-language readers particularly fortunate to have Robert Brower's annotated translations of seventy-eight tales (*The Konzyaku monogatarisyu: An Historical and Critical Introduction*, 1952), followed by Susan Wilbur Jones's *Ages Ago: Thirty-Seven Tales from the Konjaku Collection* (1959), Marian Ury's *Tales of Times Now Past: Sixty-Two Stories from a Medieval Japanese Collection* (1979), Yoshiko Kurata Dykstra's *The Konjaku Tales, Indian Section* (1986), and others. So significant are the *Konjaku* tales to early Japanese literature that selections from them appear in nearly all English-language anthologies of the classical Japanese corpus, most recently Haruo Shirane's *Traditional Japanese Literature: An Anthology, Beginnings to 1600* (2007, abridged version 2011).

Naoshi Koriyama and Bruce Allen's masterful, elegant translations of ninety extraordinary tales from the *Collection*'s twenty-one volumes on Japan—many of which appear here for the first time in English translation—beautifully complement these venerated predecessors. Contributing significantly to understandings of premodern Japan, the present volume stands out in giving readers an unprecedented glimpse into the daily lives of early Japanese commoners, who are for the most part obscured in *The Tale of Genji* and the other celebrated court classics that have been of greatest interest to compilers of English-language world literature anthologies.

As Koriyama and Allen point out in their introduction, among the aspects of life in early Japan featured in the *Konjaku monogatari shu* is the relationship of Japanese communities with the natural world. Most significantly in our age of ecological crisis is how the tales grapple with major human changes to the Japanese countryside, revealing the tensions between religion's spiritual callings to preserve nature and people's need to hunt, fish, and farm to survive. East Asian literatures are famous for celebrating the beauties of nature and depicting people as intimately connected with the natural world. But in fact, because the region has a long history of transforming and exploiting nature, much of its creative work—including the *Konjaku* collection—highlights the complex, contradictory interactions between people and the nonhuman environment. In this and many other ways *Japanese Tales from Times Past* opens exciting and invaluable new windows on early Japanese society.

Karen Thornber
Professor of Comparative Literature
Professor of East Asian Languages and Civilizations
Harvard University

Introduction

These ninety tales from medieval Japan have been selected and translated from the *Konjaku monogatari shu* (Collection of tales from times now past), which is believed to have been compiled around the year 1120, at the end of Japan's Heian Period (794–1185). The *Konjaku monogatari shu* is a huge collection of 1,039 tales that were gathered from India, China, and Japan. It thus ranks among the world's largest collections of tales. In the past, many scholars had believed that it was compiled by Minamoto no Takakuni (1004–1077). Recent scholarship, however, argues against this claim, particularly because it is now thought that some of its stories were composed after Takakuni's death.* It seems likely that the unknown compiler (or compilers) was either a Buddhist monk or an aristocrat. Although, for several hundred years, the *Konjaku monogatari shu* was not regarded as high literature in Japan, its value was rediscovered in the Meiji period (1868–1912) by critics and writers including Ryunosuke Akutagawa (1892–1927). Today, the *Konjaku monogatari shu* is highly regarded in Japan, along with works such as *The Tale of Genji* and *The Tale of the Heike*.

The original collection consists of thirty-one volumes, of which volumes 8, 18, and 21 are missing. The first five volumes are devoted to tales about India, the next five to tales about China, the next ten to Buddhist tales from Japan, and the remaining eleven volumes to secular tales from Japan.

We have selected what we feel to be the best and most interesting among the tales concerned with Japan. Certainly, the tales about India and China also have considerable historical and literary

---

* Shirane, Haruo. "Introduction to Anecdotal (*Setsuwa*) Literature," in *The Demon at Agi Bridge and other Japanese Tales*, ed. Haruo Shirane, trans. Burton Watson (New York: Columbia U. Press, 2011) 23.

interest, but we chose to concentrate on the Japanese tales—both to give our collection a clearer focus, and because we felt that these selections have the greatest originality and literary appeal. Some, particularly the earlier selections, are closely connected with the Buddhist way of living and thinking in medieval Japan, while others are more secular and even vulgar in theme and language. But each of them reveals some striking aspects of the imagination, fantasy, and creativeness of medieval Japanese. They appeal, too, as powerfully entertaining tales, filled with keen psychological insight, wry sarcasm, and barely veiled critical commentary on the doings of clergy, nobles, and peasants alike. They suggest that there are, among all classes and peoples, similar susceptibilities to pride, vanity, superstition, and greed—as well as aspirations toward higher moral goals. At the same time, these tales provide a clear look into the lives and thinking of common people—peasants, farmers, soldiers, and common traveling monks of the medieval period—showing a face of Japan that was largely missing or obscured in the more well-known court tales and poetry collections such as *Genji*, *Heike*, the *Manyoshu*, and the *waka* and *renga* verse of the period. In the *Konjaku* tales, we can observe a wide range of human life—the low life and the high, the humble and the devout; the drinking, flirting, farting, and fornicating, as well as the yearning for wisdom, transcendence, and compassion—that are all parts of our shared human nature.

Although written almost a thousand years ago, the *Konjaku* stories have a striking freshness and a sense of connection to our modern personal and social cares and to our creative imagination. Late Heian society was in the midst of a chaotic and deeply troubling period of change. The decline of aristocratic society gave way to the rise of a countrified warrior class. Murder, theft, rape, and such troubles were on the increase. There was a general belief, supported by the Buddhist doctrine of *mappo* (final days of the Buddhist Law), that the world was undergoing a period of inevitable degeneration, and that the age was headed toward an end. Buddhist teachings began to change in emphasis. They dealt with themes ranging from praising the wonders of the world, to offering advice for living in the present world, and gaining redemption in the world to come. Buddhist teachers used such parable-tales (*setuswa*) as are found in this collection to transmit these ideas, along with practical advice, to the peasants and common folk. They drew on a rich mixture of old mythology, local tales, Shinto lore about local gods and demons, and actual historical figures and events. The stories were intended to offer advice for survival when dealing with devils, tricksters, phonies, demons, and other common troubling beings and events—whether human or supernatural.

Many of the stories refer to the benefits of following the teachings of the *Lotus Sutra*. Similar in some ways to the *Konjaku monogatari shu*, the *Lotus Sutra* is also composed of a wide range of parable-stories. These parables relate Buddhist teachings to the practical concerns of daily life, through the use of concrete examples. They are written in a narrative style that is understandable by a wide range of people, including the common folk.

There is a formulaic narrative structure that is evident in these tales, suited to their original use as religious parables. They all start with a set phrase; "In olden times . . ." and end with a moral message and a rather set ending, usually something like; ". . . and such is the tale as it has been handed down." Although some modern readers may, at least at first glance, find the morals at the end of the stories to be simplistic and didactic, we should remember that the stories' original function was as a parable. If we accept such stylistic requirements of the genre, we can also see the great artistic creativity and imagination of the tales. Many readers are likely to find considerable wry sarcasm, skepticism, paradox, and wit in these morals. Even, for example, when they overtly warn against such evils as the danger or stupidity of women, there is often a strong undercurrent of parody and satire, as well as ample possibility for reading intended ambiguities and opposing interpretations. The complex psychological insights and portrayals of dreams, greed, and lust give these stories particular modern appeal.

The Meiji era Japanese writer Ryunosuke Akutagawa—known particularly for his attention to psychological details and for his

Edgar Allan Poe–like fascination with and descriptions of the darker aspects of life—wrote a number of short stories based on the tales from the *Konjaku monogatari shu*. His story "Rashomon" is based on the tale in our collection titled "A Robber Climbs to the Upper Structure of Rashomon Gate and Finds a Corpse." Film director Akira Kurosawa based his famous movie *Rashomon* on Akutagawa's adaptation of another tale included in our collection: "A Man Traveling With His Wife to Tamba Province Gets Tied Up by a Young Man at Mt. Ohe." In all, Akutagawa wrote more than ten short stories based on tales from the *Konjaku monogatari shu*. The writer Sonoko Sugimoto (1925–) has written forty-four short stories based on tales from the collection.

The *Konjaku* tales deal mainly with rural culture and nature. Along with the decline of the nobility's power and the spread of Buddhist teachings to the common folk in rural areas, major ecological changes were transforming nature and culture in the countryside. Forests—along with their resident gods, spirits, ogres, demons, and other supernatural beings—were being cut down and pushed away to clear the land for cultivation. Rivers were being diverted, and waterways disturbed. This disruption of nature was accompanied by deep feelings of ambivalence. People felt an uneasy tension between their practical and spiritual callings. On the one hand, they faced basic survival needs through hunting and killing animals, and increasingly, by clearing forests and carrying out land-engineering projects that controlled and disrupted nature. On the other hand, they still held to traditional Shinto beliefs of respect for nature's deities, along with a faith in the more recent Buddhist teachings regarding the sanctity of all sentient, and even all non-sentient beings. Buddhism not only urged abstinence from or restraint in eating animal meat, it also taught that "trees, grasses, and earth all become Buddhas" (*somoku kokudo shikkai jobutsu*).[†] Many of the tales in the *Konjaku monogatari shu* express feelings of the tension in being

---

† Shirane, Haruo. *Japan and the Culture of the Four Seasons: Nature, Literature, and the Arts* (New York: Columbia U. Press, 2012) 124.

torn between competing strains of necessity and compassion toward animals, plants, people, and places. Examples of the many stories included in our collection that express the ambivalence toward humans' relations with animals include, as their titles imply: "How a Man Copied the *Lotus Sutra* to save a Dead Fox," "A Man from Michinoku Province, Who Catches Hawks' Chicks, Is Saved by Kannon," and "On Seeing a Wild Duck Mourning the Death of the Drake He Shot, a Man Becomes a Monk." In the story "The Governor of Sanuki Province Destroys Manono Pond," we can see an early example of a cautionary tale about how human greed can result in ecological and societal destruction. In the *Konjaku* tales, we see evidence of, and reflection on, how the worlds of humans, animals, plants, and places are inherently interwoven and interdependent.

The *Konjaku* tales have had a lasting influence on many aspects of Japanese culture. A popular, often-performed Noh drama is based on the *Konjaku* tale "A Monk of Dojoji Temple in Kii Province Brings Salvation to Two Snakes by Copying the *Lotus Sutra*." It is an eerie story about a woman who loved a young monk so deeply that she turned herself into a snake when the monk didn't come as promised to see her. In the form of a snake, she pursues the young monk, who hides in a temple bell. She burns the bell with the angry fire of her unrequited love, and the monk perishes in the flames. Then a high-ranking elderly priest from Dojoji Temple "dreams a dream" that a snake appears and begs: "I am the monk that hid in the bell. The wicked woman became a snake, and I was forced to become her husband . . . Please, I pray, show your great, merciful heart and copy the chapter on the Buddha's life from the *Lotus Sutra* with your clean mind and body, and dedicate it to the Buddha to save us two snakes and release us from our sufferings." And at that, the snake goes off, and the elderly priest awakes from his dream. The two snakes are saved by virtue of the elderly priest's meritorious work.

In a number of other tales, the female bodhisattva, Kannon, saves people in miraculous ways. In one tale about a greedy county administrator of Tamba Province, Kannon gets her chest pierced with an arrow on behalf of a sculptor of Buddhist figures and thus saves his life. In another tale, she becomes a huge snake and helps carry a man up a cliff and allows him to return home safely.

In several tales, we find references to the close and respectful relations that existed between Japanese and Koreans in medieval times, such as in "A Turtle Repays the Kindness of Gusai of Paekche" and "A Human Skull Repays the Kindness of Doto, a Priest from Korea." Such stories touch on a largely underreported history of positive Japanese-Korean relations and suggest possibilities for establishing bridges of reconciliation amidst the ongoing tensions between these countries in recent times.

In the final story of our collection, "The Great Oak Tree in Kurimoto County of Ohmi Province," we see a clear expression of the ambivalence that people of the time felt toward the rampant deforestation that was occurring in Japan, and in particular, toward the cutting of the last giant trees. This short, compact tale tells of an enormous oak tree "three thousand feet in circumference" that casts its huge, dark shadow on three provinces, such that it restricts the farmers' ability to grow crops. The farmers petition the emperor for permission to cut down the tree. When granted permission, they quickly chop it down, and this results in rich, abundant harvests. This event, we can imagine, heralds the historical triumph of agriculture and the increasing control of humans over nature. Yet the story also expresses a poignant whiff of nostalgia, mixed with feelings of awe and respect for the giant old trees that had once been respected and protected by the emperors and the people alike. Such feelings of ambivalence in the face of modernization are likely to strike sympathetic chords among readers today as we, too, face similar anxieties, compromises, and ambiguities in our relations with the natural world.

Steeped in such thematic and local variation, these tales encompass a great creative space as they deal with a wide range of psychological, religious, social, ecological, and practical everyday concerns. They cast new light on previously hidden aspects of medieval Japanese society and nature, while at the same time they possess a creative spirit that can excite and challenge contemporary readers. We translators sincerely hope our readers will fully enjoy these extraordinary tales of old Japan.

Naoshi Koriyama and Bruce Allen

1
Kume, the Hermit with Magical Powers, Builds Kume Temple

In olden times, there was a temple called Ryumonji in Yoshino County of Yamato Province. Two hermits cloistered themselves within this temple, practicing the arts of living timelessly and flying through the sky. One was named Azumi and the other Kume. Now as it happened, Azumi obtained his magical powers first and he became a supernatural hermit who could fly.

Later on, Kume, too, became a supernatural hermit with magical powers of his own and he also became able to fly through the sky. One day while flying along, he happened to notice a young woman washing clothes by the bank of the Yoshino River. In doing so, she had tucked her skirt up, revealing her pure white calves. Seeing those white calves, Kume's heart was inflamed with desire and as a result, he lost his supernatural powers and tumbled from the sky, landing right in front of the woman. Thereupon, he took the woman for his wife and they lived together. How this hermit had once practiced the supernatural arts was inscribed on the door of Ryumonji, and it still remains there. Kume, the once-supernatural hermit, had become an ordinary human being. Nonetheless, it is said that when he sold his horse, he still signed his name as *Kume, former supernatural hermit.*

In the meantime, while Kume the once-supernatural hermit was living with his wife, the emperor decided to build a palace in Take-chi County of the province and he called for laborers from around the country to do the work. And so Kume, too, was summoned to work as a laborer. The other laborers called him Supernatural Hermit. When the officials heard of this, they asked the laborers, "Why is it you call him Supernatural Hermit?" In reply, they explained, "In past times, Kume used to shut himself up in Ryumonji and practice the arts of living timelessly and flying through the sky as a supernatural hermit. He had already mastered the arts, but one day while flying about, he happened to see a woman washing her clothes in the river. When he looked down at her pure white calves, he lost his magic powers, and fell down, and he landed in front of her. And so, he took the woman for his wife. That's why we call him 'Supernatural Hermit.'"

Half joking, the officials suggested, "Well then, if he used to have magical powers and he's learned the arts of supernatural living and he's lived as a supernatural hermit, he should still have some magical powers. So, rather than having you carry all that lumber yourselves, why don't we just ask Kume to carry it through the sky." Hearing this, Kume pleaded, "But I've forgotten all the arts of supernatural hermits. Now I'm just an ordinary human being. I shouldn't try to use magical powers." But, in his heart, he thought, "Once I learned the arts of the supernatural hermit, but because I had an ordinary man's passions and they stained my heart, I lost my magical powers. Still, if I pray sincerely, the Buddha might help me regain my powers." And so he said to the officials, "I will pray and try." Hearing this, the officials thought, "This guy is talking nonsense," but they said to Kume, "Well, that's certainly a great idea."

After that, Kume retreated to a quiet hall, purified his body and mind, fasted, and worshiped the Buddha for seven days and seven nights, praying with all his soul for this one thing: that he might regain his magical powers. And thus, seven days passed. The officials laughed at Kume, who hadn't appeared, but they also wondered what had happened to him. Then on the morning of the eighth day, suddenly the sky grew overcast and then it turned dark as night. Thunder rumbled, rain began to fall, and nothing could be seen. While people were wondering about these strange circumstances, the thunder ceased, and the sky cleared. When they looked about, a huge assortment of lumber, in both large and small sizes, came flying through the sky from the mountains in the south. It all settled on the site where the imperial palace had been planned.

From then on, the many officials who had witnessed this gained great respect for Kume. They reported it to the emperor, and he, too, was deeply impressed and paid respect to Kume. Soon after this, he presented Kume with seventy-two acres of rice fields, free of tax. Kume was overjoyed. He used the fields, and in the countryside, he built a temple, now known as Kume Temple.

After that, Great Master Kobo of Koya Temple had three, sixteen-foot statues of Medicine Master Buddha sculpted in copper and installed in the temple. Great Master Kobo discovered the *Mahavairocana Sutra* in the temple and consequently he thought, "This sutra will surely give us the power to attain Buddhahood." And thus, he went to China to learn the teachings of the Shingon sect. This is how Koya grew to become an important temple. And such then is the story as it has been passed down to us.

Vol. 11, Tale 24

2

One of Emperor Tenchi's Princes Builds Kasagi Temple

In olden times, in the reign of Emperor Tenchi, there lived a wise and learned prince who had a great love of literature. It was during this time that the composing of poetry began to flourish in our country. The prince also enjoyed hunting and would hunt wild boar and deer from morning to night. He was always equipped with bow and arrows, and accompanied by his men. Together, they roamed the mountains hunting wild animals.

One day, the prince went off hunting in the mountains of the eastern part of Kamo Village in Sagara County, Yamashiro Province. Chasing a deer, while mounted on a fine horse, he climbed the slope of a mountain. When the deer ran off toward the east, he continued to pursue it. Standing in the stirrups, he drew his bow and aimed at the deer, but suddenly he lost sight of it. He thought he'd hit it, but the deer wasn't there.

"Well," he thought, "The deer must have fallen over the cliff." And so, throwing the bow aside, he pulled on the reins and tried to stop the running horse, but he couldn't stop it quickly. In fact, the deer had already fallen over the high cliff. Because of its speed, the horse, like the deer, could easily have fallen over, but managed to strain its legs and stop at the very edge of the precipice. The prince could neither turn his horse around nor get off it, and the gorge below lay steep and deep, right beneath the stirrups. There was no space to dismount. If the horse had moved even a bit, it would have fallen off the cliff into the gorge below, more than a hundred feet deep. When the prince gazed down into it, he felt dizzy. He couldn't even see its bottom, nor could he tell east from west. Scared out of his wits, and with his heart thumping, he thought he was going to die there with his horse. And so, making a wish, the prince sadly beseeched, "If there are gods in these mountains, please save my life, and I will carve a statue of Maitreya Buddha here in the rock." And at that, suddenly, a miraculous thing occurred: the horse stepped backward and stood on a wider space.

Dismounting his horse, and in tears, the prince bowed down and worshiped the gods. To mark the spot for another visit, he placed his rush hat there and left. A day or two later, he returned and searched for the hat he'd left as a mark.

From the crest of the mountain, he descended the slope until he reached its base. When he looked up, he couldn't see the summit; it seemed as high as the clouds in the sky. The prince was worried. Gazing at the mountainside, he thought of carving a statue of Maitreya Buddha, but it seemed impossible. At that very moment, an angel came to his aid. Sympathizing with him, it promptly fashioned a statue. During that time, dark clouds covered the area, and it grew dark as night. In the dark, sounds from small pieces of flying rock were heard. A while later, the clouds vanished, and the mist cleared.

When the prince looked up at the cliff, he saw that a statue of Maitreya Buddha had been freshly carved. Gazing on it, he bowed deeply, broke into tears, and then returned home. From that time on, the temple has been called "Hat-marked Temple," or just "Hat-marked," for the spot had been marked by a hat.

Verily, the statue was a rare and precious one in an age of decadence. People around the world should worship it with all their hearts. They should look on it with the conviction: anyone who should care to visit this place and bow his head will surely be born in the inner hall of the Tosotsu Heaven, and meet the coming of the Maitreya Buddha.

It is said that Bishop Rouben discovered this temple some time after the statue of Maitreya Buddha was carved, and that he worshiped the statue as the main object of devotion. It has also been said that halls and monks' living quarters were built after that, and that many monks came to dwell there. And such, then, is the story as it has been handed down to us.

Vol. 11, Tale 30

3

The Kegon Buddhist Service
Held at Todaiji Temple

In olden times, Emperor Shomu built Todaiji Temple and he held a dedication ceremony to consecrate its new statue of the Buddha. At that time, there was a man named Bishop Baramon, who came from India. The noble priest, Gyogi, knew of Baramon and recommended that he serve as the lecturer at the dedication ceremony. The emperor, however, wondered, "Whom shall we ask to read the sutras?" Then he dreamed a dream in which a noble person appeared and said, "Someone will show up in front of the temple on the morning of the dedication ceremony. Whether he be a priest or a layman or of high rank or low, this person should be the reader." Then the emperor awoke from his dream.

The emperor believed firmly in what he had seen in his dream and so he sent a messenger to the gate of the temple on the morning of the dedication ceremony to look for the person. As it happened, an old man came along carrying on his back a bamboo basket filled with blue mackerel. The messenger took this old man back to the emperor and reported, "This is the first person who showed up at the temple." The emperor thought, "There must be something wondrous about this old man," and so he asked that the man be dressed in religious robes and serve as the reader. "But," the old man protested, "I am not qualified for such a task. I'm just a fishmonger who sells blue mackerel to earn a living." The emperor, however, would not accept his refusal.

When the time for the dedication ceremony came, the emperor had the fishmonger take a seat on the dais, beside the lecturer. The basket filled with blue mackerel was placed on the dais, and the staff on which he had carried the basket was placed standing on the east side of the hall. When the dedication ceremony came to an end, the lecturer came down from the dais. Then, in an instant, the reader vanished from the dais.

"This is as I expected," thought the emperor. "As my dream told me, that couldn't have been just an ordinary human being." And then, when he looked into the basket, he saw eighty volumes of the *Flower Garland Sutra* there, in place of the blue mackerel. With tears streaming from his eyes, the emperor bowed and said, "My most fervent wish has come true; the Buddha has appeared." And so, from then on, he believed in Buddhism even more deeply than ever. These events happened on March 14, 752.

After that, the emperor designated that date as a day for a yearly religious service and he had lectures given on the *Flower Garland Sutra*. This service is still held even today and it is called the "*Flower Garland Sutra* service." The monks of the temple keep their robes ready and are asked to attend the religious service every year. The emperor calls on the court nobles to provide music. Those who believe in the Way of the Buddha should visit this temple and pay homage to the sutra.

The staff with which the old man shouldered the basket still remains in the garden on the east side of the main hall. The staff no longer grows, and no leaves appear on it. It retains its withered appearance. And such, then, is the tale as it has been handed down to us.

Vol. 12, Tale 7

4

The Copper Statue of the Buddha at Jineji Temple Is Destroyed by a Robber

In olden times, in the reign of Emperor Shomu, there was a robber in Hine County of Izumi Province. He lived by the road, where he made his living by killing people and robbing them of their possessions. The robber had no belief in the Principle of Causality. He often went to temples looking for copper statues and secretly he stole them. He melted them down and made them into copper blocks that he sold for income. For this reason, he became known to others as a coppersmith.

At that time in that county, there was a temple called Jineji, and it had a copper statue of the Buddha. One day this statue suddenly disappeared, and the people in the neighborhood cried out, "It must have been stolen by a robber."

A while later, a man was passing along a northern road on horseback and he heard someone crying, "Oh! Oh! It hurts! It hurts! Someone, please help me! Save me from this man!" Hearing this voice, the traveler urged his horse to go faster. As he continued on, the voice called out as before. When he turned around and went back, the voice stopped. Then, when he went forward again, the voice cried out and groaned as before. When he turned around and went back, the voice stopped. When he went forward, the voice cried out again as before. When he went back, it stopped. The man thought this very strange and so he stopped his horse. As he listened carefully, he heard a sound, somewhat like that of a blacksmith at work. Hearing this, it occurred to him that someone might be killing a person. He walked around for a bit and then he sent his servant to secretly check out the place. The servant came to a wall and looked through a peephole into the house. There, a copper statue of the Buddha was laid out on its back. Its hands and legs had been cut off, and a man was chipping away at its head with a cold chisel. Seeing what was going on, the servant rushed back to his master and reported. Hearing of it, the master thought, "Surely this man must have stolen that statue and now he is destroying it. The voice must have been the voice of the Buddha." At that, he broke into the house and tied up the man who was destroying the statue of the Buddha. When he demanded that the man tell the details, the coppersmith confessed, saying, "I stole this copper statue of the Buddha from Jineji." Accordingly, the man sent his servant to the temple to investigate. It turned out that the statue of the Buddha had been stolen from the temple. The servant reported this to his master.

When the monks and patrons of the temple heard about this, they were all astonished. They rushed to the robber's house and saw the broken statue of the Buddha. Wailing and in tears, they cried, "How horrible! How terrible! What did our Buddha ever do to meet such a fate at the hands of a robber?" Their sorrow was boundless. And so the monks of the temple made a sacred palanquin, decorated it, and carried the desecrated statue back to the temple. The monks did not punish the robber, but the man who caught the robber, took him off to the capital and, accompanied by his servant, delivered him to the police office. When the officers questioned the robber, he confessed everything in detail. Those who heard the story, praised the event as a miracle and were aghast at the robber's crime. Promptly, they put him in jail.

When we think of it, the statue of the Buddha could not actually have felt pain. But it raised a voice of pain to show this miracle to the people. And this is how the story of these strange events has been handed down to us.

Vol. 12, Tale 13

5

Two Men from Kii Province Are Saved by the Buddha while Drifting at Sea

In olden times, during the reign of Emperor Shirakabe, in Hidaka County of Kii Province, there lived a man named Kimaro. He neither believed in the Principle of Causality nor respected the Three Treasures of the Buddha, the Dharma, and the Sangha.* He lived for many years by the sea and earned a living by going out to sea and catching fish in his nets.

Kimaro had two men in his employ. One, named Mumakai, was from Kibi Village in Ate County, and the other, named Ohojimaro, was from Hamanaka Village in Ama County; both in the same province. The two men worked diligently for Kimaro, following his instructions day and night for many years, going out to sea and catching fish in their nets.

It so happened that on June 16, 775, the winds blew hard, and the rains fell heavy. Because of the bad weather, a high tide rose, and many trees of all sizes were washed away and swept down the river. Kimaro ordered Mumakai and Ohojimaro to go out and collect some of the drifting trees. As instructed by their master, the two men went down to the river, collected a lot of trees, made a raft from them, and then floated on it down the river. The river grew rough, and the rope that tied the raft together snapped, and the raft fell apart. Both of the men were washed out to sea. They grabbed

---

* In Buddhism, the "Three Treasures" refer to the Buddha (the historical person), the Dharma (the Buddhist teachings), and the Sangha (the priesthood, or more broadly the entire community of practicing believers).

hold of trees and floated on them as they drifted about in the sea. Finally, they lost sight of each other. Thinking they had no way to reach land, and that they would soon die, they each cried out, "Save me, dear Buddha, I pray of you!" But no matter how loudly they cried out, there was no one to save them. Slowly, five days passed. With nothing to eat, they lost all their energy and their eyesight as well, until they could no longer tell east from west.

Toward the evening of the fifth day, unexpectedly, Ohojimaro washed up on a beach at a place named Tanoura on the south side of Awaji Province, where the villagers were making salt by boiling off seawater. As for Mumakai, he too drifted to the same place at about five o'clock in the evening of the sixth day. The villagers looked at them and questioned them about what had happened, but they were too weak to talk. Finally, after some time, they explained in small voices and faint breaths, "We are from Hidaka County of Kii Province. Following our master's instructions, we went out to collect drifting trees from the river. We made a raft, and while we were riding it, the waves got rough, and the rope that held the raft together snapped, so it broke apart, and we were washed out to the sea. Each of us grabbed onto a tree and drifted on the waves for several days until we were washed up here, unexpectedly, like in a dream." Hearing this, the villagers felt pity for them and fed them. Gradually, the two men regained their health and strength.

When the villagers told the provincial governor about the two men, he summoned them and met with them. Feeling sorrow for their plight, he fed and cared for them. With a feeling of repentance, Ohojimaro explained, "I used to work for a man who killed animals for many years and committed countless sins. If I return to that place now, I will be used as before and will have to kill animals. Therefore, I would like to stay here, instead of going back to that place." And after that, he went off to the provincial temple of the area and there he lived under the guidance of the priest.

As for Mumakai, after staying for two months, he went back to his home, for he was anxious to see his wife and children. His family was dumbfounded when they saw him. "We thought you had drowned in the sea, so we held a memorial service on the forty-ninth day after you disappeared. But now you have returned, unexpectedly. Is this a dream? Or are you a ghost?" they asked. Mumakai told them everything that had happened and then said, "I returned because I wanted to see you so much. Ohojimaro decided he could stop slaughtering animals if he stayed at the provincial temple, so now he's living there, training himself in the Way of the Buddha. I, too, would like to live like that." Hearing this, his wife and children were happy. And so he renounced the world and decided to go to a mountain temple and train himself in the Way of the Buddha. People thought it amazing when they heard his tale.

When we think of how those two men managed to survive after drifting in the sea for days, we come to realize that it was all made possible by the wondrous virtue of praying to the Buddha. It was also because of their deep faith.

When we come on a crisis, we should calm ourselves and pray to the Buddha with all our soul. Then we will certainly receive blessings. And so it is that this story has been handed down to us.

Vol. 12, Tale 14

6

Fish are Turned into the *Lotus Sutra*

In olden times, there was a temple built on the side of Mt. Yoshino in Yamato Province. The place was known as Amabeno Peak. In this temple, there was a priest who had lived there for many years. This was during the reign of Empress Abe. The priest kept his mind and body clean and followed the Way of the Buddha.

In time, this priest fell sick and became worn out and weak, such that he could no longer get up or down easily, nor could he eat or drink easily. Wondering how he could go on living, he thought, "I am so sick that I cannot follow the Way of the Buddha. First, I need to cure my sickness, and then I will be able to practice the Buddhist way of living again with ease. I've heard that nothing is better for curing sickness than eating fish or meat, so I would like to try eating some fish. Surely, eating fish isn't such a serious sin." And so, in secret, he told his disciple, "Since I am sick, I would like to survive by eating some fish. Won't you please go and get some fish for me."

Hearing this, the disciple sent a boy to the seaside in Kii Province to buy some fish. Accordingly, the boy went off and bought eight fresh mullets. He placed them in a small box and was on his way back when he met three men he knew. One of them asked, "What do you have in your box?" Instinctively, the boy answered, "I have the *Lotus Sutra*," because he didn't want to say, "I have some fish." But the men saw something dripping from the box and it smelled. Certainly its contents had to be fish. The men claimed, "That's no sutra; surely it's fish." Still, the boy insisted, "It's the sutra." They walked along, arguing with each other, and finally they came to the market. Taking a rest, the men stopped the boy and said, "What you have isn't the sutra, it's fish." The boy continued to insist, "It's not fish, it's the sutra." Not believing him, the men demanded, "Open that box and let us see." The boy tried to prevent them from opening it, but they opened it by force. The boy felt terribly ashamed, but when they looked into the box, lo and behold, there were eight volumes of the *Lotus Sutra!* Seeing the sutra, the men were astonished. The boy also was amazed and he went on his way happily.

Still feeling skeptical, one of the men decided he would look into this, and so, secretly, he followed the boy. The boy arrived at the mountain temple and told the priest all about what had happened. At first, the priest doubted him, but then he became happy. "This all happened," he reasoned, "because heaven wanted to help and protect me." And so the priest ate the fish. Seeing him eat the fish, the man who had come after the boy faced the priest and, prostrating himself, said, "Truly, it was in the form of fish, but as it was food for you, who are a saint, it turned into the sutras. I am ignorant and wicked and, because I didn't know the Principle of Cause and Effect, I doubted it and I troubled the boy many times. Please, forgive me for my faults. From now on, I will hold you as my master and will earnestly respect you." The man returned home, crying.

After that, this man became an important supporter of the priest. He regularly visited the mountain temple and took part in the services with all his heart. It was a wonderful thing.

When we think about it, we can see that eating keeps one's body well and able to follow the Way of the Buddha. Even if one eats poison, it turns into medicine, and even if one eats meat, it can't be a sin.

And so, as we can see, even fish can turn into a sutra in an instant. We should never criticize such things. Such then is the story as it has been handed down to us.

Vol. 12, Tale 27

A Clerk from Higo Province Escapes from a Demon's Scheme

In olden times, there lived a clerk in Higo Province. For many years he went to his office and worked there from morning to night. One day, on account of some urgent business, he left home particularly early in the morning. Because he had no attendants, he went off alone, riding a horse. As the distance between his home and the office was not even a mile, he could have reached his office in no time, but on that day the further he rode, the longer his way seemed to grow, and he couldn't reach the office. Along the way, he became lost and he came on an open field he did not know. Having traveled all day, night was already falling. With no place to lodge, he was alone in the field.

Worrying over his plight and hoping he might find a village, he reached the top of a low hill. Surveying the view, he noticed a well-built house. "I must be close to a village," he thought, and he took heart. He hurried to the house, but could find no sign of humans there. He walked around it and called out, "Is anyone home? Would you please come out. What is the name of this village?" From inside the house, a woman's voice replied, "Who is speaking? Come in, quickly." When the clerk heard the voice, he sensed something sinister, but he responded, "I have gotten lost. As I have some urgent business, I can't stop here now. Would you please show me the way." The woman replied, "Then wait a moment, and I'll show you." With the woman just about to come out, he felt so afraid that he prepared to escape. Then the woman appeared and said, "Hey, stay a while." When he looked at the woman, he saw that she was as tall as the eaves of the house, and her eyes glinted brightly. "Now I know," he thought, "I've come to a demon's house," and so he tried to escape, whipping his horse. The woman cried out, "Why are you running away? Stop, immediately!" When he heard this voice, his fear was indescribable indeed. Frightened out of his wits, he looked at the demon, whose height was about ten feet and whose eyes and mouth were spouting fire, like lightning. The demon chased after him, opening her big mouth and clapping her hands. He almost fell from his horse, but he kept racing away, whipping the horse and praying in his thoughts, "Please save me, O merciful Kannon. Please save my life today!" Rushing, his horse stumbled, and the clerk was pitched off and he landed in front of the horse. "Now I'll be caught and eaten by the demon," he thought.

Suddenly, he noticed the opening of a cave that contained some graves, and so he dashed into it frantically. The demon cried out, "Where'd he go?" Listening as he hid, the clerk heard the demon biting away and eating the horse. Hearing the sounds, the clerk thought, "When the demon has finished eating my horse, surely it will come and will eat me. But it must not realize I'm here in this cave," and so he prayed without ceasing, "O merciful Kannon, please save me, I pray of you."

When the demon had finished eating the horse, it walked up to the mouth of the cave and called out, "That man is supposed to be my meal for today. Just catch him and give me his flesh. You always treat me so unfairly. I've had enough of this!" When the clerk heard this voice, he thought, "Ah, so the demon knows I'm hiding in this cave." Then a voice from inside the cave called out, "This man is *my* meal for today, so I can't give him to you. You've already eaten his horse." Hearing this, the clerk concluded, "either way, I can't save my life. I thought the demon outside was the worst one, but now the one here in the cave is even more dreadful and it's set on eating me." In his despair, he thought, "I prayed to Kannon, but my life is now fated to come to its end. This must be owing to the karma from my previous life."

Meanwhile, the demon outside continued demanding to be allowed to eat the clerk who was inside the cave. But the demon inside wouldn't listen. So the demon outside finally gave up, reluctantly, and went back home. "Now the demon inside the cave will catch me and eat me," thought the clerk. But then, a voice from within the cave spoke, "You were to be eaten by that demon today, but because you prayed devoutly to Kannon, you saved yourself from the disaster. From now on, you must worship the Buddha with all your heart and read the *Lotus Sutra* earnestly. But first of all, do you know who I am, talking to you like this?" "No," answered the clerk. The voice replied, "I am not a demon, by any means. In ancient times, in this cave there lived a saint. He erected a stupa on the peak to the west of this place and in it he placed the *Lotus Sutra*. With the passage of many years, both the stupa and the sutra decayed and vanished. Only the very first word, 'wonder,' has remained. It is this word, 'wonder,' who is now speaking. I reside here, and so far, I have saved 999 persons who were about to be eaten by the demon. Now the number has reached one thousand including you. You must leave here and return home quickly. And you should worship the Buddha ever more devoutly, and read and accept the *Lotus Sutra*." On saying this, the voice summoned a courteous young man and had him lead the clerk back to his home. He bowed tearfully and then he was able to return, following the boy. On delivering the clerk to the doorway of his home, the boy told him, "You must read and accept the *Lotus Sutra* with all your heart," and then he vanished into thin air. After that, the clerk bowed tearfully and entered his home at midnight. He told his parents, wife, and children everything that had happened. Hearing it, they all rejoiced and were most deeply moved. From that time on, the clerk became ever more pious. He read the *Lotus Sutra* and worshiped Kannon devoutly.

Just think, even the one word, "wonder," that remained undecayed, was able to save human beings like this. How much more then may it save those who, with honest hearts, copy the entire

Lotus Sutra? In this life, divine favor is like this. Therefore, isn't the divine favor that helps human beings escape the sufferings after death even more wonderful? And such then is the story that has been handed down to us.

Vol. 12, Tale 28

8

Enku, a Monk of the Tendai Sect, Hears a Flying Hermit Chanting a Sutra

In olden times, there was a monk named Enku who lived in the West Tower on Mt. Hiei. Enku was a disciple of Bishop Shoku. Enku had left home at the age of nine to enter the temple and become a monk. There, studying under the master, he learned the scriptures of both exoteric and esoteric Buddhism. He believed devoutly in the *Lotus Sutra* and recited it day and night. His voice was filled with solemnity and was beyond compare. All those who heard him chant the sutra were certain to weep. When, in time, he went down into the city of Kyoto to recite sutras, his reputation continually rose and he was welcomed into the imperial court and nobles' residences.

After that, however, he decided to confirm his religious faith anew. Renouncing worldly success, he went off to Mt. Atago and settled in a place called the Valley of the Southern Star. There he practiced spiritual exercises in self-renunciation, blew on the trumpet shell day and night, repented his sins six times a day, and recited the *Lotus Sutra*.

Later, one October, he went to Mt. Kazuragi to practice spiritual exercises for seeking salvation through Buddhism. He climbed the mountain peak, carried out spiritual practices, and chanted the *Lotus Sutra* with all his heart. On this mountain was a very tall cedar tree. He spent a night at the foot of this tree, where he hung an image of the Buddha and recited the *Lotus Sutra*. The moon shone brightly. Around midnight, he could faintly see something flying about around the top of the cedar. The tree was so tall he couldn't see clearly what the thing was. "It must be some devil trying to confound a faithful reader of the sutra," he thought. He felt terribly afraid, but counting on the virtue of the sutra, he recited it in a loud voice. When day was about to dawn, the being that seemed to be at the top of the tree chanted nobly in a low, faint voice:

> *The virtuous deeds*
> *this man has done*
> *are inestimable;*
> *as boundless,*
> *as infinite*
> *as space.*

After reciting these words, the being in the tree flew away. The sutra-chanting monk wondered who it could have been and he looked up, but he could see no one. The voice flew off like a shadow. The sutra-chanting monk thought to himself, "When I was reciting the *Lotus Sutra*, a superhuman hermit must have heard me and sat respectfully on the treetop all night long. Those words must have been the words of his chanting when he flew away." He bowed down in deep reverence. On his return, when he told Head Priest Genshin about the occurrence, the priest was so deeply touched with awe and reverence that he wept.

It has been said that when Enku came to the end of his life, he passed away in a noble manner, reciting the *Lotus Sutra* on the Peak of the Southern Star. And such then is the story as it has been handed down to us.

Vol.12, Tale 38

9

A Monk from Kazurakawa Meets the Hermit of Mt. Hiranoyama

In olden times there lived a monk who trained himself in the Way of the Buddha. He secluded himself in a place called Kazurakawa, where he refrained from eating grains and ate only wild plants and practiced his religious training with all his heart for many months. One day he dreamed a dream in which a noble priest appeared and said to him, "There is a superhuman hermit who lives on the peak of Mt. Hiranoyama and recites the *Lotus Sutra* continually. You should visit him and make contact immediately." On waking from this dream, he went off to Mt. Hiranoyama immediately and searched for the hermit, but he couldn't find him.

Continuing his search day after day, in time, he heard a low voice off in the distance chanting the *Lotus Sutra*. The voice sounded so solemn and beyond compare. The monk was delighted and he scurried about in all directions. But he could only hear the voice. He could not see its source. After searching for the source of the voice with all his might all day long, finally he found a cave. By the opening to the cave stood a large pine tree that looked like an umbrella. When he peered into the cave, he saw the saint. His body had but little flesh. It was mostly just skin covering bones. His clothing was made of green moss. The saint said to the monk, "Who is it that has come to this place? This cave has never been visited by a human being." The monk said in reply, "When I was doing my religious practices, secluding myself by Kazurakawa, I dreamed a dream in which I was told to come here and to meet you." The hermit replied, "You must not come close to me. Keep a long distance between us. I cannot bear the human smoke that gets in my eyes. It makes tears stream from my eyes. After seven days have passed, you may come close to me."

And so, as instructed by the hermit, the monk took shelter, keeping himself ten or twenty yards away from the cave. All this time the hermit continued chanting the *Lotus Sutra* day and night. Listening to it, the monk was so deeply impressed that he felt as if all his sins from the past had been absolved. When he looked about, he saw that many deer, bears, monkeys, and other beasts and birds had brought various fruits and offered them to the hermit. Then the hermit sent a monkey to bring fruit to the monk. After seven days had passed like this, the monk visited the cave of the hermit.

At that time, the hermit said to the monk, "Formerly, I was a monk called Renjaku, living at Kofukuji Temple. I was diligently studying the tenets of the Hosso sect as a scholar when I came across a passage in the *Lotus Sutra* that read, 'If you don't accept the *Lotus Sutra* now, you will certainly regret it later on.' Ever since that time, I have eagerly sought enlightenment. When I read the passage 'If you read the sutra in a place that is free of any human voice, I, the Buddha, will reveal myself in a body that is pure and radiant,' I left the temple, went into the mountains, learned the Way of the Buddha, accomplished virtuous deeds and was able to become a superhuman hermit, quite naturally. Owing to my fate from my previous existence, I came to this cave. Since the time when I left the human world, the *Lotus Sutra* has been my parents, and the Buddha's words my protector. The sutra is the eye that lets me see things in the distance, mercy is the ear that lets me hear various voices, and my mind is able to understand all things. I have risen to Tosotsu Heaven and now I see the Maitreya Buddha. I also visit many different places and have gotten to know the saints. The Devil doesn't even come close to me. I don't even hear of fears and disasters. I can see the Buddha and hear the Law of Buddhism as I please. And this pine tree here in front is like an umbrella, sheltering the entrance of the cave from the rain. On hot days it gives me shade and on cold days it protects me from the wind. Things proceed like this so naturally. Your visit to this place has also come about through the

Law of Cause and Effect. Therefore, I advise you to remain here and practice the Way of the Buddha."

When the monk heard this, he was deeply moved by the hermit and he was attracted by his way. But in the end, he decided that he wouldn't be able to endure such a strict discipline in learning the Way of the Buddha, and so he declined the hermit's offer. He thanked him, bowed deeply, and left the place. With the help of the hermit, he was able to return to Kazurakawa on that very day. When he told his friends about all that had happened, they were immensely impressed.

And so it has been said that by training oneself in the Way of the Buddha, with all one's heart, one can become a superhuman hermit like that. Such then is the story as it has been handed down.

Vol. 13, Tale 2

10

A Monk from Shimotsuke Province Resides in an Old Cave

In olden times, there was a monk named Hoku who lived in Shimotsuke Province. Previously he had lived in Horyuji Temple, where he studied the texts of both exoteric and esoteric Buddhism. He also believed in the *Lotus Sutra*, and unfailingly he recited three of its sections by day, and another three by night.

In time, Hoku grew tired of this world. Suddenly, one day he was seized with a deep wish to seek the Way of the Buddha, and so he left the temple, and returned to his native province. In the course of traveling through various mountains in eastern Japan and training himself in religious practices, he heard that there was an old cave in a remote, untrodden mountain that had once been used by a hermit. He searched for the place, and on finding it, he peered into the cave. Mosses of various colors covered its ceiling, door, partition, and floor. The front yard also was covered with moss. When Hoku looked at the place, he was happy and he thought, "This is the place where I will learn the Way of the Buddha." He secluded himself in the cave and chanted the *Lotus Sutra* with all his heart for many years. During that time, a beautiful woman suddenly appeared and brought him excellent food and offered it to him. Hoku felt afraid and suspicious, but he ate the food. Its fine taste was without compare. Hoku asked the woman, "Who on earth are you? From where did you come? This place is secluded and far from the human world. I feel very suspicious." The woman answered, "I am not a human being. I am a female demon, but as you were devoutly chanting the *Lotus Sutra*, I came to serve you." When Hoku heard this, he was deeply impressed. Since she continued to serve

46

him like this, he was never in want for food or drink. In the meantime, various birds, bears, deer, and monkeys came along to listen to him chant the sutra in the front yard.

At about the same time, there lived a monk named Rogen. He had no fixed residence and he traveled about visiting holy places in different provinces, reverently chanting mystical spells. One time, when he was wandering and carrying out his religious practices, he lost his way and happened on this cave. When Hoku saw Rogen, he thought it strange and he asked, "Who are you, and from whence have you come? This place is deep in the mountains, secluded from the human world, and is not easily visited by human beings." Rogen replied, "While I was in the mountains doing my training in the Way of the Buddha, I got lost and I ended up here. And, may I ask, who are you and how did you come to reside here?" In reply, Hoku told him all about himself.

The two lived together in the cave for several days. When Rogen saw the female demon who came to serve the sutra-chanting monk, he asked, "This is a secluded place, far from the human world. How is it that such a beautiful woman comes and serves you? Where does she come from?" The saint answered, "I have no idea where she comes from. Because she enjoys my chanting of the *Lotus Sutra*, she comes like this all the time." Seeing the beautiful woman, Rogen thought, "She must be a woman from the village who respects this believer of the sutra and brings him food." Increasingly, feelings of lust arose within his heart.

At this, the female demon sensed the feeling in Rogen's heart and said to the saint, "A depraved and shameless person has come to this quiet, clean place. He deserves an immediate punishment of death." The saint replied, "You must not punish him immediately and kill him. Let us save his life and just send him back to the human world." At that moment the female demon abandoned the form of a beautiful woman and turned herself into a hideous, angry woman. Seeing the sudden metamorphosis, Rogen was nearly scared to death. The demon grabbed Rogen, lifted him into midair, and quickly took him to a village, though it would have taken an ordinary person a week to get there on foot. Dropping him there, she returned. Rogen remained as still as a dead person for some time. After a while, he awoke. He realized that he had let lust for a female demon rise in his heart, and this was because he was still a common mortal, bound by earthly passions. Regretting his sin and repenting, he quickly embraced anew a firm resolve to follow the Way of the Buddha. He was hurt in mind and body, yet he was able to remain alive and return to his native village, where he told the villagers about this experience. He believed more deeply in the *Lotus Sutra* and studied and chanted it with all his heart.

All this came about because of Rogen's foolishness.

From this, we should realize that the female demon was, without a doubt, a guardian spirit of the *Lotus Sutra*. And such then is the story as it has been handed down.

Vol.13, Tale 4

11

Unjo, a Sutra-chanting Monk, Escapes a Snake's Attack by Chanting the *Lotus Sutra*

In olden times, there lived a sutra-chanting monk named Unjo. For many years since his youth, he had chanted the *Lotus Sutra* day and night. One day, he thought to himself, "I'd like to visit different parts of the country and make pilgrimages to the holy places," and so he set off for Kumano. On his way, traveling through Shima Province, the sun went down, and he looked around for lodgings for the night, but his search was in vain. There was a high cliff by the ocean, and in it, he spotted a cave, so he went inside to spend the night. The place was far away from any villages. Trees grew densely on the cliff above the cave. Unjo sat there and chanted the *Lotus Sutra* with all his heart. The cave smelled terribly fishy, and Unjo was filled with apprehension. At midnight, a breeze began to blow, and he sensed an eerie presence. The fishy smell grew even stronger. Unjo felt terribly scared, but there was no way he could leave the place. The night was pitch dark, and he had completely lost his bearings. All he could hear was the sound of the waves on the sea. Then he sensed something big descending from the upper part of the cave. Surprised, and wondering what it could be, he took a closer look and realized that it was a large poisonous snake. There, at the entrance to the cave, it was poised, ready to swallow Unjo. Staring at it, Unjo thought, "I am in danger of being devoured by this snake and losing my life, but I wish to be saved from Hell by the virtue of the *Lotus Sutra* and be reborn in the Pure Land." And so he began to chant the *Lotus Sutra* with all his heart. At that moment, suddenly, the snake disappeared. Then a heavy rain began to fall, strong winds began to blow, lightning flashed, and a flood engulfed the mountains. After a time, the rain stopped, and the sky cleared.

Then a man appeared. He entered through the mouth of the cave and sat down, facing Unjo. Unjo had no idea who it could be. No one could have been expected to be there, so he thought, "This must be a demon-god," but it was dark, and he couldn't see the figure clearly. Unjo felt terribly afraid, but the man bowed respectfully to him and said, "I have lived in this cave for many years, killing living things and eating the humans who came along. I was planning to gulp you down too, but when I heard you chanting the *Lotus Sutra* it immediately changed my evil mind for the good. The heavy rain that fell, and the lightning that flashed tonight were not real weather. The rain was the tears that streamed from my two eyes. To atone for the sins I've committed, I shed tears of remorse. From now on, I will never allow evil thoughts to arise." And saying this, the man disappeared, all of a sudden.

After escaping the danger of a snake attack, Unjo chanted the *Lotus Sutra* ever more fervently so that he might pray for the good of the poisonous snake. Hearing him chanting the sutras, the snake must have gained a good heart. At daybreak, Unjo left the cave and went to the temple at Kumano. No traces of a rainstorm or lightning could be seen outside the cave.

When we think of this, we can realize that we should not stay in such unfamiliar places. It is said that Unjo gave this kind of advice to the people. And such then is the story as it has been handed down to us.

Vol.13, Tale 17

12

A Shameless, Depraved Monk Recites the Chapter on the Buddha's Life from the *Lotus Sutra*

In olden times, there was a temple called Koryuji, to the east of Ninnaji Temple. In this temple there lived a priest named Joju. There was also a monk who was Joju's disciple. Although this monk looked like a monk, he didn't believe in the Buddha, the Dharma, or the Sangha. Nor did he understand the Principle of Causality. He behaved like a layman. He always carried a bow and arrows and kept a sword at his side. He was fond of committing all kinds of evil deeds. When he saw birds and animals, he shot and killed them. When he saw fish, he ate them. In his heart, he had deep-seated carnal desires, and he always lusted to touch women. He neither held the prayer beads in his hands nor wore the surplice over his shoulders. Truly, he was a depraved monk. Nevertheless, he honored the chapter in the *Lotus Sutra* on the Buddha's life and he recited it once every day—even if his body was unclean.

After a time, this monk left Koryuji Temple and went to Hoshoji Temple to become a disciple of Genshin, the head priest. He lived in the building where they kept the wagons. Obediently, he followed the head priest and served him. One day he got very sick and suffered for several days. The head priest felt very sorry to see him so sick and so he gave him the Buddhist precepts. The monk received the precepts with all his heart. Then he got up, rinsed his mouth, and recited the chapter on the Buddha's life from the *Lotus Sutra* with all his heart. When he came to the passage, "When you enter into the Supreme Way you will promptly become a Buddha," he passed away peacefully.

Although he had led a depraved life for many years, he met with good fortune toward the end and received the Buddhist precepts. Because he passed away while reciting the *Lotus Sutra*, people believed reverently that he must have been saved from falling into the evil realm. And such then is the story as it has been handed down to us.

Vol. 13, Tale 37

13

Biwa no Otodo Copies the *Lotus Sutra* and Saves a Precept Master

In olden times, at the temple on Mt. Hiei, there lived a man called the Precept Master Muku. When he was very young, he went to the mountain temple and became a monk and he never broke any of the commandments. He was also very honest and deeply inclined to follow the teachings of the Buddha. He was promoted to the rank of *sogo*, one of the higher ranks, but he renounced the pomp and fame of the world, seeking enlightenment in the future life. Therefore, he confined himself within the temple, chanting prayers to Amitabha ever diligently. This he did as his lifework. He was always in want of clothes and food, and he lived in dire poverty. Much less did he have any savings.

However, by some twist of fate, he happened to obtain an enormous amount of money. At the time, the precept master thought, "When I die, my disciples will surely be in want, so I will secretly hide this money and save it for their use after my death. At my dying hour, I will let them know about it." And so the monk secretly hid the money in the ceiling, and his disciples never learned about it. In time, the precept master fell sick, and while he was suffering greatly in bed, he completely forgot about the money he had hidden. And so he passed away without telling anyone about it.

At that time there lived a man named Biwa no Otodo, whose common name was Nakahira. For many years, he had had close relations with the precept master as a disciple. He had consulted closely with the precept master on all matters, and so, when the precept master died, Otodo was terribly saddened. Then he dreamed a dream. In it, the precept master appeared wearing dirty clothes and looking

53

feeble and wretched. He spoke to Otodo, saying, "When I was alive I chanted prayers to Amitabha with all my heart as my sole work, believing, 'Surely I will be reborn in Paradise.' But since I didn't have any savings, I secretly hid a large amount of money in the ceiling for my disciples, thinking, 'My disciples will surely be in want after my death.' And I thought, 'At my dying hour I will let my disciples know about this,' but when I was in anguish in my sick bed, I completely forgot about it, and so I died without telling them about it. Nobody will ever know about this. As retribution for my sins, I was reborn as a snake and am suffering indescribable anguish in the place where the money is. When I was alive, my relationship with you was very close, so please, would you look for that money, take it, and use it for copying and honoring the *Lotus Sutra*, and thus, may you also rescue me from this anguish." Then Otodo awoke from his dream.

Otodo grieved terribly. Without sending a messenger, he himself traveled to the temple at Mt. Hiei and went to the precept master's chamber. He asked someone to search the ceiling for the money, and there they found it, just as he had been told of in his dream. Among the coins was a snake, coiling itself around the money. On seeing the human beings, the snake slithered away. When Otodo told the precept master's disciples about his dream, they were immensely moved and shed tears. Otodo returned to Kyoto and soon used the money for copying Part I of the *Lotus Sutra* and for honoring it. Some time later, the precept master vividly appeared again in one of Otodo's dreams bearing an incense burner and saying to Otodo, "By virtue of your good deeds I was able to be released from the snake's world and now I am about to be reborn into Paradise, by virtue of the prayers I have chanted to Amitabha for many years." And on saying this, he flew away toward the west. Then Otodo awoke from the dream.

It is said that Otodo was filled with joy and that he spread the story widely among the people. And such then is the story as it has been handed down to us.

Vol. 14, Tale 1

A Monk of Dojoji Temple in Kii Province Brings Salvation to Two Snakes by Copying the *Lotus Sutra*

In olden times, two monks set off on a pilgrimage to visit the shrines in Kumano. One of them was old and the other was young and particularly handsome. When they reached Muro County, they came to a house and asked if they could stay there overnight. The landlady was a young widow and she had several female attendants.

Looking at the handsome young monk, the woman felt her sexual passions aroused and she treated him particularly kindly. When night fell, the monks went to sleep. Later, at about midnight, the woman crept secretly to the bedside of the young monk, draped her robes over herself and the monk, and lay by his side. Then she woke him up. The monk was surprised and bewildered. "I have never let other men stay at my house," the woman told him, "but from the first time I saw you today, I made up my mind that I must make you my husband. That's why I allowed you to stay here tonight. I thought, 'I'll let this man stay here tonight and make my wish come true,' and so now I've come to you. I lost my husband and now I'm a widow. Please, have pity on me."

Hearing this, the monk was deeply troubled. He sat up and said to the woman, "As I've been following a long-held wish, I have kept my body and mind clean and I have come a long way to visit the shrines of the deities in Kumano. If I were to break my vow, both of us would commit a grave sin, so please give up this idea right away." And with such words he firmly refused her.

The woman greatly resented his refusal and clung to him through the night, trying to entice him. But the monk, using various excuses, tried to dissuade her from her temptation. "I'm not completely rejecting your request," he said, "but first I must visit the shrines in Kumano, light the lanterns, and make offerings for a few days. Then, on my way back, surely I will accept your request." And so, counting on this promise, the woman went back to her own room. When dawn broke, the two monks left the house for Kumano.

From then on, the woman waited anxiously for the day of his return. She counted the days, ever yearning for the young monk and holding nothing else in her heart. She prepared all sorts of things for him. On their way back, however, the two monks felt afraid of the woman's temptation and so they escaped by taking a different road.

Wondering what was taking the monk so long and growing tired of waiting, the woman went out to the road and questioned people who passed by. After a while, she found a monk who was returning from Kumano and asked him if he had seen a young monk wearing a robe of such and such a color returning from Kumano, and accompanied by an older monk. The monk replied, "Those two monks, they left a few days ago." Hearing this, the woman clapped her hands in anger and cried, "They must have gotten away, taking a different road!" Enraged, she returned to her house and confined herself in her bedroom. After a period of silence, she died.

When her attendants discovered this, they grieved and as they cried, suddenly, a snake, some thirty feet long, crept out from the bedroom. It slipped out of the house and onto the road, where it rushed off as if it were following the path of those returning from Kumano. The people who saw the snake were horrified.

In the meantime, the two monks were walking along far ahead, but somehow someone alerted them, saying, "Something strange is going on behind you. A snake—it's about thirty feet long—has appeared and it's following you, going through the fields and mountains." Hearing this, the two monks thought, "Surely the woman of that house has wicked intentions. She must have become a poisonous snake, and now she's chasing after us because we broke our promise." And so they ran faster until they reached Dojoji Temple. Having seen them running, the monks of the temple asked, "Why on earth were you running like that?" Then the young monk told them all about the story and asked for help. The monks of the temple gathered and discussed the matter. They took down the temple bell, hid the young monk under it and then closed the gate of the temple. The older monk hid with the monks of the temple.

A short time later, a huge snake made its way to the temple. Even though the gate was closed, the snake slipped over the fence, went around the temple buildings a couple of times, and then it came to the door of the hall in which the young monk was hiding under the temple bell. The snake struck the door with its tail a hundred times or so. Finally, it broke down the door and went in. It coiled itself around the bell and kept striking on the crown with its tail for several hours. The monks of the temple were all terrified, but they were also puzzled about the snake's actions, so they opened the doors, gathered around, and looked at the snake. They saw the poisonous snake shedding bloody tears from its eyes. Finally, it raised its head, licked its lips, and then rushed off in the direction from which it had come. While the monks of the temple were watching, the large bell was covered with flames and was burned in the poisonous heat from the snake. They dared not approach it. Eventually, they were able to pour water on the bell and cool it down. When they removed the bell to look for the monk, he had been completely burned up. Not even a speck of bone was left. Only a few ashes remained. The older monk who had been with him cried in sorrow and then went off on his way home.

A while later, a high-ranking elderly priest of the temple dreamed a dream in which a snake even larger than the previous one appeared and said to him, "I am the monk that hid in the bell. The wicked woman became a snake, and I was forced to become her husband. I have taken on this wretched body, and my sufferings are limitless. Much as I wish to be released from my pains, I am utterly helpless, even though while I was alive I believed in the *Lotus Sutra*. I eagerly wish to be saved from these sufferings by the virtue of your profound goodness. Please, I pray, show your great, merciful heart and write out a copy of the chapter on the Buddha's life from the *Lotus Sutra* with your pure mind and body, and dedicate it to the Buddha to save us two snakes and release us from our sufferings. How else can we be saved, except by the power of the *Lotus Sutra*?" And in saying this, the snake went off, and the old priest awoke from his dream.

After that, this dream inspired a religious fervor in the old priest's heart. He copied the chapter on the Buddha's life from the *Lotus Sutra*. He lay aside all his possessions and invited all the other monks to hold a day-long service so that the two snakes might be released from their sufferings.

Some time later, a woman and a monk appeared in one of the old priest's dreams. Smiling and full of joy, both of them came to Dojoji Temple and bowed to the old priest and said, "By virtue of your purity and good deeds, we two were able to discard the snakes' forms instantly and enter into the Pure Land. I have been reborn in Tori Heaven, and the monk has gone up to Tosotsu Heaven." Having announced this, they parted from each other and ascended into the sky. And then the old priest awoke from his dream.

After that, the old priest was filled with joy and he was even more moved by the power of the *Lotus Sutra*. Mysterious indeed is the power of the *Lotus Sutra*. For it was all owing to the power of the *Lotus Sutra* that the two could discard their snake forms and be reborn in the heavens. All those who had seen or heard of this were inspired to believe reverently in the *Lotus Sutra* and to copy and read it. And the spirit of the old priest, that too was commendable. It must have resulted from his good deeds in a previous life. And when we think of it, the desire that the wicked woman felt for the monk—that too must have been the result of her deeds in a previous life.

In this story we can see an example of the fearful strength of a wicked woman's heart. It is for that reason the Buddha has warned us to keep a distance from women and to avoid them. Such then is the story as it has been handed down to us.

Vol. 14, Tale 3

15

How a Man Copied the
Lotus Sutra to Save a Dead Fox

In olden times, there lived a handsome young man. We are not even sure of his name now, but it seems he was from a samurai family. One day, appearing from somewhere, he was walking by the corner of Nijo Street and Shujaku Avenue in Kyoto. As he passed in front of the Shujaku Gate, he noticed a stunningly beautiful young woman, fine of figure and about seventeen or eighteen years of age. Dressed in exquisite layers of kimono, she was standing by the side of the street. Unable to pass her by with merely a glance, the man approached and took her hand.

He led her to an area within the gate where there were no other people, and there they sat down, and he started talking; "It must have been fate that led me to meet you like this, so please, won't you give me your love? And do listen to me—for I speak from my heart." The woman replied, "It is not that I would say no. Indeed I would wish to do as you ask, but if I were to follow your request I would lose my life, without a doubt." Unable to appreciate the meaning of her words, the man thought, "She must be just trying to brush me off," and so he began to embrace her forcibly. In tears, the woman said, "You have a wife, children, and a home in this world. For you, this is just a casual affair, but for me—it would be too sad to lose my life just for a fling with you." And so the woman tried to resist the man's approaches, but finally she gave in to his persuasions.

When the sun had set and night fell, they rented a cottage nearby for the night. They slept together and exchanged love again and again, all night long. At the break of day, before leaving, the woman said, "No doubt I will lose my life because of you. So I ask this of you: please write out a copy of the *Lotus Sutra* for me, dedicate it, and have memorial services carried out for my future life." The man replied, "It is only natural for a man and woman to make love. What makes you say you will surely die? But if you should die, I promise I will make a copy of the *Lotus Sutra* and dedicate it for you." The woman said, "If you wish to find out whether I really die or not, go to the Butokuden Hall tomorrow morning and look. There you will find proof." And on saying this, she took the man's fan and departed in tears. Not quite believing what she had said, the man walked off and returned home.

The following morning, wondering if what the woman had said would prove true, the man went to Butokuden Hall and looked around. A gray-haired old woman came along, crying bitterly and looked at him. The man asked her, "Who are you, and why are you crying?" In reply the old woman said, "I am the mother of the woman you saw by the Shujaku Gate last night. She has already passed away. I am here to tell you of it. The dead one is lying right over there." Pointing to the spot with her finger, she vanished instantly.

The man thought this very strange and so he went closer. There, in the courtyard, he saw a young fox lying dead, with a fan covering its face. The fan was the very one he had held the previous night. Gazing at it, he thought, "The woman I saw last night was this fox—and I had intercourse with it." And thus, he realized what he had done. Filled with emotions of pity and strangeness, he went on his way back home.

From that day, he copied out the first part of the *Lotus Sutra*, and once every week he had memorial rites performed for the woman's future life. When the forty-ninth day after her death approached, the woman appeared before the man in a dream. She was dressed as a heavenly maiden and surrounded by thousands of other women, similarly attired. She said to the man, "Since you have saved me by honoring the *Lotus Sutra*, I was able to be absolved from my sins forever and now I have been reborn in Tori Heaven. Your kindness is immeasurable. I shall never forget this, ever." And on saying this, the woman rose up into the sky. During that time, exquisite music sounded from the heavens. Then the man awoke from his dream. With a feeling of exalted wonder, he rededicated his faith in honoring the *Lotus Sutra*.

The man's heart was uncommonly magnanimous. For even though the woman had clearly stated her last wishes, it was admirable that he kept his word and performed memorial services for her future life. Surely, the two must have remained close friends in eternity in the sphere of the Buddha since departing from their previous lives.

It is said that the man told this story to others. And so this is how the story came to be handed down to us.

Vol. 14, Tale 5

16

A Nun Who Was the Mother of the High Priest Genshin Goes to Heaven

In olden times, there was a high priest named Genshin who lived in Yokawa Temple. Originally from Kazurakinoshimo County in Yamato Province, he went off to Mt. Hiei to become a monk when he was still very young. Genshin studied very diligently and eventually he became an excellent learned priest. And so, one day he was invited to attend a series of eight lectures on the *Lotus Sutra* sponsored by the Dowager Empress Sanjo. After attending the eight lectures, he was presented with some gifts by the empress. Some of these gifts he sent to his mother in his native province of Yamato with a message saying, "The empress bestowed some gifts on me after I attended eight lectures. Since this is the first time I have been presented gifts, I thought I would send some of them to you."

His mother wrote in reply, "I am happy to receive the things you sent and happy to know that you have become such an excellent, learned monk. That, however, was not my true hope when I sent you off to become a monk. Now I see that you are going about and doing things such as attending those eight lectures. You may find it fitting to do so, but I feel rather differently about it. I have many daughters, but only one son. Even before you celebrated your coming of age, I let you enter the temple on Mt. Hiei. I had hoped you would attain great learning and become as great as the saint of Ta-muno Peak, and that you might even save me in my life to come. It was not my hope that you should be going about ostentatiously as a famous priest. I am now an old woman and I've been hoping I might see you become a saint while I'm still alive, and then I might die with my heart at peace."

When Genshin opened and read this letter, his eyes filled with tears. Sobbing profusely, he wrote in reply, "I have no ambition to become a famous priest. It is just that I wanted to let you know that I had heard the eight lectures attended by the members of the imperial family. It pains me to receive such a message from you, yet at the same time, I feel so grateful. Therefore, I will seclude myself in the mountains and train myself, following your advice. And when you can say, 'Now that my son has become a saint, I would like to see him,' I will come down and see you. Otherwise, I will never come down from the mountain. Truly, you are both my mother and my best teacher." To this, his mother wrote in reply, "Now I feel relieved and can look toward the other world with ease. I am so very, very happy. Please do not neglect your religious practices." He looked at the letter again and then tucked it in among his Buddhist scriptures. From time to time, he looked at it and again broke into tears.

Genshin secluded himself in the mountain temple for six years and then, in the spring of the seventh year, he wrote to his mother. "I have been here in the mountains for six years. It has been so long since we have met, I wonder if you might be wishing to see me. If that is so, I would like to see you, even for just a short time." In reply she wrote, "I too would very much like to see you, but do you think that sin will diminish if we were to meet? I will be happier to hear that you are still secluding yourself in the mountains. Unless I ask you first to come to see me, please don't come down from the mountain." Looking at the letter, Genshin thought to himself, "This nun, my mother, is truly an extraordinary woman. No other mother in the world could say such a thing."

And so, in time, nine years came to pass. Then one day, for some reason, although his mother had previously written, "Unless I ask you first to come to see me, please don't come down from the mountain," Genshin suddenly felt pangs of loneliness and longed to see his mother. He thought deeply to himself, "My mother might pass away soon—and I too might even die soon." In the midst of this sadness, he decided, "Even though she told me not to go to see her, I must go now anyway." And so he set out on a journey. When he reached Yamato Province, he met a man carrying a letter. The high priest asked the man, "Where are you going?" The man answered, "I'm carrying a letter from a nun to her son, the high priest in Yokawa Temple." He replied, "That person could only be me." And so, still seated on his horse, Genshin took the letter and opened it.

Genshin saw that the handwriting was so weak it hardly looked like his mother's. He felt a lump in his throat as he read it and wondered, "What could have happened?" The letter read, "I have been quite well, but now I'm afraid I have caught a cold and I have been feeling weak for the past few days; perhaps it's because of my age. Although I told you firmly not to come to see me unless I should ask you, now that the end of my life is closing in, I feel terribly afraid that I might die before seeing you again. I long to see you, so would you please come quickly to see me now."

As he read the letter Genshin thought, "Somehow the uneasiness in my heart must have been because of my mother's condition. Truly the bonds between a parent and child are special, and my mother's faith has been so deep that she strongly urged me to continue training myself in the Way of the Buddha. This is why she must have felt this way." As he contemplated these things, his tears fell like rain. Genshin had several student clerics traveling with him. He said to them, "This must all be a presentiment." And so they spurred their horses on, to the effect that they arrived by nightfall. Rushing to her side, Genshin found that his mother was terribly weak and in critical condition.

"Mother, I am here," Genshin announced loudly. His mother answered, "How could you have arrived so soon? It was only at dawn that I sent out a messenger." He replied, "Your condition must have prompted me to think of you these past days, so I was already on my way when I happened to meet your messenger." Hearing this, Genshin's mother said in a faint voice, "How happy I am! I was afraid I might not be able to see you in my dying hour, but now I am seeing you like this. Our relation must have been wonderfully close since our former life." Genshin asked, "Did you chant the prayer to Amitabha?" His mother replied, "In my heart I wished to do so, but I was too weak, and there was no one to help me." Then Genshin told her wonderful stories and urged her to chant the prayer to Amitabha. His mother, the nun, was profoundly inspired and she chanted the prayer to Amitabha hundreds of times. While she was doing so, she breathed her last at dawn, as if fading away.

Genshin reflected, "If I hadn't come, my mother would not have passed away in this way. Our relation as mother and son has been so close, and my coming here and urging her to chant the prayer has inspired her religious spirit. Since she passed away chanting the prayer to Amitabha, I am sure she has gone to Paradise. What is more, she met her death so nobly, by virtue of her good heart. And that has also led me to the Way of the Buddha. In this way, mother and I have given the very best guidance and we have led each other to the Way of the Buddha." In tears, Genshin, the high priest, returned to the temple of Yokawa.

Hearing this story, the other high priests at Yokawa were deeply moved by the wonderful relation between the mother and her son. They broke into tears, for they were profoundly touched. Such then is the story as it has been handed down.

Vol. 15, Tale 39

17

A County Administrator of Tamba Province Has a Statue of Kannon Made

In olden times, there lived a county administrator in Kuwata County of Tamba Province. He had been thinking of having a statue of Kannon made to fulfill a long-standing wish, and so he went to Kyoto to commission a sculptor of Buddhist figures to make him the statue. He had prepared the sculptor's expenses and he spoke with him earnestly. The sculptor accepted his request and received the payment. The county administrator was pleased and returned home.

The sculptor was a kindhearted man who earned his living by making statues of the Buddha and, since childhood, he had cherished the chapter on Kannon in the *Lotus Sutra*. He read its thirty-three verses every day without fail. Furthermore, on the eighteenth day of every month, he faithfully held a service in honor of Kannon and he also followed the dietary proscriptions.

As it turned out, the sculptor was able to complete the statue in just three months after receiving the order—much sooner than the county administrator had expected. He created a most beautiful statue of Kannon and delivered it to the administrator's house. It was common for a sculptor to finish his work much later than the appointed time, even if the expenses had been paid in advance. But in this case, not only was the statue finished so unexpectedly soon, but also it was beautifully done, just as the administrator had hoped. Extremely pleased, he thought, "What kind of extra reward should I give this sculptor?" But he was not so well off and he had almost nothing he could offer. All he had was a horse. It was a black one, about five or six years old, with a gentle nature and strong legs. It walked well and ran fast on the roads. It neither scared nor tired easily. When people saw it, they all wished they could own it, but the county administrator considered it his priceless asset and he had taken care of it for many years. But as he was so pleased with the splendid work of the sculptor, he decided to give it to him. And so he brought the horse out and presented it. The sculptor was very happy to receive the horse. He placed a saddle on it and rode off, leaving the county administrator's house for his home in Kyoto. He had his assistant take the horse he had ridden when they came.

The county administrator had always cared for the horse and had kept it close. Now, when he looked at the grass scattered about the stable, he fondly remembered the horse and missed it dearly. His regret at having given the horse away was indescribable. He could not bear his regret even a moment longer and he couldn't remain still, so he told one of his close assistants, "Although I gave away my horse to reward the sculptor for his wonderful work, now I deeply regret it. If you can understand my feelings, won't you help me get it back? Pretend you're a robber, shoot the sculptor, and then bring the horse back to me." His assistant replied, "I should be able to take care of that quite easily, sir." So he took a bow and some arrows and rode off on a horse.

Since the sculptor was traveling by the main roadway, the administrator's man took a shortcut and went ahead to a place called Shinomura, where he waited in ambush in a chestnut grove. A while later, the sculptor came riding along on the horse. Although the administrator's man's first thought was, "How can I do such a wicked thing?" he could not refuse the order of his master, on whom he had been relying. So he put a sharpened arrow to his bow, had his horse charge directly toward the sculptor, bent the bow powerfully, and then shot the arrow from a distance of about forty feet. How could he miss his target from such a distance? The arrow struck above the sculptor's navel and the arrowhead was visible where it emerged from his back. The sculptor fell on his back, along with the arrow. His horse ran free, so the administrator's man chased after it, caught it, and took it back to his master. The administrator was overjoyed to see his horse. He tied it close to him and stroked it with affection.

After that, several days passed, but no inquiry came from the sculptor's home. Wondering about the situation, the county administrator sent his man to the sculptor's home, instructing him to ask, "How is the sculptor doing? As my master has been out of touch for some time, he is wondering about him." So the county administrator's man left for Kyoto and went to the sculptor's house, quite unconcernedly. The sculptor's house was set back from the street and there was a plum tree in front of it. The horse was tied to the tree, and two men were giving it fodder and rubbing it affectionately. The sculptor was sitting on the porch, looking at the horse. The horse looked even glossier and more robust than before. Looking at the scene, the assistant was terribly astonished. There was the sculptor he thought he had killed, and there, too, was the horse he thought he had taken to his master. He doubted what he was seeing and so he stood there looking carefully at them. Certainly, the sculptor was there, and so was the horse. He was completely dumbfounded and his mind was troubled. Though he felt terribly apprehensive, he asked the sculptor what his master had instructed him to say. The sculptor replied, "Well, I've been fine. Many people would like to buy the horse, but it's such a wonderful one I'm going to keep it for myself."

The county administrator's man thought this was very mysterious, and so he ran back to his master as fast as he could to tell him of what he had seen. Hearing it, the administrator, too, thought it strange and so he went out to the stable—only to discover that the horse was gone! He felt afraid and went to the statue of Kannon so that he might repent. When he looked at the statue of Kannon, he saw that an arrow was sticking out from Kannon's chest, and from it blood was flowing. He called his assistant immediately and showed him. They both prostrated themselves on the ground and wept on and on. After that, they both cut off their topknots and became monks. They went off to a mountain temple and trained themselves in the Way of the Buddha.

The scar left by the arrow on the statue of Kannon has never healed, even to this day. People come to see and admire it. As the sculptor was a merciful person, Kannon took the arrow on his behalf, as she had previously vowed. This was truly a wondrous thing.

It is said that this is a Kannon that all thoughtful people should visit and worship. And such then is the story as it has been handed down.

Vol. 16, Tale 5

18

A Man from Michinoku Province, Who Catches Hawks' Chicks, Is Saved by Kannon

In olden times, in Michinoku Province, there was a man who earned his living by catching the chicks of hawks. He took them from their nests and then sold them to falconers who raised them for their work. For years, he had searched for the spots where hawks built their nests and he had taken their chicks. As a result, the mother hawk must have been very disturbed and so she didn't build a nest in the same tree again. Instead, she found a place that no human being would be able to reach. There she built a nest and laid her eggs. Beside it was a steep precipice, and below it was a rocky shore, bordered by the bottomless sea. Far beneath the top of the precipice was a tree that hung out over the great sea. The hawk laid her eggs in a nest in this tree. No human being could get near it.

When the season for catching hawk chicks came around, the hawk chick catcher went to the tree where the hawk used to build her nests. But how could he have found a nest this time? And indeed, there was no sign there of a nest having been built. The hawk chick catcher felt terribly disappointed at not finding a nest, and so he scurried around, and looked some more, but it was in vain. "I wonder," he thought, "has the mother hawk died or has she built a nest somewhere else?" So he searched all around the mountains, every day. At last he spotted a new nest, far off in the distance. Eagerly, he climbed closer and looked with a glad heart, but finally he realized that the nest could not be reached. If he were to go down from the top, it was right by the perpendicular cliff. If he were to climb up from the bottom, there was the rocky shore by the bottomless sea. Even if he could locate the nest, he would not be able to reach it. The hawk chick catcher was afraid he would no longer be able to make a living.

So the hawk chick catcher told his neighbor about it and complained, "I used to catch the chicks of hawks, and sell them to the falconers, and earn enough money for the year. But this year, the hawks built their nest in such a dangerous place that I'll have no way to get any chicks." Then his neighbor suggested, "Perhaps we could work out a good plan such that you might be able to catch some." So they both went to the place where the nest was located. When he saw it, the neighbor suggested, "We can set a large stake at the top of the cliff, tie a rope several hundred meters long to it, attach a big basket at the end of the rope, and then you can sit in the basket. I'll lower you down to the nest and you can catch the chicks."

The hawk chick catcher was very pleased to hear this suggestion and he went home happily to get a basket, a rope, and a big stake. Together, they went to the spot above the nest. As planned, they drove in the stake, tied the rope, attached the basket to the rope, and the hawk chick catcher climbed into the basket. Then his neighbor lowered the rope and basket to the nest far below. The hawk chick catcher got out of the basket, positioned himself by the nest, caught the chicks, tied their wings with string, and then put them in the basket. He had his neighbor lift the chicks in the basket while he remained below. He planned to go up next when the basket came down again, but although his neighbor lifted the basket and took the chicks, he didn't lower the basket again for the hawk chick catcher. He just left him there and returned home. He went to the hawk chick catcher's home and said to his wife and children, "When I was lowering your husband in the basket, the rope broke and he fell into the sea and died." Hearing this, the wife and children cried inconsolably.

The hawk chick catcher remained by the nest, waiting for the basket that would lift him back up. He waited, expecting that it would come down any minute, but several days passed and the basket never came. The spot was so narrow that if he moved even a little from the hollow of the rock he would fall into the sea far below. He had nothing to do but wait for death. But, although the hawk chick catcher had committed sins for many years, he had been reading the chapter on Kannon in the *Lotus Sutra* on the eighteenth day of every month. Now he prayed, "For many years I caught the chicks of hawks that flew in the sky, tied their legs with string, and then sold them, and let them catch other birds. For this sin I have received retribution and now I am about to die. But please, merciful Kannon, do not let me fall into the River of Three Crossings. Please receive me into the Pure Land by virtue of my worshiping you over the years."

As he prayed in this way, a large poisonous snake with eyes like iron bowls emerged from the sea, licked its lips, and crept up the cliff. As it seemed about to swallow him, the hawk chick catcher thought, "I would rather fall into the sea than be swallowed by this snake." And as he was thinking this he drew his sword and stuck it into the head of the snake, just as it was about to attack him. Surprised, the snake continued creeping up the cliff. Sitting astride the snake, the man easily rode it to the cliff's top. Then, in an instant, the snake vanished.

At that moment he thought, "Kannon must have transformed herself into that snake and rescued me." In tears, he praised Kannon and then returned home. As he hadn't eaten anything for several days, he was weak, and starved, and he was barely able to walk home. When he arrived and stood by the doorway, he saw that the door was posted with a sign that read "In Mourning," and so he guessed that his family must be holding a memorial service on the seventh day after his death. He knocked on the door, opened it, and entered. His wife and children were overcome with joy, seeing him safely returned. After that he told them all about what he had experienced.

Some days later, the eighteenth day of the month arrived, and so he bathed himself to make himself completely clean. He opened the sutra box to chant the chapter on Kannon in the *Lotus Sutra*. There he found a sword stuck in the scroll of the sutra. It was the same sword he had stuck into the snake's head at the hawk's nest. Realizing that the chapter on Kannon had rescued him by transforming itself into a snake, he felt an immeasurable sense of gratitude. Immediately, he was inspired with religion. He cut off his topknot and became a monk. After that, he trained himself in the Way of the Buddha ever more devoutly and he renounced his evil ways.

People living near and far heard about his story and all were deeply moved. But how ashamed his neighbor must have been! And yet the hawk chick catcher didn't bear any grudge toward him. Kannon works her miracles in such wonderful ways. It has been said that all those throughout the world who hear this story should pray to Kannon with all their hearts. And such then is the story as it has been handed down to us.

Vol. 16, Tale 6

19

A Believer in Kannon Goes to the Dragon's Palace and Returns Rich

In olden times, there was a young man who lived in Kyoto. His name has not been recorded, but he must have been a samurai. He was poor and he faced difficulties in making ends meet. Nonetheless, this man took his meals religiously at the appointed hours on the eighteenth day of every month and he worshiped Kannon devoutly. On those days he visited hundreds of temples and worshiped the Buddha.

Living in this manner for many years, he continued visiting temples on the holy day of September eighteenth, as ever. In those days there were not so many temples, and it so happened that on one of these occasions, as he was passing through Minami Yamashina, he met a man about fifty years old on the road in a remote, place deep in the mountains. The man had something hanging from the end of his stick. Wondering what it was, the young man looked and saw that it was a small spotted snake, about one foot long. As he passed by, he noticed the small snake moving. He asked the man with the snake, "Where are you going?" The man replied, "I'm headed for Kyoto. And, if I may ask, what about yourself?" The young man answered, "I'm on my way to visit temples and worship the Buddha. And, if I may ask, what are you going to do with that snake?" The man with the snake replied, "I use snakes in my work, so I caught it and I'm taking it with me." The young man asked, "Would you please give me that snake? It's a sin to kill living things. Please let it go today, for the sake of Kannon." The man with the snake said, "Kannon grants her blessings to human beings, too. Since I have a use for snakes, I caught it and I'm taking it with me. I don't particularly wish to kill living things, but we human beings have to use various means to earn our living in the world."

The young man continued, "What are you going to do with it, anyway?" The man with the snake replied, "I have been making maces for monks for many years. To straighten a cow's horn to make a mace, I use the fat of such small snakes. Therefore, I caught this one for such use." The young man asked, "What do you do with the maces?" The man with the snake replied, "Why are you asking such foolish questions? I make maces and sell them to those who need them, and that supports me to buy my clothes and food." The young man said, "I see that you can't help doing that for your living. But I'm not asking you to give me the snake for nothing. I'll offer any of the clothes I'm wearing in exchange for the snake." The man with the snake asked, "Which of your clothes will you give me?" The young man replied, "Whichever you like—the upper garment or the pleated trousers—you can have your choice." The man with the snake said, "I don't want either." Then the young man said, "Well then, you may take this quilted kimono I'm wearing." The man with the snake replied, "All right then, I'll take it." So the young man took off his quilted kimono and handed it to the other man. He took the kimono, gave the snake to the young man, and was about to leave, but the young man asked, "Where did you get that snake?" The man answered, "I got it at the small pond over there," and walked away.

After that, the young man took the snake to the pond, looked for a suitable place, and released the snake in a cool spot. The snake slipped off into the water. After making sure it had gotten away safely, he walked toward a temple. When he had gone about two hundred yards, he met a pretty young maiden, about twelve or thirteen years in age, dressed in lovely clothes. The man thought it strange to find her in such a remote mountain place, but the maiden said, "I was deeply touched by your kind heart and so I came here to express my gratitude." The man replied, "For what reason do you feel grateful to me?" The maiden said, "Since you saved my life, I told my parents about it and they said to me, 'Go and welcome him, quickly. We must express our gratitude to him.' And so I've come to welcome you."

The man thought this maiden must have been the snake and so he felt sorry for her, yet he also felt afraid. He asked her, "Where are your parents?" She answered, "Over there. I'll take you there," and so she led him toward the pond. He was so afraid that he wanted to run away, but the maiden said insistently, "We will never do any harm to you." And so he followed her to the pond, though with reluctance. The maiden said, "Please, would you wait here for a while. I'll go and let my parents know of your coming, and then I'll be back." Suddenly, she vanished. While the man was standing by the pond, filled with apprehension, the maiden reappeared and said, "Now I'll take you there. Please close your eyes and go to sleep." He did as he was told, and while trying to look like he was asleep she said, "Now open your eyes." So he opened his eyes and saw a beautifully decorated gate—one far beyond compare with any castle in our country. The maiden continued, "Would you please wait here for a moment. I'll go and tell my parents," and then she went inside the gate. After a short while she returned and said, "Please follow me." So he followed her, still feeling apprehensive, and then he saw many splendid buildings standing side by side, all built with seven precious stones and shining in perfect resplendence. When he came to the main part of the palace, he saw a central hall, decorated with various precious stones and beautiful drapes, all sparkling brilliantly.

"This must be Paradise," he thought. After a short while, a dignified-looking man, about sixty years old, handsomely attired and with long sideburns, appeared and said, "Now, would you step up here, please." The young man wondered to whom the man was speaking, but then he realized it was he, himself, who was being addressed. The young man said, "I am most grateful to you, but could you please tell me what reason you have for requesting me to be here?" The older man replied, "Why are you here, you ask? Come now, you must realize that we have reasons for meeting and welcoming you. Please, come up immediately." So the young man went up the steps, struck with awe. The older man continued, "We are deeply impressed by your kind heart and we are very grateful to you. We have welcomed you here to express our gratitude." The young man replied, "Could you please tell me what you are talking about?" The older man spoke again, "There are no people who do not love their children. We have many children, and today our daughter, the youngest of our children, went to the pond nearby to play. We told her strongly not to go, but she wouldn't listen, so we just let her go and play. Later, our daughter came back and said, 'Today I was caught by a man and he was going to kill me, but another man came along and saved my life.' Therefore, we are extremely grateful to you and so we welcomed you to express our profound gratitude."

Hearing this, the young man realized that the man must be the father of the snake. When the older man called his followers, several dignified-looking men appeared. He said to them, "Serve this guest with the utmost care." They brought out delicious food and set it before him. The older man ate some of the food and then asked the young man to help himself. He still didn't feel quite at ease, but he ate the food. Its delicious taste was indescribable. When they were clearing the table, the head of the palace said, "I am the Dragon King. I have lived here for a very long time. To repay your kindness, I would even like to offer you a magic ball that can grant you whatever you wish. But since we know the people in Japan are wicked, I'm afraid they couldn't be trusted with it for long." Then he said to his men, "Bring me that box over there," and so they brought him a lacquered box. They opened it, and inside there was a lump of gold—about three and a half inches thick. The older man took it out of the box and broke it into two. He placed one half back into the box and gave the other half to the young man, saying, "Don't spend this all at once. If you use it by breaking it off bit by bit, according to your needs, you will never be in want, all your life." Thereupon, the young man accepted the piece and placed it inside his kimono.

Then the young man announced, "Now I must be going," and the maiden who had brought him there came to him and led him back to the gate he had passed through earlier and said, "Please go to sleep again, as before." While he was sleeping, they reached the side of the pond. The maiden said, "I have brought you back to this place. Please return home from here now. I will never forget my gratitude to you." And then she vanished in a flash.

When the man returned home, people asked him, "Why didn't you come back for such a long time?" He thought it had been just a short time, but, in fact, many days had passed. After that, he kept the broken half of the gold lump in secret, never telling others anything about it. By breaking it off little by little, just to get what he needed, he was never in want. He was rich in everything and he became well off. No matter how often he broke off pieces from the end, the gold resumed its original shape. He remained wealthy throughout his life and he continued to worship Kannon, as devoutly as ever. When he passed away the lump of gold vanished too. His children could not inherit it.

As the man had worshiped Kannon earnestly, he was able to see the Palace of the Dragon King, and obtain the lump of gold, and become a rich man. When it was that this took place, no one knows for sure, but such is the story as it has been handed down to us.

Vol.16, Tale 15

20

A Woman from Yamashiro Province Is Saved from the Danger of a Snake by the Grace of Kannon

In olden times, there was a man who lived with his daughter in Kuze County of Yamashiro Province. His daughter started to read the chapter on Kannon in the *Lotus Sutra* when she was seven years old. On the eighteenth day of every month she devoted herself especially to her religious practices and chanted the prayer to Kannon. When she was twelve, she had finished memorizing one volume of the *Lotus Sutra*. Although young, she was merciful, compassionate, and had no wickedness in her heart.

One day, when she was out walking around, she met a man carrying a crab, all tied up. The woman asked the man, "What are you going to do with that crab?" The man with the crab told her, "I'm going to eat it." The woman pleaded, "Won't you give me that crab? If you need food, we have plenty of fish at our house. I'll give you some fish in exchange for the crab." And so, the man accepted the woman's request and gave her the crab. The woman took the crab, went to the river, and set it free.

Some time later, when the woman's father was out working in their rice field, a poisonous snake came along and was about to swallow a frog. Seeing this, the father felt sorry for the frog and said to the snake, "Please set the frog free. If you follow my request and set the frog free I'll let you marry my daughter." He said this quite carelessly, on the spur of the moment. Hearing this, the snake looked at the man's face, released the frog, and crept off into the bushes. The man reflected on what he had said and sorely regretted it. He couldn't even eat. His wife and daughter said to him, "Why aren't you eating? You look worried about something." The man replied, "I'll tell you the truth. I saw a snake about to eat a frog and so, on the spur of the moment, I said to the snake, 'If you let that frog go free, I'll let you marry my daughter.' Now I regret it deeply." But his daughter said, "Please eat your meal. You needn't worry about it." And so the man ate, following his daughter's assurance, and he stopped worrying about what he had said.

That night, around ten o'clock, someone knocked on the door. The man, worried, said to his daughter, "Oh no, that must be the snake." The daughter said to her father, "Tell him to come back in three days." When the woman's father opened the door and looked out, there he saw a man dressed like a nobleman of the fifth rank. The man said, "I have come according to the promise you made this morning." The woman's father replied, "Would you please come back in three days." Hearing this, the nobleman of the fifth rank left.

After that, the daughter had a storage barn built with thick boards and had it securely enclosed. On the evening of the third day, she entered the storage barn, closed the door tightly, and said to her father, "When the snake comes and knocks on the door tonight, please open it quickly. I will pray earnestly to Kannon to save me." And after saying this, she confined herself in the storage barn.

Around ten at night, the nobleman of the fifth rank came and knocked on the door. The door opened. When he saw that the woman had confined herself in the storage barn, he grew furious and resumed his former shape as a snake. It encircled the storage barn and pounded on the door with its tail. The woman's parents were scared to death watching it. At midnight, the knocking sound ceased. At that time, a crying call from the snake was heard. Then it too ceased. When they looked at the place at dawn, a large crab—the leader—and tens of thousands of smaller crabs were swarming all around the snake and they gnawed it to death. Then all the crabs crept away.

The woman opened the door of the storage barn and said to her father, "While I was reciting the chapter on Kannon through the night, a handsome priest came and said to me, 'Fear not. Just rely on the prayer and let the power of your prayer to Kannon banish the poison gas and the fire from the poison snakes and the scorpions and all.' It was the protection of Kannon that saved me from the danger." Hearing this, her parents were indescribably happy.

After that, they buried the dead snake and built a temple there. They erected a statue of the Buddha and made a copy of the *Lotus Sutra*, and they kept it there to save the snake from further agonies and to save the crabs that had killed the snake. The temple was named Kanimata Temple, which means "temple full of crabs," and it still exists today, but people now call it Kamihata Temple, for easier pronunciation. They don't know the real story behind it. "Kani" means "crab," while "kami" means "paper." When we think of it, we can realize that the young woman of that house was not just a usual human being. It is said that people throughout the world were deeply impressed by the miraculous power shown by Kannon. And such then is the story that has been handed down to us.

Vol.16, Tale 16

21

Kaya no Yoshifuji of Bitchu Province Marries a Fox and Is Saved by Kannon

In olden times, there lived a man named Kaya no Yoshifuji in Ashimori Village of Kaya County, Bitchu Province. Yoshifuji had made a fortune from the business of moneylending. He was profligate by nature and known for his amorous affairs.

In the autumn of 896, while his wife was away in Kyoto, he remained at home—a temporary widower, so to speak. One evening, while out strolling, he spotted a beautiful young woman he had never seen before. Roused with carnal desire he approached her and set out to make her his conquest. The woman looked as if she were about to escape, so he walked up and took her hand and said, "May I ask who you are?"

The woman, dressed very attractively, replied, "I am no one at all." This she said most charmingly. Yoshifuji then asked her, "Won't you please come to my place?" The woman replied, "I'm afraid that wouldn't be proper," and she seemed to be getting away. "Well then, where is your house?" he asked, "I'll go along with you." "It's right over there," she replied and walked on. Yoshifuji walked along with her, holding her hand.

Not far away was a beautiful house. On taking a closer look, he could tell that it was well constructed and finely appointed inside. "Strange," thought Yoshifuji, "I can't recall ever having seen such a place before." Inside the house, there were men and women of different ranks, all scurrying about. "Our young lady has returned," they announced. "Well then, she must be the family's daughter," thought Yoshifuji. And so, happily, he proceeded to spend the night with her.

The next morning, a man who appeared to be the master of the house came and said to Yoshifuji, "You must have come here directed by some bond of fate determined by a previous life. Now, by all means, you must stay with us." The man welcomed him most cordially. Yoshifuji had fallen completely in love with the young woman and vowed to stay with her forever. He remained by her side all the time and he completely forgot about his own house and children.

Back at his home, when Yoshifuji didn't return home in the evening, the people there thought, "Looks like he must be off spending time with a woman, as usual." When night came, and he still hadn't returned, some grew angry. "Enough of this. We'll have to go looking for him." But since it was past midnight, much as they searched the neighborhood, they couldn't find hide nor hair of him. "He couldn't have gone too far, since his traveling outfit is still here. He went off in casual wear," they said. And while they were still making a great fuss like this, the dawn broke. They had searched for him in every imaginable place he could have gone, but still, they couldn't find him. "If he were young, he might have gone off and renounced the world and become a monk, or jumped off a cliff, or something like that. But knowing him, this is just strange."

In the meantime, in his new household, the young woman became pregnant and easily gave birth to a child at full term. And so the relation between the two grew ever deeper. Months and years seemed to flow by, fulfilling all their wishes.

Back at his own house, people continued to search for Yoshifuji, including his elder brother Toyonaka, who was the county mayor; his two younger brothers Toyokage, who was a county official; Toyotsune, who was the priest of Kibitsuhiko Shrine; and Yoshifuji's son Tadasada. Lamenting Yoshifuji's disappearance, they thought, "At least we should find his body." As Yoshifuji's brothers were wealthy, they vowed to make a statue of the eleven-faced Kannon. So they cut down a yew tree and carved out a statue the same size as Yoshifuji. They bowed to it and prayed, "Please, at least let us see his dead body." Ever since the day he disappeared, they said prayers and read a sutra, praying for Yoshifuji and hoping to assist him in his future life.

In the meantime, at the place where Yoshifuji was staying, a strange man suddenly appeared, carrying a stick. The master of the house and all the other men and women were terribly frightened by his appearance and they all ran away, terrified. Then the man jabbed at Yoshifuji's back with the stick and shoved him out of the house through a narrow passage.

Around that time, on the evening of the thirteenth day after his disappearance, the people at Yoshifuji's home were reminiscing about him sorrowfully. "What a strange way he vanished," they said, "and it was just about this hour." And then, from under the storehouse in front, a dark-looking thing, something like a monkey, crept out with its rear end lifted up. "What's that!" they all exclaimed. "It's me," the thing replied, and its voice was exactly like that of Yoshifuji. His son Tadasada, thinking this most strange since the voice was truly his father's, demanded, "What's all this about?" He jumped down to the ground and pulled the creature up.

"Back when I was living alone, I always longed for women. Then, quite unexpectedly, I became the husband of a noble woman and lived with her for many years. Since then, we've had a son. He's very handsome, and I hold him in my arms all the time, morning and evening. I regard him as my first son and heir. Tadasada, you now come after him. It's because I love his mother so." Hearing this, Tadasada asked, "And so, where is this son of yours?" Yoshifuji replied, "He's over there," pointing toward the storehouse.

When Tadasada and all the other people of the household heard this, they were astonished. When they looked at Yoshifuji, they saw he had grown terribly thin, like a very sick man. When they looked at his kimono, it was the one he had worn when he disappeared. When they searched under the storehouse, they found many foxes, all scattering and running away. That was the place where Yoshifuji had lived. Looking at it, they finally realized that Yoshifuji had been bewitched by a fox, married it, and lost his sanity—and that was why he was saying such crazy things.

So they called on a prominent priest and asked him to recite prayers for him. They also invited a yin-yang diviner and had him conduct a purification ceremony. They had him bathe over and over again, but still he did not return to his former appearance. After that, gradually he regained his sanity. He was terribly ashamed of himself and felt it all most strange.

Yoshifuji had been under the storehouse for thirteen days, but to him it seemed as if it had been thirteen years. Furthermore, the space between the ground and the beam supporting the storehouse was barely six inches high, though Yoshifuji had thought it amply high and wide and thought the storehouse was spacious enough to go in and out of easily, as if it were a big mansion. All of this was owing to the witchcraft of the foxes. And as for the layman who came along with a stick, he was the transformed figure of the Kannon, who had been made for his well-being.

And so we can see that people throughout the world should worship Kannon with all their hearts. After that, Yoshifuji remained in health for more than ten years and he died at the age of sixty-one.

It has been said that this story was told by Miyoshi no Kiyo-tsura, who was then the governor of Bitchu Province. Such then is the story as it has been handed down to us.

Vol. 16, Tale 17

The Kannon of Ishiyama Temple Helps a Man Compose a Tanka Poem

In olden times, there was a mayor of Ikago County in Ohmi Province who was married to a young and beautiful wife. She was also very sensible and more talented in the arts than any other. And so, one provincial governor after another fell in love with her and tried to win her affections. Though they tried mightily, she was very chaste and she vowed never to give her love to any other man but her husband, no matter how wonderful the person might be. She would not answer letters from even the governor of the province.

In the meantime, a certain governor assumed the post and started to rule the province. When he heard of this beautiful woman, his desire to win her was stronger than that of any previous governor. But he couldn't just say to her husband, "Give me your wife." Nor did he try sending her love letters, because he knew his predecessors had all been rejected. He tried to think of all sorts of schemes, until finally he hit on an idea. He summoned the county mayor, sending the message, "Report to the governor's office, for there is urgent business." The county mayor rushed to the governor's office, wondering what sort of business it could be. The governor said to the mayor, "Come forward." Feeling quite apprehensive, the mayor knelt on the floor respectfully.

The governor continued, "Of all the people in our province, you are the most knowledgeable. Therefore, I have summoned you here to ask you about things past and present." The man felt quite relieved, finding he had not been summoned to be punished for something he had done. While he was telling the governor about things of the past the governor said to him, "Have some of this," and offered him sake freely.

When the man had grown more relaxed, the governor confided, "Actually, I have something to ask of you. Would you kindly listen to me?" The county mayor replied, "How could I object to the governor's request?" In turn the governor said, "I'd like to propose that you and I have a contest. I suggest that you put all your efforts into it, without any restraint. If you win, I'll let you govern half the province. If I win, I will get your wife, no matter how sad you might feel about it." The county mayor replied humbly, "How could I ever hope to be the victor over the governor in a contest? Even so, could you please tell me what this is about?" He was trembling. Then the governor said, "It is by no means definitely decided that you will lose the game. You might win. You can never predict the outcome of a game."

The county mayor thought to himself, "I can't expect to defeat the governor, yet I could never give away my wife, whom I've loved so deeply for all these years. Even so, what can I say now?" Then the governor had an inkstone brought to him and he wrote something. On finishing it, he had it sealed in an envelope and had a seal affixed to it. He had this placed in a letterbox and had a seal stamped on the box as well. He said to one of his men, "Give this to him," and then said to the county mayor, "You must not open it now. In it is the first part of a tanka poem. Even though you don't know what the first part of this tanka poem says, you must complete it by adding an appropriate ending that has the same sentiment. So take this home and bring it back within seven days from today. If you can bring back an appropriately completed poem, you will win and you will receive half of the province. If you commit a fault in completing the tanka poem, your wife will be mine."

Utterly confounded by the proposal, the county mayor returned home. He looked very sad indeed. Wondering what was the matter, his wife asked, "What business was it that summoned you to the governor's office?" As he continued to look so deeply depressed, she worried greatly and asked, "What was it that happened there?" He did not answer for a long time, but in tears kept on looking at his wife. Seeing her husband in this state, the woman, now terribly alarmed, asked again, "Won't you tell me what happened at the governor's office?" Hesitantly, the husband said, "I've never left your side all these years and I have loved you with all my heart. But now, I am sorry, I have only several more days to see you." His wife replied, "This is so strange. You must tell me more about it." Through his tears the husband said, "The governor ordered me to complete a tanka poem I've never read by adding an ending part. I can never hope to supply a second part to such a poem within seven days. I have no doubt I'll lose the game and I'll have to part with you soon."

His wife responded, "This may be beyond the power of humans, but I'm sure that Buddha can grant requests to humans, and Kannon, especially, pities all beings just like her own children. Therefore, you must make a visit to the Kannon of Ishiyama Temple in our province and ask for her blessing." She continued, "You must stop eating fish and meat today and come back seven days from today." And so she saw that her husband refrained from eating those things.

All the members of the house purified their bodies and minds, and on the third day the husband went to visit Ishiyama Temple. He stayed there overnight, but he was unable to have even a single dream. Terribly grieved, he thought, "I may not have been destined to receive the great compassion of Kannon. This must be my destiny, because of my previous existence." And so he left the temple before dawn and started for home with a sad look on his face. He saw many people going to and from the temple. One kindhearted person asked him, "What is making you so sad?" In reply he just said, "Nothing." As he was making his way homeward, a graceful woman, not so young in age and wearing a sedge hat and accompanied by a few women, walked toward him. She looked at him, stopped, and asked him, "Why do you look so sad on your way home?" He replied, "I am not sad. I come from Ikago County." The woman continued, "Something must be troubling you. Won't you please tell me?" Then, thinking that this might even be Kannon, pitying him and talking to him in the form of a woman, he said, "To tell the truth, I have to complete a tanka poem by supplying an appropriate ending. So I went to visit Ishiyama Temple and I stayed there for three days and nights, hoping to receive help from Kannon. But I never even had a dream. So I've resigned myself to fate and now I'm returning home like this." The woman said, "Why didn't you tell me about this sooner? That is quite a simple matter. You can complete the poem by just supplying these words:

> *do I feel attracted by that person,*
> *though I've never even seen her before?*

When he heard these lines, his joy was overwhelming. He thought to himself, "This must have been granted to me by Kannon," and he asked the woman, "Where do you live? I cannot express my gratitude in words." The woman replied, "What shall I say I am? I'm just glad I thought of those lines." And in saying this, she walked on toward the temple.

And so the man returned home. His wife was waiting for him and asked, "How did it work out?" Her husband said, "This is what happened," and he went on to tell about what had taken place. His wife said, "Ah, it is just as I thought," and added the ending part to the poem and placed it in the box, which he then took to the governor's office on the evening of the seventh day.

Hearing of his arrival, the governor thought, "This is quite remarkable that he has come on the appointed day. But he won't have been able to complete the poem with an appropriate ending," and so he said to him, "Come here." So the man presented the box containing the final part of the poem. When he opened the box and looked at the poem, he saw that the ending was perfect. He was deeply impressed and so he gave the man many gifts. He said, "I must admit that I have lost the game." And so he let him govern half of the province, as he had promised.

The first part of the poem in the box read:

> *By the Bay of Ikago*
> *in Ohmi Province,*
> *why indeed*

and then it was followed by:

> *do I feel attracted by that person,*
> *though I've never even seen her before?*

It was wonderful. But how could it have been inept, when the blessed Kannon had deigned to add the ending part? From that day on, the county mayor shared half of the province and ruled over it. He held a one-day Buddhist service at Ishiyama Temple to thank Kannon for all the blessings he had been given. This service is still carried out as a traditional ceremony. It has been observed from generation to generation by the offspring of the county mayor. And so it was that this story, telling how mysterious is the miraculous work of Kannon, came to be handed down to us.

Vol. 16, Tale 18

A Woman Traveling to Chinzei Escapes from Bandits with the Help of Kannon

In olden times, there was a man from Chinzei who went off to Kyoto to do some business and stayed there for several months. He found it dreary living there alone. In the house next to the one in which he was staying, there was a maid. This maid introduced him to a young woman with a good figure who was serving at the imperial court and this led to their getting married.

From then on, the man always kept the woman by his side. When the time came for him to return to his native province, and he told her he would take her back with him, she said she was "happy to go" because she had no one in Kyoto she really knew or could rely on. So the woman prepared for their departure. The maid in the neighboring house was happy too and said, "I'm glad I brought you two together." And so the man took the woman back with him to his native land. The man was well off, and for several years they lived free from any financial difficulty.

The truth be told, the man's occupation was robbery, although he tried to keep this fact hidden from his wife. Gradually, however, she came to sense the reality. She hoped nothing terrible would happen in this new place. As her husband loved her dearly, she pretended not to know anything about what he was doing. Sometimes she even thought she might stop him from doing the dishonorable work, but as he was a man of fierce temperament, she dared not speak to him of it. Nonetheless, she continued hoping she might help put an end to his shady business. And so, one night when they were alone lying together and talking, she said to her husband, "I have something to tell you. Would you listen?" The man replied, "Gladly. On my life, I would never refuse to listen to what you say. Just tell me what it is." The woman was glad to hear this and so she said, "I have seen your dubious work. Won't you please stop doing it?" Hearing this, the man changed color and stopped talking.

The woman regretted what she had said, but what had been said could not be taken back. She had nothing more to say. After that the man changed the expression on his face and would not come near her. The wife regretted her action and thought, "I've said a foolish thing. Now surely, I'll be killed by him." But since she had been reading the chapter on Kannon in the *Lotus Sutra*, she recited the prayer silently to herself; "Please save me, merciful Kannon."

Several days later the man said to his wife, "Why don't we go to the hot springs nearby? Come on, let's go." The woman thought, "He's going to kill me today," but as she had no way to escape she acceded to his request. He placed his wife on his horse and then he too mounted it, shouldering a quiver of arrows, and they set off at about five in the afternoon, taking a couple of men along. In tears and fearing an imminent death, the wife couldn't even see her way. She recited a prayer to Kannon from the bottom of her heart; "I will soon be coming to an end in this world. Please save me in the next world."

While they were passing along a narrow path with a mountain on one side and a pond-like marsh with reeds on the other, the wife said to her husband, "Would you please excuse me. I have to re- lieve myself, so I'd like to get down from the horse." Disgruntled, the man said to one of his attendants, "Well then, let her down." And so the man came and helped her dismount. Since the man who helped her dismount was standing very close by her, she said to him, "You shouldn't be so close to me. Move away!" Her husband too was standing about twenty yards away, holding the horse. Then the woman thought, "I would rather drown in that marsh than be killed," and so she took off her clothes and placed her straw hat over them, making it look like she was still there squatting. Then, completely naked, she slipped secretly into the marsh, without the men noticing anything.

The surface of the marsh was like mud, and on it reed-like grasses were growing thickly, but its bottom was deep. As she got into the marsh, she crept farther away. "I will die soon," she thought, but as she crept along the bottom she said her prayers to Kannon. Then, as she listened from beneath the water, she heard the harsh voice of a man shouting in the distance, "What's holding you up so long? Get her back on the horse!" As he still heard no word from her, he shot an arrow at her hat, but still he heard no sound. The arrow just flew through the air, and there was no response. The man said to his attendant, "That's strange. Go take a look." His attendant went and looked, but the woman was not there. Since there was nobody to be seen, he said to his master, "There is no one there, sir." The master dismounted from his horse to look for himself and he found only the clothes and the hat, not his wife. Surprised, the man first searched the mountain for her, but it was in vain. He couldn't imagine that she had gone into the marsh. In the meantime, the sun went down and it grew dark. Furious, the man scratched his head, but there was nothing he could do, so he went back home.

The woman crept out farther into the marsh. After continuing all night long, at dawn she came to a shallow place. A short distance away, she could see land. Seeing a place that looked like a village, she was glad and finally she reached the land. As her body was all covered with mud, she cleaned it off with water. Since it was March, it was very cold. Quivering with chills, she thought she should go to a house and ask for help. As the sky grew lighter, an old man, walking with a stick, came along and saw her. He called out, "Who is this person, all naked?" The woman replied, "I came on some robbers. What shall I do?" The old man replied, "Oh, how terrible! Come with me," and he took her to his house and said to his old wife, "Look at this person. How pitiful she is!" His wife, being a very kindhearted person, felt sorry for her and clothed her in a humble, lined kimono and then took her back to an inner room where she warmed her by the fireplace. As she lay there, she felt revived and as if she had been brought back to a new life. They gave her food, and after they had cared for her for several days, they realized that she was really a very beautiful woman. How fortunate that she had gotten away, far from the place where she was about to be killed!

At this time, there was a young unmarried son of the governor of the province. The daughter of the old couple was serving at the residence of the governor. She happened to make a visit back to her family home from the house where she was employed, and there she saw the woman. They got to know each other and they talked together for several days. When the daughter went back to the governor's residence again to work, she mentioned the woman. Hearing of her, the son of the governor soon made a visit to the small house. On entering, he saw the beautiful woman, who looked so good in every way, although she was just wearing a humble, lined kimono. He approached her and moved to embrace her and she didn't resist, and so they became intimate with each other. After that the man gave her new clothes and asked her to live with him in the residence of the governor.

After they had been living there together for several days, in tears, the woman told him everything about what had happened. The man thought about her story and then, without making any reference to the woman, he said to his father the governor, "There is a man named so and so living in that province and for many years his occupation has been robbery. He married a woman from Kyoto a while ago. He planned to kill her, but she managed to escape and is alive. That man should be caught immediately." On hearing this, the governor sent a messenger to the province to tell the people about it. In that province there had already been rumors about the man. Finding the rumors substantiated by this message, the people went off and soon they caught the man and had him brought back. When they interrogated the man, he wouldn't confess his crimes for some time, but as they inquired persistently into his past, at last he told his whole story. Watching from behind a reed screen, his previous wife felt sorry for him. Then they dragged the robber out into a field and cut off his head.

The woman and the son of the governor continued living there together as a married couple, and later they went to Kyoto and lived there for a long time. She believed that this had all come about through the grace of Kannon's help and she served the merciful Kannon ever more devoutly.

In such ways do those with honest hearts receive the Buddha's blessing. And it is thanks to this woman's telling her story that it has come down to us today.

Vol. 16, Tale 21

A Woman Who Could Not Speak Is Healed, Owing to the Grace of the Kannon of Ishiyama

In olden times, there lived a daughter who came from a family of considerable means, although its name has not been recorded. The woman was beautiful of figure, but ever since her birth she had been unable to speak. Her parents grieved constantly over the misfortune, but they could do nothing to help her. For some time they suspected, "It must be a curse from a god or the act of an evil spirit." So they prayed to the gods and to Buddha, and they called in a noble priest and had him pray to heal their daughter, but still she remained unable to speak as she grew up. In time, her parents neglected her, leaving only her wet nurse to care for her. And then, both parents passed away, one after another.

The nurse pitied her more and more, and grieved over her handicap, and thought, "I must help her to marry a man and let her bear children for her future life. Since she has such a good figure, someday, a man may come along and take her for his wife." In tears, the nurse talked to the woman about the situation and got her to understand. And so one day, the nurse introduced her casually to a high-ranking courtier who was handsome and kindhearted. From then on, the man visited the woman day after day. Because he found her so beautiful, he loved the woman and wanted to be by her side all the time. He talked to her about everything, but she never replied, so at first he just thought she must be bashful. But when he saw her trying to talk and her eyes filling with tears, he realized that she must be unable to speak. Although he still loved her, he came to visit her less frequently, because now he knew that she was handicapped. The woman felt terribly sad. And so she went away, leaving no trace behind.

When the man went to her house, he found she wasn't there. Now that she was gone, he remembered her image fondly and worried. Longing dearly for her, he searched for her everywhere, but his efforts were in vain. He passed his time in tears. The woman had gone to Ishiyama Temple to visit a monk who was a relative of her wet nurse. With her, she took a waiting woman and a maid. There, she thought, she would become a nun and confine herself in the hall with the statue of Kannon. She prayed, "I understand that Kannon listens and, among all the Buddhas, most readily grants humans' difficult wishes. And so, I pray, please deliver me from my infirmity. If you cannot save me because of my evil deeds in my previous life, then I shall die immediately. If that is the case, please save me in my future life, I pray."

While she was confining herself in the temple and praying in this manner for several days, a master priest came from the East Tower of Mt. Hiei. He was an excellent practitioner of ascetic rituals. People at that time all respected him and followed his teaching. When he visited Ishiyama Temple and, in its hall, saw the woman who could not speak, he inquired, "May I ask who you are? And why are you confining yourself here?" As the woman was unable to speak, she explained her situation by writing on paper. The master priest said, "I will try to help you to speak. Help will come through the blessings of Kannon for all living beings." In writing, the woman expressed her happiness again. The master priest chanted his prayers devoutly in front of the statue of Kannon, for three days and nights, without stopping. But no effect was noticed and the master priest became angered and prayed tearfully. Then, as he continued praying, the woman vomited for about two hours. After that she became able to speak, although not articulately. Soon after, however, she became able to talk like a normal person. An evil spirit had been preventing her from speaking.

In tears, the woman bowed deeply to the master priest and, as a token of her gratitude, offered him a rosary of crystal beads that she had kept for many years. After accepting the rosary, the master priest returned to his own mountain temple.

While the woman was still at Ishiyama Temple, the high-ranking courtier, who had been searching in vain for her, experienced a religious inspiration that arose suddenly in his heart. And so, he went to visit holy places. When he visited the central hall of the temple at Mt. Hiei, he called on the master priest, whom he knew. He was given food and he was taking a rest when he happened to notice a rosary of crystal beads hanging on the wall. Immediately, he inquired of the master priest, "Where did you get that rosary?" The master priest replied, "I was given it when I healed a woman who could not speak and who had shut herself in Ishiyama Temple." When the young man heard of the woman who could not speak, he felt troubled at heart and asked for more details. Then he learned the full story. After hearing it, he knew without a doubt that this must be the woman. With a joyous heart he hurried back toward Kyoto.

On his way he visited Ishiyama Temple and looked for the woman. Though at first she tried to hide her identity, when the man talked on insistently about his past, she saw his genuine heart. Finally, they were reunited. They both wept, and talked about those past years, and then they went back to Kyoto together. They exchanged deep vows, became man and wife, and lived together. They realized that this all had been granted through the blessings of Kannon, and so they served Kannon ever more devoutly, with all their hearts.

From this we can realize how wonderful are the blessings of merciful Kannon. And such then is the story as it has been handed down to us.

Vol. 16, Tale 22

25

A Poor Woman Who Worships the Kannon of Kiyomizu Temple Is Saved

In olden times, there lived a young woman in Kyoto who was poor and had no way to earn a living. For many years, she had been visiting Kiyomizu Temple, but had found no sign of receiving divine favor.

Nonetheless, she continued going to Kiyomizu Temple as usual and she prayed to the Kannon of the temple, saying, "I have been visiting this temple for many years now, counting on your blessing, but I am poor and I have no money to live on. Even if I am destined to this lot because of my deeds in my previous life, please, I pray, grant me your divine favor." On saying this, she prostrated herself on the floor and fell into sleep. In a dream, she saw a noble-looking priest who said to her, "When you return to Kyoto, you will meet a man who will speak to you. You must do as he tells you." Then she awoke from her dream.

After that, the young woman prayed to Kannon and hurried home to Kyoto all alone late at night, and she met no one on her way. But when she came to one of the Great Gates, she met a man. Because it was so dark, she couldn't tell who it was. The man approached her and said, "I have something in mind. Please do what I tell you." Placing her faith in her dream, she listened to him and decided she shouldn't run away, even at such a time of night. She asked, "Where do you live? May I ask your name? It's strange that I should meet you here." The man grabbed her forcefully and pulled her toward the east. She couldn't help but follow him. He took her to the inner precincts of Yasaka Temple and pulled her into the tower, where they lay together. Soon the day broke and the man said, "All this must have come to pass because of a deep relationship in our previous life. Please stay here. You are the only person I know here. I will rely on you from now on." After saying this, from behind a partition he brought out ten rolls of beautiful twill and ten rolls of silk and cotton fabrics and gave them to the woman. The woman said, "I, too, have no one else I can rely on and so I will depend on you." Then the man said, "I have to go out and take care of something now, but I'll be back by evening, so just stay here please." And at that, he went out.

When the woman looked about, she saw an old nun. She thought it very strange that the man should live here in this tower. In the distance she could see piles of all sorts of goods and merchandise. Then the woman thought, "This man must be a robber. He has no place to live. That's why he lives secretly in this tower." She felt terribly scared and prayed to Kannon, "Please save me." When she looked around, she saw the nun open the door slightly, peep out, and after making sure no one was around, place a wooden bucket on her head and go out. The woman thought, "She must have gone to draw water. I'll run away before she comes back." Slipping the rolls of twill and silk fabrics inside of the front of her kimono, she ran away as swiftly as she could. When the nun returned, she saw that the woman had gone, but as she had no way to chase after her, she gave up.

The woman made her way toward the center of Kyoto, hiding the things in the front of her kimono. But thinking it unwise to walk through the middle of Kyoto like this, she stopped in at the small house of a person with whom she had a slight acquaintance, who lived near the corner of Gojo Street and Kyogoku Avenue. Just then, she saw a lot of people coming from the west. Hearing them cry out, "A robber was caught and he's being taken away," she opened the door quietly and looked out, only to see the man who had slept with her being dragged along by some low-ranking officers of the police department. Seeing this, the woman was scared, almost to death. So—just as she had suspected—he was a robber.

The officers were taking him to the tower of Yasaka Temple to make an on-the-spot inspection of the stolen goods.

The woman thought to herself, "If I had stayed there, what would have become of me?" She felt terribly scared and wondered what she should do. Nonetheless, she felt that all that had happened had come to pass through the help of Kannon. Her gratitude was boundless. A while later, she reached the center of Kyoto and, little by little, sold off what she had taken. Using the sales as start-up money, she built up some savings. Eventually, she found a husband and they lived happily together.

Such is the mysterious work of Kannon. It is said that this story took place in recent times. And such is the story as it has been handed down to us.

Vol. 16, Tale 33

A Man from Kii Province Falsely Accuses His Wife and Is Punished

In olden times, there was a temple named Sayadera in Kuwahara Village, in Ito County of Kii Province. In this temple, there lived several nuns.

These nuns thought of offering prayers for the fulfillment of their religious lives and so, during the reign of Emperor Shomu, they held a Buddhist service at the temple. They invited Daie, the Zen priest of Yakushiji Temple in the Ukyo district of Nara and held a meeting of repentance in front of the Eleven-faced Kannon.

At that time, in the village, there lived a wicked man whose name was Fumino Imiki, but who went by the common name of Uedano Saburo. Being wicked, he didn't believe in the Buddha or the Dharma or the Sangha. He had a wife named Kamitsukeno Kimi, whose nickname was "Woman of the Big Bridge." She was beautiful in appearance and she also knew the Buddhist Law of Cause and Effect. One time, while her husband was away, she observed the commandments for a day and a night and attended a meeting of repentance with all the other participants. While she was there, her husband returned home and found her gone. He inquired of the servants, "Where is she?" They answered, "She went to a meeting of repentance." Hearing this, the husband got very angry and stormed off to the temple, where he loudly called out his wife's name. Seeing what was going on and feeling compassion, the priest tried to instruct the man. The husband, however, wouldn't listen and he shouted at him saying, "You're a bandit priest who wants to make a conquest of my wife. I'll break your head immediately." He called his wife and dragged her back home. When they got back, he said to her, "No doubt, you've been violated by that priest." In anger, he dragged her off to bed and they lay together. Soon, he started having intercourse with her, and right away, his penis began to feel as if it were being bitten by ants. He grew ill with the pain, and soon after he died.

When people heard the story, they remarked, "Even if he didn't hit the priest, it was outrageous for him to have such a wicked heart, and to abuse the priest, and embarrass him in public. That's why he got such a punishment." They despised him and railed on and on about him.

Therefore, as you can see, one should not abuse a priest. It is said that this was a punishment imposed on a man who interrupted people who were attending meetings of repentance in front of Kannon. And such is the story as it has been handed down to us.

Vol. 16, Tale 38

A Monk from a Temple on Mt. Hiei Receives Enlightenment with the Help of the Bodhisattva of Boundless Space

In olden times, there was a young monk who lived in a temple on Mt. Hiei. After he became a monk, he desired to learn more about Buddhism, but as he was also much given to pleasure and playing around, he didn't study seriously. He tried to learn the *Lotus Sutra*, but did so only half-heartedly. Nonetheless, he maintained this desire to learn about Buddhism more deeply, so he visited Horinji Temple in Kyoto and offered prayers to the Bodhisattva of Boundless Space. But still, he couldn't set his mind on studying seriously, so he remained an ignorant monk.

Regretting his condition, the monk made another visit to Horinji in September. He had intended to return home soon, but he got carried away talking with the other monks he knew at the temple. The sun was about to set, so finally, he started back in a hurry. When he reached the western part of Kyoto, the sun had already gone down, so he stopped at the home of a person he knew. But the master was away in the country, and there was no one else there except for the maidservant, so he decided to visit the home of another person he knew.

On his way, he came on a house with a Chinese-style gate. By the gate there stood an attractive young woman dressed in many-layered clothing. The monk walked closer to her and said, "I have come down from Mt. Hiei on a visit to Horinji and now I'm on my way back. But since the sun has set, might I ask you to let me stay here overnight?" The woman replied, "Would you wait a moment, please. I'll go and see what the mistress says." Soon, she came out again and said, "We would be pleased to accept your request. Please come in right away."

The monk was very happy and so he entered the house. He was shown to a special room for guests, where they had lit a light for him. The room had a four-foot high folding screen, and a few tatami mats, stitched with Korean-style patterned hems, had been laid out. Soon the attractive young woman dressed in many-layered clothing brought in a tall container of food. The monk ate it all, drank some sake, washed his hands, and was just sitting there when someone opened the sliding door and stood by the curtained screen. A woman's voice said, "May I ask who you are and how you got in here?" The monk replied, "I came down from Mt. Hiei and visited Horinji, and while on my way back the sun went down, so I asked if I might stay overnight." The woman continued, "Well then, if you often visit Horinji, please drop in whenever you please." After saying this, she closed the sliding door, but a part of the curtained screen got caught in it and the door didn't close neatly.

By now, it was late at night and the monk went outside. While strolling about in front of the latticed shutters on the south side of the house, he noticed a hole in the shutters. He peeped in through the hole and saw a lady who seemed to be the mistress of the house. She lay by the low lamp stand, reading a book of stories. She looked to be about twenty and her beauty was beyond compare. She was wearing purple-twilled silk and her hair looked as if it reached the bottom of her kimono. Two women were lying in front of her, behind the curtained screen. At a short distance, was a young girl—no doubt the one who had brought him the food. The room looked impeccable. On a two-tiered shelf, a gold-lacquered case for combs and an inkstone case had been laid out. It seemed there must have been incense in the burner, for there was a fragrance in the air. Looking at the mistress of the house, the monk forgot himself entirely. In ecstasy he thought, "What merit from my past existence could have brought me into this house and led me to meet this person?" He continued thinking; "Of what worth is my life if I don't fulfill my wishes?"

And so, when he thought everyone was quiet and the woman had fallen asleep, he opened the sliding door that had not quite closed, approached her secretly, and lay beside her. The woman was sound asleep, so she was unaware of his presence. As he moved closer, the fragrance was most wonderful. Thinking of how she might be shocked and cry out, he was quite worried. Praying earnestly to the Buddha, he opened her kimono and placed his hand inside the opening. The woman awoke in surprise and demanded, "Who is this?" He replied, "It's me." The woman said, "I let you stay here because I thought you were a noble monk. Now, seeing your conduct, I regret it." The monk attempted to move closer to her, but she protected herself with her kimono and showed no hint of yielding. At this point, the monk was suffering in great anguish and agony. At the same time, he was afraid that people might hear them, so he gave up his forceful behavior.

The woman continued, "I am not necessarily saying that I could never accept you. My husband passed away in the spring of last year and many men have approached me, but I have remained a widow, vowing to myself, 'I could never accept any man who is not appropriate.' I've been trying to respect such a fine monk as you. Therefore, I am not saying that I could never accept you. Let me ask you; can you recite the *Lotus Sutra* by heart? Is your voice beautiful? If you can recite the sutra by heart in a noble voice, then we may be able to enter into an affectionate relationship with each other while you are reciting the sutra. What do you think of this?" The monk replied, "Although I have studied the *Lotus Sutra*, I can't yet recite it by heart." The woman asked, "Is that because it's difficult to learn it by heart?" The monk answered, "How could I not have learned it by heart if I had tried hard enough? But my mind was given over to pleasures, so I can't recite it by heart." The woman said, "Then go back quickly to the temple on Mt. Hiei, and learn the sutra by heart, and then come back. Then we may enter into an affectionate relationship, secretly, just as you please." Hearing this, the monk felt his desire subside, and when dawn broke he said goodbye and slipped out of the room. The woman gave him breakfast and then let him depart on his way.

The monk returned to his temple on Mt. Hiei. Recalling the woman's looks and behavior, he could not forget her. He resolved, "I will learn the sutra by heart soon and then I will go back to see her." And so, he made efforts to learn the sutra quickly and he was able to learn it by heart in twenty days. While he was learning to recite it by heart, he could not forget the woman and he kept writing letters to her. Along with her replies she sent such things as an unlined kimono and some dried boiled rice. So the monk thought, "She must be considering me as her husband," and his happiness was immense.

Because he could now recite the sutra by heart, the monk visited Horinji, as before. And then on his way back, as before, he went to the house. And as before, he was given food, and the women who served the mistress of the house came out and they talked together. When it grew late at night, they retired. The monk washed his hands and began to read the sutra. His voice sounded most beautiful. His heart, however, was not in his reading; it was somewhere else. When the night was far advanced, and everyone in the house seemed to have gone to sleep, the monk opened the sliding door, as before, and sneaked to her side without anyone noticing. As he snuggled up closer and lay by her side, she awoke. Thinking she must have been waiting for him, he was very happy and then he tried to get into her kimono. But with her kimono, she protected herself from his advances and said, "I have several things to ask you. I need to make sure about this. I can see that you have learned to recite the sutra by heart now. But if we were to enter into intimate relations only on account of this, and if we were to find it difficult to separate from each other, it would be very troubling to be regarded by others as having just indulged in physical intimacy. I would not like to be with a man who is satisfied merely with being able to recite the sutra by heart. And in regard to your studies, it would be better if you could serve the court and the imperial family. If you just confine yourself in the temple and read sutras, that will not be sufficient. I will be happy to be near you, but it would be much better if you were to become a learned priest. Then we could live together. And so, if you truly love me, devote yourself to your studies at the temple on Mt. Hiei day and night for about three years. Become a learned priest, and then come back. Then I may have an intimate relationship with you. There is no other way I could possibly accept your request, even if I were killed. I will write to you during your stay at the temple on Mt. Hiei. If you should have any problems, I will help you."

Hearing this the monk thought, "Yes, that sounds reasonable. If I were to force my way on a woman who can see into the future, it would be sad, indeed. What is more, I am poor, and it wouldn't be bad to get ahead in the world, relying on her kind help." And so, with these thoughts in mind, he promised to follow her suggestions and he left her room. When day broke, he was served food and he went back to Mt. Hiei.

After that, he began his studies immediately and devoted himself diligently to his learning, day and night. His desire to see the woman made this feel as urgent, as if he were brushing fire from his head, and he studied with all his mind. At last, in about two years, he became a learned priest. He was by nature very intelligent and so he was able to become a learned priest in such a short time. And within three years, he truly became an excellent learned priest. Every time he took part in symposiums in the presence of the emperor and gave lectures on the thirty chapters of the *Lotus Sutra*, he was acclaimed more than any other priest. His fame as the most learned priest among his peers spread through all the temples on Mt. Hiei.

And so, the three years passed. During the period of his secluded studies, letters from the woman came regularly, and so he was able to continue with—for the most part—a peaceful mind, because he trusted her kindness. Now that he had become a learned priest after three years he visited Horinji Temple, as before, to see the woman. On his way back, he went to her house toward evening, as before.

As he had notified her in advance of his visit, he was shown to the same room and, through the curtained screen, he asked about what had happened in the past years. The woman had not talked to others about their relationship and she had told her maid to give him a message that read; "You may think it strange now, for in the past I didn't speak with you directly when you visited, but this time I will talk with you now." The priest was excited when he read the message, but he replied, simply, "Thank you." The woman said, "Please come in." Entering the room with a glad heart, he looked around and saw a clean tatami mat on the far side of a curtained screen that stood by the bedside where she was lying. On the tatami mat, was a round straw cushion. On a stand, there was a lamp facing the other way, behind a folding screen. It seemed there was a maid seated by the woman's feet. When the priest came closer and sat on the straw cushion, the woman said, "How have you been since I last saw you? And have you become a learned priest?" Her voice was most enchanting. Hearing it, the priest was overwhelmed with joy and his body trembled. "It's not worth mentioning," he replied, "but I was praised when I took part in the Thirty Lectures and Symposiums." The woman commented, "That is wonderful to hear, but now I would like to ask you several questions. A person who can answer these questions must be a truly learned priest. One who does nothing but read the sutra does not interest me at all."

And in saying this, she went on to ask some discerning, abstruse questions, starting with ones about the opening chapter of the *Lotus Sutra*. The priest answered the questions according to his learning. In response to his answers, she asked some even more difficult questions. This time, he thought out the questions by himself and was able to answer like an ancient sage. And so the woman said, "I see you have become such an excellent learned priest. I wonder how you accomplished this in just a few years. You must be very intelligent." The priest thought to himself, "Even though she is a woman, she knows the Way of the Buddha, deeply. I never expected this. If we should get married, it will be very good to talk with her. She would surely urge me to keep on learning."

While they were talking, the night advanced and the priest lifted the curtained screen and moved closer to her. She just lay there without saying anything. The priest lay down by her, feeling very happy. The woman said, "Please, just remain as you are for a while." And so, they just held hands together. And while they lay beside each other and talked, the man fell asleep, owing to his fatigue from walking all the way from Mt. Hiei to Horinji.

In surprise, he awoke from his sleep and thought, "I fell sound asleep. I didn't even get to tell her my feelings." As he looked about, he saw himself lying on crushed pampas grass. "This is strange," he thought. Raising his head and looking about, he found himself lying alone in an unfamiliar field, with not a soul around. Amazed, his heart thumped and his fear was immense. When he got up and looked around, he saw some clothes scattered about. He picked up the clothes and held them to his chest. Standing there for a while and looking about carefully, he realized he had been lying in a field in the eastern part of Sagano. This seemed so incredible. The morning moon was bright, and it was March, so it felt very chilly. He was shivering from the cold and he couldn't even think. He couldn't decide which way to go. Then he thought, "Horinji Temple must be the nearest place. I'll go there and spend the night," and so he ran off in that direction. First he went to Umezu and started to cross the Katsura River, but the stream was as deep as his hips and he was almost washed away by the current. Finally, he managed to wade across. Shivering, he arrived at Horinji Temple, where he entered the main hall, prostrated himself, and said, "I have just had a harrowing experience, so please have mercy on me." As he lay there he fell into sleep.

In a dream, an imposing-looking young monk with blue hair appeared, sat by the priest, and said, "You were bewitched tonight, but it was not by a fox or a badger; it was by me. You are intelligent, but you have been interested in playing around and in sensual pleasures, not in studying, so you couldn't become a learned priest. However, you came to me and asked, 'Please let me gain learning. Bestow wisdom on me.' So I wondered what I might do and then

I thought, 'This man is especially interested in women, so I might be able to take advantage of this nature to promote his studies.' And so, I bewitched you. Therefore, there is no need to fear. Go back to the temple on Mt. Hiei quickly, and learn the Way of the Buddha with all your heart, and work hard all the time." On hearing these words, the priest awoke from his dream.

From this, the priest realized, "the Bodhisattva of Boundless Space appeared in the form of a woman and contrived to help me all these years." He felt immensely ashamed of himself. In tears, he repented his past. When the day broke, he went back to the temple on Mt. Hiei and pursued his learning ever more diligently. He became a truly wonderful, learned priest.

Since these were all the doings of the Bodhisattva of Boundless Space, how could they possibly have failed? The *Sutra of Boundless Space* tells us, "Anyone who counts on me shall receive my help. And when a person, toward the end of his or her life, grows sick and suffers pains or becomes sightless and deaf and unable to pray to the Buddha, I will appear in the form of the father, mother, wife, or child of that person and I will sit together and help in praying to the Buddha."

And so in this way the Bodhisattva of Boundless Space took the form of a woman, according to the needs of the man's character, and encouraged him to pursue his learning. Because this was done just as written in the sutra it is especially impressive. It is said that this story was told by the priest, himself. Such then is the story has it has been passed down to us today.

Vol. 17, Tale 33

The Monk Koku Is Saved from Death with the Help of Fugen Bodhisattva

In olden times, in the Province of Ohmi, there was a mountain temple named Konshoji. In this temple, lived a monk named Koku who was very devoted to chanting the *Lotus Sutra*. He had lived in the temple for many years chanting the sutra night and day, ever diligently. His voice was beautifully delicate, and everyone who heard him chant was deeply moved. This devoted chanter had a compassionate heart and he cared deeply for all people.

At the same time, in a certain county of the province, there was a brave, strong man named Hyo Heisuke, who belonged to the venerable clan of Taira no Masakado. He had a wild heart and he lacked compassion for animals. He would go out into the fields in the morning hunting deer and birds, and to the bays and rivers in the evening catching fish and clams. Evil as he was, he was impressed by the beauty of Koku's chanting of the *Lotus Sutra*. At first, he listened to Koku's teaching in the mountain temple, but later, he respectfully invited Koku to his home and asked him to chant the sutra there. This, he continued to do for many years. Heisuke, however, had a young wife, and one of his attendants told him that the monk was carrying on an affair with her when he came to chant the sutras.

Hearing this, Hyo Heisuke immediately grew furious and, without checking on the credibility of the story, decided to kill this sutra-chanting monk. And so, he said to the monk, "Let's go visit the mountain temple," and he led him off into the mountains. Suddenly, he took hold of the monk and tied him to a tree. Having no idea what this was about, the monk became immensely frightened and grieved at the sudden turn of events. Hyo Heisuke shouted out, "Shoot at his side!" And so, his most skilled archer took up his bow, fixed an arrow to the bowstring, pulled it hard and aimed at Koku's side and shot. But the arrow fell to the side, without hitting the monk. "That's strange," he said, and then he shot at him again. But again, the arrow fell aside, as before. The monk remained calm, thinking of the fortunate consequences of his previous life, and thought, "Although I am innocent, I almost lost my life," He raised his voice and chanted the *Lotus Sutra* as follows:

> *When you come to the end of your life*
> *you will go directly to the world of peace*
> *and sit in the middle of the lotus flower*
> *where Amida Buddha is surrounded*
> *by the many great bodhisattvas.*

When the monk chanted like this, even some among Hyo Heisuke's followers were deeply touched and felt like crying, but they were afraid of their master. When the arrow failed to hit the monk the second time, Hyo Heisuke got angry and said, "It's because you are such a poor bowman," and so, he took up the bow himself and shot an arrow. But it, too, fell to the side, as before. Surprised and suspicious, Hyo Heisuke threw away his bow and arrow and exclaimed, "This is extraordinary! Even when the arrow was shot from such a short distance, it missed the mark three times. This must be because of the protection of guardian deities." He felt terribly afraid and released the sutra-chanting monk. He said to the monk, "Just now I made a grave mistake. From now on, I will never have an evil heart toward you." And so, vowing thusly, he wept tears, repented his sin, and took the monk home.

That night, Hyo Heisuke dreamed a dream, and in it, he saw golden-colored Fugen Bodhisattva riding on a white elephant. And stuck in the body of the bodhisattva he saw three arrows. Then in the dream, he asked, "Why are those arrows stuck in your body?" Fugen

Bodhisattva answered, "Yesterday, you falsely accused the sutra-chanting monk and tried to kill him, and so I took these arrows on his behalf." And while thinking on this, he awoke from his dream.

· After that, Hyo Heisuke felt still more afraid and he thought, "On a false charge I was about to kill the chanter of the *Lotus Sutra*. That is what Fugen Bodhisattva was telling me." Turning to the monk, he shed tears of repentance and told him all about the dream. He punished the man who had told him the false story and banished him permanently.

For a few days, the monk thought about what had happened and he came to feel very tired of the world. Thus, he planned to leave the house secretly at midnight and take the statue of the Buddha and the *Lotus Sutra* with him. Hyo Heisuke dreamed a dream, and in it, Fugen Bodhisattva appeared and said, "You have held services for me for many years. On account of the merit of your services, I would like to take you into Paradise. However, you were going to kill me on a false charge. Many Buddhas have told us to distance ourselves when seeing evil and to come closer when seeing good. Therefore, I wish to leave this house now and go to another place, for good." Thinking on these words, Hyo Heisuke awoke from his dream. Surprised and suspicious, he lit a light and glanced quickly at the place where the monk had been, but he wasn't there. Nor was the statue of the Buddha or the sutra there. The monk had left without his noticing. When day broke, he searched from east to west, but he couldn't find where the monk had gone. After that, he felt so sorry. In tears, he greatly repented his previous mistakes. For many years, he continued to search, but never was he able to find the monk.

And so, when we consider these events, we can realize that, no matter what other people might tell us, we should never believe a thing until we have checked out its truthfulness. It is also said that we should never commit evil acts in a fit of anger. Such then is the story as it has been handed down to us.

Vol.17, Tale 40

On Seeing a Wild Duck Mourning the Death of the Drake He Shot, a Man Becomes a Monk

In olden times, in Kyoto there was a young samurai. The exact period when this story took place is not certain, but in any case, the man was very poor and he was having difficulty making ends meet.

As it happened, his wife had given birth to a baby and she wished to eat some meat. Being poor, he didn't know how he could possibly get any meat for her. He knew no one in the countryside he could visit, and he had no money with which to buy meat in the market. After much thought, he went out of his home before dawn with a bow and a couple of arrows. He thought he would go to a pond and shoot a duck for his wife. He wondered for a while just where he should go, and then he thought, "Mimidoro Pond is far away from people's houses. I'll go there and see." So he went to the edge of the pond and hid himself in the grass and looked about. There, he saw a couple of wild ducks approaching him, quite unaware of his presence. He shot an arrow, and it hit the drake. He was very happy and he went into the pond and retrieved it. He hurried home, but the sun had already set and he arrived home after nightfall. He told his wife about it and thought gladly, "I'll dress it and cook it tomorrow morning and I'll have my wife eat it." So he hung the duck on a rack and went off to bed.

At midnight he awoke, hearing the sound of the duck on the rack flapping its wings. Wondering if the duck had come back to life, he lit a lamp and went to the rack and looked. There he saw the dead drake hanging on the rack, but a live female duck was also there at its side. It was fluttering its wings beside the drake. "Now I see," he thought, "The female, who was feeding together with the male yesterday, saw her husband shot, and in grieving for him, she must have followed me all the way back here." Suddenly, he felt his religious sensibilities touched. His pity and sorrow were beyond description.

When the man approached carrying the lamp, the female duck just stayed there with her husband, unafraid of losing her own life. Seeing this the man thought, "Even such a humble creature has followed her husband, longing for him, all the way to this place, unafraid of death. As for me, I was born a human being. Since I cared for my wife, I killed the bird." He felt guilty about giving his wife the meat of the bird and so he woke her and told her about what had happened and had her look at the ducks. Seeing them, his wife also felt terribly sorry. Even when day broke, she never ate the meat of the duck. Her husband thought more about this and his religious feelings were further inspired, so he went off to the well-respected mountain temple on Mt. Atago, cut off his topknot and became a monk. Some time after that, he became a high priest and performed his duties ever-diligently.

We can realize that the man's sin in killing a creature was grave, yet through this experience, his religious sense was kindled and he became a monk. It has been said that all this came about as a result of his doings in his previous life. Such then is the story as it has been handed down to us today.

Vol. 19, Tale 6

30

Snakes Are Seen in a Vat of Sake Made from Rice Cake Offerings

In olden times, there was a monk who had lived in a temple on Mt. Hiei. Since there wasn't much for him to do in the mountains, he left the temple and returned to his home village in a certain county of Settsu Province, where he married a woman. When the people of his village held memorial services or lectures on the sutras, they often called on this monk to preside over the functions. Although he was not particularly learned, he knew how to conduct such events. For their New Year's services, they always invited him as the preacher.

For this work, the monk received many rice cakes. These he didn't give away to others, but kept at home. His wife reasoned, "Rather than giving away these cakes to children and servants, it would be better to gather the old dried hardened cakes, break them into pieces, and brew some sake from them." When she told her husband, the monk, of this plan he replied, "That sounds like a good idea," and so they used the cakes and brewed sake from them.

Some time later, when they thought the sake must be about ready to drink, the wife went to the vat and opened it. On taking the lid off, she saw something wriggling about in the vat. She thought this strange, but since it was dark in the vat, she lit a light and lowered it down inside to look. There she saw numerous snakes, large and small, wriggling about in the vat and raising their heads. "How abominable! What brought all these creatures?" she cried, and then put the lid back on the vat, and ran away. When she told her husband about this, he thought, "That's strange, indeed. My wife may have been mistaken about what she saw. I'll go

117

and take a look myself." So he lit a lamp, lowered it into the vat and looked inside. There, he too, saw many snakes, all wriggling about. The husband, also, was startled and stepped away. After that, they put the lid back on the vat and decided, "We'll take all this, vat and all, to a distant place and just throw it away." So they brought it outside, took it to a faraway place, and secretly left it in an open field.

A couple of days later, three men happened to walk by the sake vat. Seeing it they wondered, "What sort of vat is that?" One of them walked up to it, removed the lid, and looked in. The wonderful scent of sake drifted out from the vat. In surprise, the man said to the other two, "This is wonderful sake," and so the other two came closer, looked into the vat, and saw that it was indeed full of sake. The three men wondered, "What could this be about?" Then one of them declared, "I'm going to drink this sake, no matter what." The other two replied, "It's been thrown away in a field like this—that's strange. There must be some reason for it. It gives me the creeps. We can't drink it." But the man who had previously vowed to drink it was a real boozer and he couldn't resist the temptation. "Well," he said, "Looks like you guys are afraid to drink it. But no matter what it is that may have been thrown away, I'm going to drink this. I don't give a damn about my life." And on saying this, the man took a cup from his side, scooped up some sake, and drank it down. Finding it a wonderful sake, he went on to drink three cups. As the other two also were fond of drinking, they too yearned to try some. Finally they said, "Today we three came here together. If one of us should die, could we ever abandon him? And then too, even if someone were to kill us, we should all die together. So let's all drink." And so, the two men joined the other in drinking the sake. It tasted so exceptionally good that the three men declared, "Let's drink our fill." Since the vat was big, and since there was plenty of sake in it, they brought it home and drank from it every day. Nonetheless, nothing bad happened to them.

The monk still had some sense and he thought, "Those offerings that were made to the Buddha, I took them all for myself. I was so wickedly selfish that I didn't give any of the rice cakes to other people. I just made sake out of them. I was so sinful that they turned into snakes." A little later, feeling thusly ashamed of himself, the monk heard some people saying, "Three men found a vat of sake in a field and brought it home and drank it all up. They say it was a most wonderful sake." Hearing this story, the monk thought, "So, they weren't really snakes. We were so sinful that the sake looked like snakes to our eyes." And so, he was even more filled with regret.

We can see that taking for oneself what has been offered to the Buddha is a grave sin. It was such a strange thing that the offerings really looked like wriggling snakes. And so, a monk should not abuse the offerings given to the Buddha by using them for himself. He should share them with other people and with other monks.

This is what was told by the three men, and by the monk himself, and this tale has been told from generation to generation. And such then is the story as it has been handed down to us today.

Vol. 19, Tale 21

31

A Turtle Repays the Kindness of Gusai of Paekche

In olden times, there lived a man in Mitani County of Bingo Province. He was an ancestor of the county's present mayor. At the time when Paekche in Korea was defeated, he went there with his men to assist, since he had some connections with that country.

His venture in Paekche, however, did not go well. He lost all his men and had to remain there alone. He wished to return to Japan, but for many years he wasn't able to do so. Longing for his homeland, he made a tearful prayer; "If ever I may return to my homeland, I will build a large temple and set up a statue of the Buddha and offer services." In Paekche, there lived a priest named Gusai. The man was a good friend of Gusai, and they had vowed to remain friends, even into the next world. When the man was finally able to return to this country several years later, he brought Gusai with him.

On arriving in Bingo Province and resuming his life there, he was very happy to fulfill his promise, and so he built a large temple. Gusai worked with him. In planning to have a statue of the Buddha made for the temple, he sent Gusai to Kyoto with many treasures to obtain the gold for it. Gusai went and purchased as much gold as he could and then started on his way back. When he reached the shore of Naniwa, he saw some fishermen who were about to kill four large turtles. Gusai felt so sorry for the turtles that he bought them and released them into the sea.

After that, Gusai set sail and was passing by Kabaneshima Island of Bizen Province when, toward evening, his ship was attacked by pirates. The pirates jumped into Gusai's ship and threw two of his boys overboard into the sea. Then they said to Gusai, "Now you jump into the sea. Otherwise, we'll throw you in, too." Clasping his hands together, Gusai pleaded with them to spare his life, but the pirates showed no mercy. And so, reciting prayers in his heart, Gusai, jumped into the sea. The pirates took everything in the ship, including all the gold he had purchased.

When Gusai jumped into the sea, he found that the water was only as deep as his hips, and that his feet were resting on something like a rock. He kept standing in the sea like this all night long until daylight broke. And then, when he looked at what was under his feet, he realized it was a large turtle's shell. When he looked around the place, he saw it was the shore of the Bay of Bingo. All this was very strange. The place where his ship was attacked by pirates had been near Kabaneshima Island of Bizen Province. His present location was on the shore of Bingo Province. That meant he had already passed by two provinces in one night. Wondering how he could have managed to come so far, he was completely dumbfounded. He went ashore and thought, "The turtles I freed into the sea the other day must have come to my help to repay their indebtedness." He felt overwhelmed with emotion.

From there he went back to his home in Mitani and told the story. When the master heard it, he said, "It's a common occurrence that people get attacked by pirates and are robbed of properties, but it's all because of the turtles' help that you didn't lose your life." While the two were reflecting happily on the incident, several men came to the house trying to sell some gold. When Gusai came out and looked at them, he realized that they were the six pirates he had encountered near Kabaneshima Island. Recognizing Gusai, the pirates were thrown into consternation and became too frightened to talk. But Gusai didn't tell the others anything about the men and he bought the gold at their asking price. The pirates thought, "Now surely we are doomed." But Gusai paid for the gold, without saying anything. The pirates left, feeling relieved.

After that, they completed the temple, made the statue, and held services. The temple is now called Mitani Temple. Later, Gusai made his home by the shore, and there, he continued helping those who passed back and forth. He died at an age of more than eighty.

This is not the first story about a turtle repaying kindness by saving a human being. It has been said that there have been other such stories, beginning with those that came over from India and China. They continue to be told in our country, to this day. And such then is the story as it has been handed down to us.

Vol. 19, Tale 30

A Human Skull Repays the Kindness of Doto, a Priest from Korea

In olden times, a priest named Doto came over to this country from Korea. He resided in Gankoji Temple. Doto thought of building a bridge over the Uji River in order to perform a meritorious deed. At the time he was engaged in this work, there was a man named Eman who lived in a place called Kita-yamashina. One time, when Doto was passing over Mt. Narasaka on his way back to Gankoji after visiting Eman's home, he found a skull along the road, and he realized that it had obviously been trampled on by people. Looking at it he pitied the skull, and he had the boy who assisted him pick it up, and place it on a tree.

Some time later, toward New Year's Eve, a man came to the gate of Gankoji and called out, "Could I please see the assistant of the virtuous priest Doto?" When the boy was summoned, he left his room and met the man at the gate, but he didn't know who this person was. The man said to the boy, "Because of the kindness accorded to me by your master, Priest Doto, I was saved from many years of anguish and now I am at peace. Tonight is the only night I could repay the kindness I owe." After saying this, the man led the boy outside. While he was being led along, the boy didn't know where he was going. In time, they arrived at a house in a village. When he entered the house, not knowing what to expect, he was served a large amount of food. The man and the boy, ate and gradually the night deepened. And so, the two spent the night at the house together. Toward dawn, they heard someone approaching.

The man said to the boy, "My elder brother, who killed me, has come. I must leave right away." Wondering what was going on, the boy asked, "What is this all about?" The man replied, "My brother and I went to various places and earned four hundred pounds of silver to start a business. When my brother and I were passing over Mt. Narasaka carrying the money, he desired all of it for himself and so he killed me. Then he went to our home and told our mother that his younger brother had been killed by robbers. After that, my skull remained in that place for many years and it was trampled on by the passers-by. But your master, the high priest, he looked at it and had mercy on it, and had you pick it up and place it on the tree. Thus, I was freed from my sufferings. Because of this, I can never forget what I owe you. Therefore, I prepared food for you in order to repay your kindness. I brought you here so you could eat this food." And then, on saying this, he disappeared.

While the boy servant was still thinking how strange this was, the ghost's mother came into the house, together with the brother who had killed him, for the purpose of comforting the spirit of the one who had been killed. Surprised at seeing the boy, they asked, "Who is this person?" and they tried to find out why he was there. The boy told them about the spirit. Hearing this, the mother was filled with anger toward the elder brother who had killed the younger brother. In tears, she said, "Then it was you who killed my dear son—and I never knew about it. You told me a lie when you said, 'He was killed by robbers.'" Amidst her tears, she lamented and bowed to the boy and gave him food. When he returned to his living quarters at the temple, the boy told his master priest about what had happened. The priest was deeply moved. And so, we can see that even the skull of a dead person can repay kindness in this way. If this is so, how then could a person who is living forget the kindness he or she owes? What one does to repay the things owed to others is blessed by the Buddha.

Today the bridge over the Uji River is the one that Doto built. It is also said that this bridge was built by angels, although it is not exactly known whether angels actually came to help Doto in building it. Such then is the story as it has been handed down to us.

Vol. 19, Tale 31

33

A Woman Haunted by a Tengu Goblin Visits the Quarters of Ninsho, the Eminent Monk of Butsugenji Temple

In olden times, there was a temple called Butsugenji in the eastern hills of Kyoto. At this temple there lived an eminent monk named Ninsho. He was a very noble monk indeed. For many years he had resided at the temple, doing his work and not going out. One day, quite unexpectedly, a woman came to this monk's cell. She was about forty years old and was the wife of a gold-leaf worker who lived in the area around Seventh Street. With her, in a bag, she brought some dried boiled rice, hard salt, and wakame seaweed. Offering them to the monk, she said, "I have heard that you are a noble monk, so I have come here to offer my services to you. I would be happy to make your robes for you so they fit you well." And then, after saying this, she left.

The monk wondered, "Who was that woman who was just here?" Then about twenty days later, the same woman came again. She brought with her a maidservant who was carrying on her head a bag that contained some polished rice, boxes of rice cakes, and appropriate seasonal fruits. In this manner, she visited several times, and so the noble monk gradually came to think favorably of her. "It must be because she respects me highly that she comes here often," he thought. Then again in July, she came with a maidservant, this time carrying some melons and peaches.

This time, the other monks in the quarters had all gone to Kyoto. Seeing the monk all by himself, the woman asked, "Are there no other monks here? I don't see anyone else." The monk replied, "The other monks had things to do in Kyoto, so they are all gone now, but they will be back soon." The woman said, "I'm glad I came today at an opportune time. In fact, it is because I have something to talk to you about that I have been coming here often. But I was not able to tell you about it, because there have always been others around. I have something important to discuss with you." So she took the monk to a place where there was no one else around. Wondering what it was she wanted to talk about, the monk moved closer to her and listened to her. The woman took his hands and said, "I've been thinking of you all these years. Won't you please help me." She moved closer and closer. Surprised, the monk demanded, "What is this about?" and tried to free himself from her grasp. Pressing herself on him desperately, the woman pleaded, "Please help me." In consternation, the monk replied, "Stop this right now. I understand your request. Certainly I will listen to what you have to say, but we can't do that unless we talk to the Buddha. First, we must talk to the Buddha." And after saying this, he attempted to walk away. The woman suspected he was going to run off, so she grabbed him and pulled him into a room where a statue of the Buddha was kept.

The monk moved to the front of the statue of the Buddha and said, "Somehow, I have been taken prisoner by a devil. Please help me, Revered Fudo, I pray of you." Saying this, the monk clutched his prayer beads so hard it seemed they would break, and he butted his head on the wooden floor so it seemed that it, too, would break. In an instant, the woman was thrown back about a dozen feet and laid out flat. With her two arms raised, she was bound by the spell of the Buddha and left spinning like a top. A while later she cried out, raising her voice as high as if it might reach the heavens. All the while, the monk clutched his prayer beads and bowed in front of the Buddha. The woman cried out again several times and butted her head against the pillar forty or fifty times, such that it seemed as if it would break. Then she screamed, "Help me, oh please, help me!"

At that point, the monk raised his head, got up, and said to the woman, "I cannot understand this. What is this all about?" Then the woman said, "Now I will tell you everything. I am a tengu goblin who haunts the Oshirakawa area of the eastern hills. When I was flying over the monks' quarters, I saw you conducting the religious services diligently, and the sound of your bell was most pleasant to hear. Then I thought, 'Why don't I debase that monk?' So I entered into the body of a woman for a couple of years and contrived to defile you. But I was bound like this by your noble, miraculous power. These past years, I have been terribly troubled, but now I have learned my lesson. Please, release me quickly. All my wings are now broken. I am completely helpless. Please, have mercy on me." As she said this, with tears in her eyes, the monk turned to the Buddha. Also in tears, he bowed deeply and then he released the woman. And at that, the woman returned to her senses and regained her former mind. Straightening her hair as she moved away, she left without saying another word.

From that time on, the woman was never seen again. It is said that the monk became even more careful, and that he devoted himself to his work ever more diligently. Such then is the story as it has been handed down to us.

Vol. 20, Tale 6

34

Empress Somedono Is Abused by a Tengu Goblin

In olden times, there was an empress named Somedono, who was the daughter of Supreme Minister Fujiwara no Yoshifusa and the mother of Emperor Montoku. She was renowned for her beauty, yet she was perpetually troubled by an evil spirit, and so various prayers were offered in the attempt to drive this spirit away. Priests who were known for having miraculous powers were called in and they conducted ceremonies for exorcism, but to no effect.

By Mt. Kazuraki in Yamato Province, at a place called Kongo Hill, there lived a noble high priest. For many years, he had trained himself in mystical practices, such that he could have a bowl fly in and bring him food, or have a jar fly about and fetch him water. Through practicing such skills, his miraculous powers came to be without compare. As his fame continued to spread, the emperor and Empress Somedono's father, the supreme minister, heard of it and thought, "Let us call him in and ask him to pray that she may be healed." So they decided to summon him to the palace. A messenger was dispatched and he went to the high priest and explained to him why he was being asked to come. The high priest declined persistently, but finally, he conceded that it would be difficult to refuse their request, and so he came.

In the presence of the emperor, the high priest offered a prayer, and soon it showed a miraculous effect. One of Empress Somedono's ladies-in-waiting immediately started crying and raving and became crazy. An evil spirit had entered her and caused her to run about and wail. While the high priest kept praying still more ardently, the woman was bound and soundly beaten. Thereupon, an old fox jumped out of her clothing, spun around, fell down, and was unable to run away. So the high priest had the fox tied up and he said a magic spell and told it to renounce its wicked ways. Seeing this happen, the empress' father, the supreme minister, was immensely happy. Empress Somedono's sickness was gone in a few days.

The supreme minister was so happy that he asked the high priest to remain at the imperial palace for a while. And so, acceding to his request, the high priest stayed on. In the summer, when a curtain was blown open by the wind, the high priest happened to catch a glimpse of Empress Somedono wearing only an unlined summer kimono. He was completely overwhelmed by her beauty, and his mind was confused, and his heart was terribly disturbed. He was consumed by a deep desire for the woman.

There was, however, nothing he could do about it, and so he just languished for her, with his heart aflame. Not even for a moment could he forget her, and owing to his deep longing, he lost his normal judgment. So one day, when there was no one around, he crept inside the curtain and grabbed the sleeping empress by her waist. The empress awoke surprised and scared. She tried to resist, perspiring heavily, but her strength was not sufficient. And so, with all his might, the high priest tried to force himself upon her. Seeing this, the ladies-in-waiting cried out and made a great commotion. Also present at the palace, at the emperor's request, was the court physician Kamotsugu, who had been called there to help cure the lady's illness. Hearing the sudden noise from the empress' sleeping quarters, he ran in, whereupon he caught the high priest trying to slip out past the curtain. He grabbed the priest and informed the emperor about the incident. The emperor was furious, and he had the priest bound and placed in prison.

In prison, the high priest said nothing and just looked up to heaven. In tears, he vowed, "I may die right now and become a demon, but while that woman is still alive in this world I will satisfy my desire with her." The prison guard overheard this and told the empress' father, the supreme minister, about it. Shocked at hearing this, the supreme minister told the emperor. They had the high priest banished to his former place in the mountains.

So the high priest went back to his temple, but his longing for the empress remained unbearable, and he prayed ardently for a chance to get near her. He prayed to the Buddha, to the Dharma, and to the Sangha to grant him the chance to get her, but it seemed impossible to fulfill his wish in this world, so he decided, "I will become a demon, as I wished for before." And so, from that point on, he stopped taking food and he starved to death within a dozen days, whereupon he immediately turned into a demon. His figure was naked and his head was bald. He was about eight feet tall, and his skin was as black as lacquer. His eyes were as large as iron bowls, his mouth open wide, and his teeth as sharp as knives. Fangs protruded from both his upper and lower jaws. He wore a red loincloth and carried a mallet at his waist. And so, this demon appeared and stood by the curtain of the room where the empress was. Those who saw the demon were frightened out of their wits and ran away, stumbling and running this way and that. Seeing all this confusion, some of the ladies-in-waiting fainted, while others lay on the floor covering their heads with their robes. No commoners witnessed this, as they were not allowed into the palace.

While this was going on, this demon stole the empress' mind and drove her insane. Thereupon, she dressed herself neatly, smiled, hid her face with a fan, entered the curtained space, and then proceeded to lay with the demon. As the ladies-in-waiting listened, the demon told the empress how he had been longing for her ceaselessly, every day. At this, the empress laughed merrily. Hearing this, the ladies-in-waiting all ran away. After a period of time, when the sun had set, the demon came out from behind the curtain and left. The ladies-in-waiting entered hurriedly, wondering what had become of the empress. Then she appeared, just as usual, as if asking, "Did anything unusual happen?" Only her eyes expressed a hint of fear.

When they reported this incident to the emperor, rather than feeling afraid, he worried deeply, "What will become of her from

131

now on?" After that, the demon continued to come every day. The empress neither looked afraid nor lost her composure. She seemed to be regarding the demon as an attractive being. Seeing this, everyone at the palace pitied her and felt immensely sad and sorry for her.

In the meantime, the demon entered into another person and declared, "I must surely avenge myself on that person Kamotsugu." Hearing of this, the physician Kamotsugu was so frightened that, before long, he suddenly died. In addition, several of Kamotsugu's sons also went insane and died. Seeing this situation, the emperor and the empress' father, the supreme minister, were so terrified that they asked important priests to pray for the demon's surrender. Perhaps as a result of the miraculous work of their prayers, the demon didn't come back for about three months, and the empress' mind recovered somewhat, and so the emperor was pleased to hear of this. He said, "I'd like to visit her once," and so, he paid a visit to her residence. It was a visit filled with far deeper emotions than usual, and all the officials and bureaucrats accompanied the emperor.

When the emperor entered her residence, he looked at her and, in tears, said some sympathetic words. The empress was deeply moved. She looked exactly as she had before. But then, the demon leaped out from a corner of the room and stepped within the curtained area. When the emperor saw this, he was astonished. Then, as before, the empress hurriedly entered the curtained area. After a while, the demon leaped to the south side of the room. On actually seeing the demon before them, the ministers, the imperial court nobles, officials, and bureaucrats were all confounded and frightened. "How incredible," they thought. Then the empress, too, came out and followed the demon. She lay with him and proceeded to engage in the most disgraceful acts, without compunction, while everyone watched. Finally, the demon got up, and so did the empress, and they went behind the curtain. There was nothing the emperor could do but grieve. And so, he went back to the palace.

This story tells us that a noble lady should not get close to such a priest. It has been said that although this story is vulgar and it shouldn't be told openly, nonetheless, it offers a lesson for future generations, showing why women should not get close to priests like that. And so, this is the story as it has been handed down to us.

Vol. 20, Tale 7

A Dragon Is Caught by a Tengu Goblin

In olden times, in a certain county of Sanuki Province, there was a large pond called Manono Pond. This pond was built by Great Teacher Kobo for the purpose of saving the common people. It was very large in circumference and had high embankments built all around it, so that it didn't look like a pond; rather, it looked like a sea. Its bottom was deep, and fish, big and small, lived in it. In it there also lived a dragon.

One day, wishing to sunbathe, the dragon emerged from the pond and coiled up in the form of a small snake and lay by the embankment, far away from any human villages. Just then a long-nosed tengu goblin, who lived on Mt. Hirano of Ohmi Province, happened to be flying over the pond in the form of a black-eared kite. When he saw the small snake lying there coiled up by the embankment, he swooped down, snatched it, and then flew off high up in the sky. Though the dragon was strong, he was caught off guard and so he couldn't do anything. He was just grabbed and carried away. The tengu goblin tried to crush the small snake into pieces and eat it, but because the dragon was so strong, the goblin couldn't crush it and so he carried him off, back to his home on Mt. Hirano. There he shoved the dragon into a narrow cave where he couldn't even move. The dragon was in anguish. There wasn't a drop of water. He couldn't fly away. And so he just waited, expecting to die in a few days.

In the meantime, the goblin thought, "I'll use this chance to go to Mt. Hiei, where I'll snatch an important monk." And so he went off at night and perched on a tall tree on the northern side of the East Tower. In front of him, were the monks' quarters, and presently one of the monks came out onto the verandah. He urinated, and then, to wash his hands, he brought out a water bottle, washed, and was about to reenter the room. At that moment, the goblin swooped down from the tree, snatched him up, and flew all the way back to the cave at his home on Mt. Hirano and shoved him into the cave, along with the dragon. The monk, with his water bottle still in hand, was dumbfounded. While the monk was still thinking, "This is the end of my life," the goblin went off, leaving the monk behind.

Then a voice sounded in the dark, asking the monk, "Who are you, and from where have you come?" The monk replied, "I am a monk from a temple on Mt. Hiei. When I was out on the verandah of the monks' quarters to wash my hands, a goblin suddenly snatched me and brought me here. So now I'm here with my water bottle. And who, may I ask, is speaking to me?" The dragon said in reply, "I am the dragon that lived in Manono Pond of Sanuki Province. When I was out on the embankment of the pond, a goblin swooped down from the sky and snatched me and brought me to this cave. It's so narrow that I can't move and I haven't even a drop of water. I can't fly into the sky." The monk said, "There may be a drop of water left in my bottle." Hearing this, the dragon was very happy and said, "I've been here for many days and I'm about to die, but now, as we've met each other, perhaps we can save each other's lives. If I could have a drop of water, certainly I could take you to your former home." The monk was very happy and he tilted the bottle to give the dragon a drop of water, and the dragon received the water.

The dragon was very happy and he said to the monk, "Do not be afraid. Just close your eyes and cling to my back. I will never forget your kindness." Thereupon, he turned himself into the form of a small child, carried the monk on his back, and kicked the cave open. When they emerged from the cave, thunderbolts rumbled and the sky grew overcast and rain fell heavily. It was all very mysterious. The monk thought, "This is terribly frightening," but as he trusted the dragon, he let himself be carried on its back. And so, in hardly any time, they arrived at the temple on Mt. Hiei. Then, after placing the monk on the verandah, the dragon flew off.

After the monks in their quarters had thought they saw lightning strike, it had suddenly turned dark as night. When it brightened up again, they saw that the monk who had suddenly disappeared the night before was there on the verandah. They thought this very strange, and so they questioned him. He told them about the incident in detail. All who heard about it were deeply impressed and filled with wonder.

After that, the dragon wanted to avenge the goblin, and so he searched for him. Finding the goblin walking around in Kyoto disguised as a rough-looking monk asking for alms, the dragon swooped down upon him and kicked him until he was dead. Thereupon, the goblin turned back into a black-eared kite with broken wings and was trampled upon in the street. The monk from the temple on Mt. Hiei chanted the sutras faithfully and performed good deeds, thus repaying what he owed the dragon.

Indeed, the dragon kept his life because of the monk's virtue, while the monk was able to return to the mountain temple with the help of the dragon. All of this must have been made possible by virtue of mysterious bonds from a previous life.

We are told that this is the tale that the monk told to his fellow monks. And such then is the story as it has been handed down to us.

Vol. 20, Tale 11

A Monk from Mt. Atago Is Bewitched by a Wild Boar

In olden times, there was a devoted monk who had been training himself for a long time on Mt. Atago in the Way of the Buddha. He devoted himself to the *Lotus Sutra*, with no interest in other matters. He didn't leave his living quarters, he had not received much education, and he hadn't studied the Buddhist scriptures.

On the west side of the mountain, there lived a hunter who made his living by hunting deer and wild boar. This hunter respected the monk highly and often visited him, occasionally bringing him gifts.

The hunter hadn't been to see the monk for quite a while, but then, one day, he visited and brought him some fruit in a bag. The monk was very pleased, and they talked about various things. Then he moved closer to the hunter and said, "A very blessed thing has been happening recently. I have faithfully believed in the *Lotus Sutra* for many years, with no interest in other matters. It may be because of this, that Fugen Bodhisattva has been appearing every night recently. Would you like to stay here tonight and worship him?" The hunter replied, "That's a wonderful thing. Yes, I'll stay and worship him."

The monk also had a boy disciple. The hunter questioned the boy; "The monk says that Fugen Bodhisattva has been appearing. Have you ever seen Fugen?" The boy answered, "Yes, I've seen him several times." The hunter thought, "Then I too might see him." And so, he sat behind the monk without going to sleep. As the date was past the twentieth of September, the night was long. While waiting eagerly, sometime after midnight, a bright light appeared from the mountains in the east, as if the moon were rising. When a gust of wind blew over from the mountains, the monk's quarters were brightened, as if lit by moonlight. As they gazed on the scene carefully, a white bodhisattva riding, on a white elephant, descended slowly. The sight was graceful and blessed. The bodhisattva approached and stood up, facing the monk's quarters.

In tears, the monk bowed to him most reverentially. He asked the hunter behind him, "And did you worship him too?" The hunter replied, "Yes, I did worship him, most reverentially." But he thought to himself, "It is natural that a monk who has been devoted to the *Lotus Sutra* for many years may see a bodhisattva, but it's strange that such people as this boy and I, who are ignorant of the sutra, might also see a bodhisattva. It shouldn't be a sin to test this situation, for I do sincerely wish to deepen my faith." And so, as he stood above the bowing and prostrating monk, the hunter fixed a sharp arrow to his bowstring, pulled the bow with all his might, and then shot at the bodhisattva. His arrow seemed to have hit the bodhisattva's breast and the light disappeared, like a fire that has been put out. It seemed to fall down into the bottom of the valley.

"Whatever did you do?" the monk asked and cried in bewilderment. The hunter replied, "Please be calm. I couldn't understand this at all, and I thought it strange. So to test it, I shot an arrow. I don't think this should be a sin." The hunter tried to comfort the monk, but his grief was not lessened. When day broke, they looked at the spot where the bodhisattva had stood and they saw that a lot of blood had been shed. They traced the marks of the blood and went down the mountainside about a hundred yards. There, at the bottom of the valley, they found a large wild boar lying dead, with an arrow piercing through it from its breast to its back. When the monk saw it, his grief subsided.

This shows us that even a monk, if he lacks wisdom, can be bewitched by animals. It also shows that even a hunter who kills animals, if he has thoughtfulness, can see through a wild boar's intentions.

And so, in such ways, do animals try to bewitch human beings. And so, also, may animals lose their lives. Some have said that these are but foolish matters, but such is the story as it has been handed down.

Vol. 20, Tale 13

37

A Man from Settsu Who Killed Cows Is Saved and Returns to This World

In olden times, there was a man who lived in Nadekubo Village of Higashinari County in Settsu Province. His family was prosperous and wealthy. The man, however, came to be haunted by an evil spirit and, to free himself from the curse, he held prayer services at which he sacrificed a cow every year. By the time he had held these services for seven years, he had killed seven cows. At that time, he fell very sick for another seven years. Although he followed the treatment prescribed by a doctor, he didn't get well. And then, when he called on a yin-yang diviner to exorcize the evil spirit, this too was of no avail. His sickness continued to get even worse, and gradually he got weaker, until he was about to die. At this point, he thought deeply, "My serious illness, my anguish, and my worries must all be the result of my sin from killing those cows." To repent his sin, he observed the precepts on each of the six precept-observing days every month, and also he sent messengers throughout the countryside and had them buy up and release birds, animals, and fish that were being held in captivity.

Nonetheless, after seven years, he finally passed away. At his dying hour he called his wife and children to his bedside and said, "When I die don't bury me right away but lay me out for nine days." And so, following this request, his wife and children did not bury him. At the end of nine days, he came back to life and recounted to his wife and children his story:

"When I died, seven beings with cow heads and human bodies came along. They tied my hair with a rope and led me off attached to the rope and guarded all around. When I looked ahead, I saw a tall building constructed in a stately fashion. When I asked, 'What kind of palace is this?' the seven beings stared at me with angry eyes without saying anything. When we got inside the gate, a dignified, important-looking person came out and had me face the seven people. He said, 'This is the person who killed you.' Thereupon, the seven people, who were all equipped with chopping boards and knives, said, 'Let's make a dish of raw flesh and vinegar and eat him. This is the enemy that killed us.' But at that moment, tens of thousands of people suddenly appeared and freed me from the rope to which I had been tied. They said, 'It is not his fault. He killed the cows to serve the demon that was haunting him. Therefore, it's the demon that is to blame.' From this point, there arose an endless dispute between the seven people and the tens of thousands of people, arguing for and against the charges, and so the King of Hell was unable to make a judgment.

"The seven persons, however, continued to insist, 'This man cut off our legs and offered them on an altar. Therefore, we'll take this man and make a dish of raw flesh and vinegar and eat him.' On the other hand, the tens of thousands of people said to the king, 'We know the situation very well. This man isn't to blame. The demon is the one to blame.' They continued to argue, and still, the King of Hell couldn't make a judgment, so he said, 'Come back tomorrow. I will make my judgment then.' And so he had them go. On the ninth day, once again, they all gathered and made their appeals, as before. The king announced, 'I will make my judgment based on the number of the people.' And so, he accepted the allegation made by the tens of thousands of people.

"When they heard, this the seven people smacked their lips, swallowed, and pretended to make a dish of raw flesh and vinegar and eat it. They were disappointed and angry, and all agreed, 'It's terrible that we couldn't get revenge. We will not forget this. We'll avenge ourselves yet,' and then, the seven left. The tens of thousands of people honored me. They took me out of the king's palace, placed me on a palanquin, and carried me along. I asked them, 'Who are you who have saved me like this?' They replied, 'We are the birds and animals you have bought and released over the years. We have not forgotten your kindness, and now we are repaying it.'"

After that, the man's religious feelings were stirred even more ardently. He paid no respect to demons and he believed ever more devoutly in the Buddha's teachings. He made a temple out of his own house, placed a statue of the Buddha in it, and diligently studied Buddhism. He also continued tirelessly to release birds and animals that were held in captivity. From that time on, he was called Natengu. In the latter years of his life, he was free from illness and he lived to be over ninety.

And thus, we are told that buying and releasing birds and animals that are held in captivity is something a faithful person should always do. And such then is the story as it has been handed down to us.

Vol. 20, Tale 15

A Man from the Old Capital Strikes a Mendicant Monk and Is Punished

In olden times, when the capital was still in the old city, there lived a man who was foolish and didn't believe in the Law of Cause and Effect.

One day a mendicant monk came to his house. The man got angry at the monk and tried to hit him. The monk ran off into the flooded rice fields, but the man caught him and began to strike him. In this predicament, the mendicant chanted a passage from a sutra and prayed, "Dear Buddha, please help me, I pray." Thereupon, the man was bound by the power of a spell. Suddenly, he began to run about and he fell into bewilderment, and so the mendicant monk was able to escape.

The man had two children. When they saw their father bound by the spell, they wanted to help him and so they went to a monastery and asked the priest to go with them and help. The priest replied, "Why are you asking me to go?" The children told him all about the incident. The priest was scared by this situation and had no wish to go. The two children, however, were eager to help their father and so they earnestly pleaded with the priest. And so finally, with reluctance, he accepted their request. During that time the father had been utterly perplexed and distraught. However, when the priest chanted the first passage of the twenty-fifth chapter of the *Lotus Sutra* the bondage of the spell was immediately released. The father's heart was filled with religious fervor and he bowed to the priest. The two children, also, were happy and they bowed to him.

Thus, it has been said that one should never despise or strike a mendicant monk, even in jest. And such then is the story as it has been handed down to us.

Vol. 20, Tale 25

39

A Man from Yamato Province Catches a Hare and Is Punished

In olden times, there lived a man in a certain county of Yamato Province. He was wild by nature and he had no sense of compassion. He loved killing animals and made his living by hunting.

One day, he went out into the fields and caught a hare, skinned it while still alive, and then left its body in a field. Not long after, pustules formed all over the man's body, his skin broke out in sores, and he suffered excruciating pains. He sent for a doctor and was prescribed some medicine for treatment, but it was to no avail. A few days later, he died. Those who saw him or heard of his fate said in rebuke, "It's clear that this must have been his punishment in this world for killing the hare."

As this story shows, human beings enjoy killing animals just for sport, but animals may value their lives even more than we human beings. Therefore, it is said that we should cease killing animals and realize that animals value their lives just as we do. Such then is the story as it has been handed down.

Vol. 20, Tale 28

40

A Man from Kawachi Kills a Horse and Receives Retribution

In olden times, in a certain county of Kawachi Province, there lived a man named Iwawake, who raised melons and made his living by selling them.

One day, he thought he would go out to sell his melons and have his horse carry them for him. But he piled on more melons than the horse could carry. The horse started out carrying all the melons, but along the way, it could no longer continue walking and so it stopped. Seeing this, Iwawake grew extremely angry, and whipped the horse, and then he piled even more melons on it. The horse shed tears from both its eyes and took on a most sorrowful expression. But because the man had no feelings of pity, he whipped it and drove it on. Finally, he finished selling the melons, but he was still very angry and so he killed the horse. In fact, he had already killed several other horses in such a way.

Following this, when Iwawake was boiling some water in a cauldron at his home, he went to the fireplace. Suddenly, both of Iwawake's eyes slipped out from his face and fell into the hot water of the cauldron. He suffered grievously, but there was nothing he could do about it. All those who heard the story agreed, "This must have been his punishment in this world for his killing of the horses."

As this story shows, we should stop killing animals and realize that animals have been our parents in our previous lives. Failing to keep this principle, the man received his punishment in this world. It is also said that we should think of the suffering to come in the next world. And so, this is the story that has been handed down.

Vol. 20, Tale 29

41

Kishi no Himaro Is Punished for Attempting to Kill His Mother

In olden times, in Kamo Village of Tama County, Musashi Province, there lived a man named Kishi no Himaro. His mother was named Kusakabe no Matoji.

During the reign of Emperor Shomu, Himaro went to Chikuzen Province following his superior, the governor of the province. He stayed there for three years. His mother accompanied him, while his wife remained in his house in Musashi Province. Longing for his wife, he thought, "I've been away from my wife for such a long time. Since I can't get permission, I can't go back to see her. But if I were to kill my mother, then I'd be allowed to go home and stay with my wife during the period of mourning."

His mother was a compassionate person and she carried out good acts all the time. One day, Himaro said to his mother, "There is a place in the mountains to the east where they hold lectures on the *Lotus Sutra* for seven days. Why don't we go and attend them?" And so in this way, he invited her to go. His mother was only too pleased to accept his suggestion and replied, "That's exactly what I would like to do. Let's go right away." Feeling her religious inspiration stirred, she took a bath, cleansed her body, and then went off with her son deep into the mountains. But there she could see no temple, such as her son had spoken of, at which to hold a religious service.

When they came to a place that was very remote from any village, Himaro stared at his mother angrily. Seeing him in this condition, his mother asked, "Why are you so angry? Have you been possessed by a demon?" Thereupon, Himaro drew his sword and was about to cut off his mother's head. But his mother kneeled in front of her son and said, "We plant a tree so that we may receive fruit and shade. We raise a child so that we may be supported by him. So why are you now about to kill me, in spite of my love for you?" Although Himaro heard these words, he would not listen and he prepared to kill her. "Wait," she cried, "I have something to tell you." And on saying this, she took off her clothes and placed them in three different places and said, "I will give this piece to you, my first son. And give this piece to my second son, your younger brother. And then, give that piece over there to my third son, your youngest brother." And so his mother announced the terms of her last will. At this point, Himaro was about to cut off his mother's head with his sword.

At that very moment, the earth was sundered apart, and Himaro began to slip into a chasm. Seeing this, his mother quickly grasped his hair and, as she looked up at the sky, she cried, "A demon has taken possession of my son. This was not his true intention. May heaven forgive his sins." Although she cried out loud, he fell and was swallowed completely by the chasm. The hair she had grasped was pulled off from his head and remained in her hands. Holding the hair, she returned home, crying mournfully. There she held a memorial service for her son. She put the hair in a box, placed it in front of the Buddha, and chanted a passage from a sutra. The mother's heart was so full of compassion, that she was able to carry out such a good deed for her son even though he had planned to kill her.

We know that heaven does not forgive the acts of an abusive son. And although, of course, we also know that people of this world should never go to such an extreme as to kill their parents, it is also stressed that we should respect our parents deeply and never treat them ill in any way, whatsoever. And so, this is the story as it has been handed down to us.

Vol. 20, Tale 33

42

A Mysterious Being Incarnated as a Beggar Refuses a Gift from Monk Gishoin

In olden times, there was a monk named Gishoin. He was the monk of Gankoji Temple and was very learned.

It was in winter that he was traveling to Gankoji from the capital. Strong winds blew over the banks of the Izumi River, and it was bitterly cold. As he was passing through the woods of Yotate, he saw a monk, with a straw mat wrapped about his waist, lying on his face in the shadow of a grave. Looking at the monk, Gishoin wondered, "Is this a dead man?" He stopped his horse and looked carefully and then he saw the body move.

Gishoin asked, "Who are you, and why are you lying there like that?" The man replied in a faint voice, "I'm a beggar." Gishoin asked, "Are you cold?" The beggar answered, "I'm too stiff to feel the cold." Gishoin felt so sorry for him that, while he remained sitting on his horse, he immediately took off one of his robes and threw it down on top of the beggar. "Put this on," he said. Then the beggar got up and removed the robe that had landed on his head and threw it back to Gishoin. The robe hit his face. Gishoin thought this was terribly rude and so he asked, "Why do you act like that?" The beggar replied, "When you give something to a person, you should dismount your horse, bow to him, and then give it. But when you threw that robe down on me from your horse, how could I accept it?" And in saying this, the man disappeared instantaneously.

Gishoin thought, "That could not have been an ordinary human being. It must have been a Buddhist sage incarnated as a human." He dismounted his horse and picked up the robe that had been thrown back to him. He bowed down to the spot where the beggar had been. But it was to no effect. He remained there long, sunk deep in thoughts, but nothing more happened. So in sadness and regret, he walked along slowly, pulling his horse behind him for a distance of about one thousand yards, until the sun went down.

Afterwards, Gishoin told others, "We should never look down on beggars like that." What he said is true even for wise monks such as he, but can fools understand such matters? Therefore, we are told that we should respect even beggars. And such is the story as it has been handed down.

Vol. 20, Tale 40

43

Vice Minister Takafuji Is Caught in a Storm and Meets a Beautiful Young Woman

In olden times, there was a man named Fuyutsugi, who was called by his title, Court Noble Kan'in of the Right. His reputation among the public was high and he was very intelligent. However, he died while he was still quite young and he left many children. The eldest son was Nagara no Chunagon, the second son was Grand Minister Yoshifusa, the third son was Minister of the Left Yoshimi, and the fourth son was Court Attendant Yoshikado. In those days, the members of important households also had to start their careers by serving as court attendants.

Court Attendant Yoshikado had a son named Takafuji. From his childhood Takafuji had loved hawking. Since his father, the court attendant, also loved hawking, Takafuji must have inherited this passion.

One day in September, when he was about fifteen years old, the young man Takafuji went off hawking. While he was tramping about around Mt. Nagisa in Southern Yamashina, suddenly, around four o'clock in the afternoon, the entire sky darkened, cold rain began to fall, winds began to blow, and thunder and lightning raged, so the men scattered in different directions seeking shelter from the storm. The young man set off swiftly on his horse, heading for a house he had noticed on the west side of the mountain. He was followed by his footman. The two of them arrived at the house, which was enclosed with a board fence made of *hinoki* cypress. This house had a small Chinese-style gate, through which the man entered on horseback. The main house had a shingled roof and a small corridor that ran along its side. He dismounted his horse, led it to the end of the corridor, and asked his footman to look after it. The young master sat down on the wooden floor. Still, the winds continued to howl, the thunder crashed, the lightning struck, and the rains continued to pour down, so they could not leave and they continued to wait out the storm there.

Soon nightfall came and they started feeling uneasy and were wondering what to do. Then a man of about forty years in age and wearing bluish-colored hunting clothes came in and said, "May I ask who you are?" The young master replied, "While we were out hawking, we were overtaken by this sudden storm. We didn't know where to go, but while on my horse and looking about for shelter, I noticed this house. We were very relieved to be able to stop here, but now we are wondering what to do." The man said, "You may stay here until the rain stops." Then he went to the footman who was tending the horse and asked him, "Could you tell me who your master is?" The footman answered, "My master is the son of the esteemed court attendant." The master of the house was very surprised to hear this. He went inside and lit some lamps and then came out again and said, "This is just a humble house, but I wouldn't want you to remain outside like this. Won't you please come inside, at least until it stops raining? Your clothes are very wet, so why don't you dry them by the fire? We will feed the horse and take care of it at the back of the corridor." The house was certainly a humble one, yet somehow, it had a look of significance. The ceiling was made of thin cypress boards, and around the room were several folding bamboo screens, and there were three or four tatami mats with clean edges decorated with flowered patterns in a Korean style. Since Takafuji was tired, he took off his clothes and lay down. The master of the house came in and offered, "Now let me dry your hunting robes and trousers by the fire," and so he took them for drying.

While Takafuji was lying there and looking about the room, a young woman, about thirteen or fourteen years of age and wearing a pale purple kimono with a deep purple pleated skirt, entered from the narrow room adjacent to the main house. She was carrying a square tray in one hand and hiding her face with a fan she held in the other. As she looked at him from the side at a distance, she seemed bashful, so he said to her, "Come closer." And so, softly, she moved closer to him. She had beautiful hair that flowed richly down over her brow, and she somehow possessed a beauty of a different sort than what could normally be expected of a woman in such a place. Then she brought over the tray on which some chopsticks had been placed. Setting this out in front of him, she retreated. Seen from behind, her hair was abundant and it seemed to reach all the way down to her knees. Then she entered again with another square tray, on which various foods had been placed. Still quite young, she could not set out the items correctly. She just placed them there and then left. On the tray were steamed rice, small radishes, abalone, dried game meat, and various other foods. As Takafuji had been out all day hawking, he couldn't resist helping himself to all of the food, even though it was the house of a humble man. Moreover, he drank all the sake that was offered. When the night grew late, he decided to go to sleep.

Takafuji, however, could not forget the young girl and he couldn't fall asleep, so he called out, "I'm afraid to sleep here alone. I'd like that girl to come here." And at that, the girl came. "Come closer," he said, and he pulled her to his side. He held her in his arms and they lay together. She looked even more attractive than when seen from a distance. Takafuji was completely taken by her and, although he was still young, he promised his unfailing love to her, and they continued to exchange their love all night long. She looked wondrously elegant, and he talked with her throughout the night. When the dawn broke, he got up and prepared to leave. He took his sword and handed it to her saying, "Take this and keep it to remember me by. Even if your parents should thoughtlessly ask you to marry someone else, you must refuse." And so, with great reluctance, he took his leave.

When Takafuji had ridden his horse about four hundred yards from the house, he met up with several men who were out looking for him. They were happy to be reunited and they went back to the house in Kyoto together. His father, the court attendant, had been worrying because his son had gone out hawking the previous day and hadn't come back. He had been worrying all night long, wondering, "What could have happened?" So at daybreak, he had sent out his men to search. When his son returned with them, he was overjoyed and said, "In youth, one can't resist the desire to go out. I, too, used to go out when I was your age, and my father didn't stop me, so I let you go freely. But when a thing like this happens, it worries me greatly, so please don't go off like this again from now on." And so from then on, Takafuji stopped going out hawking.

The men who had gone hawking with the young man hadn't seen the house he visited and none of them knew about it. Only the footman who had taken care of his horse knew the house. But the footman had since taken leave from his work and returned to his hometown, so now there was no one there who knew of the place. Although Takafuji longed for the young woman, he was unable to send her messages. As time passed, his longing only increased. And so, still longing for her, several years passed.

During this time, his father, the court attendant, died at a rather young age. Consequently, the young man went to his uncle's place and lived there. The young Takafuji was very handsome and kind-hearted, and his uncle Yoshifusa was very fond of him. "What a wonderful young man," he thought. Takafuji now had no father and he felt lonely and could only think of that young woman. And so, in this way, about six years passed.

One day, he heard that the man who had taken care of his horse had come to the capital from the countryside, so he called him in, pretending that he wanted to have him attend to his horse. He asked, "Do you remember the house we once visited when we went hawking and took shelter from the rain?" The man replied, "I certainly do." The young master continued, "Well, I'd like to visit that house today. Let's go there, as if we're out hawking. I'd like you to keep that in mind, all right?" And so they set off and crossed over Amida Peak, taking with them a low-ranking guard with whom the master was on friendly terms. They arrived at the place at sunset.

As it was near the twentieth of February, the plum blossoms in front of the house were falling, and a bush warbler was singing beautifully on a treetop, and the petals of the blossoms were floating along on the stream in the garden. The whole atmosphere was most enchanting. They entered the yard, with Takafuji riding on his horse.

When he called to the head of the house, the man came out, happily surprised by this unexpected visit. Takafuji asked if the young lady was still there, and the answer was, "Yes." He was very happy. Then he was led to a room where she was sitting by a curtained screen, as if hiding bashfully. When he came closer and looked carefully, he saw that she had grown more mature and even more attractive than before. He wondered how there could be such a beautiful woman in the entire world. And by her side, was a beautiful young girl, about five or six years old. "Who is this little girl?" he asked. Glancing downward, the woman looked as if she were crying. As she didn't seem to answer readily, Takafuji called her father, who came in and prostrated himself. The young master asked him who the child was. Then the father answered, "My daughter has never been close to any man since you visited here that time. She was quite young and had never been with a man, but after you came she became pregnant and then she gave birth to this child." Hearing this, Takafuji was terribly surprised. And then, when he looked at the bedside, he saw the sword he had left with her. Realizing that she had so faithfully kept her promise, he was overwhelmed with emotions. And when he looked at the little girl, it seemed that she looked just like him. And so he stayed there overnight.

The following morning, he had to leave, but he said, "I will be back and I will take you with me." And so he left. He wanted to know who the head of the house was, so he made some inquiries and found that his name was Miyajino Iyamasu and that he was the mayor of the county. He thought, "This woman is the daughter of such a humble man. She must have had a deep connection with me in our previous existence." And so the next day he came back, accompanied by two samurai, with a carriage covered with straw mats and hanging reed screens. He had the woman and the little girl ride in the carriage. And since it would have looked inappropriate if there had been no attendant, he asked the woman's mother to accompany them, and he had her ride in the carriage, too. She looked to be a bit over forty years in age and was dressed very neatly and she seemed a very suitable wife for the county mayor. She wore a stiff, light yellow dress and her hair was hanging down and covered in the back beneath a robe. He took them all to his residence and there he lived with this woman and paid no attention to other women. Soon after, two sons were born to them, one right after the other.

Takafuji was a very fine man, and steadily he got ahead in the world. In time, he became Chief Councilor of State. When Emperor Uda was still on the throne, the daughter of Takafuji became the empress. Shortly after, she gave birth to a son and he became Emperor Daigo. The older of their two sons, Sadakuni, became General of the Right under the Chief Councilor of State. He was also called the General of Izumi. Their younger son, Sadakata, became the Minister of the Right. He was also called Minister of the Right of Sanjo. The boys' grandfather, the mayor, was promoted to a fourth-ranking noble and he served as the director in charge of repair work. When Emperor Daigo was enthroned, his grandfather Takafuji, who was at the time the chief councilor of state, was made vice minister.

The house of Iyamasu was turned into a temple and it is now known as Kanshuji Temple. Beyond it on Mt. Higashiyama, Iyamasu's wife built a temple, which is called Ohyakedera temple. The family must have thought fondly of this area where Iyamasu built his house, since they built the mausoleum nearby for Emperor Daigo.

And so we can see how taking shelter temporarily from a rainstorm brought about this happy result, all because of providence from the couple's previous existence. And such then is the story as it has been passed down to us.

Vol. 22, Tale 7

44

Tachibana no Norimitsu, a Former Administrative Officer of Michinoku Province, Kills Three Bandits

In olden times, there lived a man named Tachibana no Norimitsu, who was formerly an administrative officer of Michinoku Province. He was not from a samurai family, but was very stouthearted, prudent, and strong. He was also handsome and his reputation was excellent, so he was highly respected by the people.

While still young and serving as an official of the Imperial Guards during the reign of Emperor Ichijo, he went off in secret from the night guards' room to visit a woman. With night already deepening, he went out from the palace gate, taking only a sword with him. As he was walking down Ohmiya Street, accompanied by a boy servant, he sensed the presence of some people near the hedge. Apprehensively, he walked on. Since the early August moon was hanging along the edge of the western mountains and the area by the hedge on the west side was covered in shadow, he couldn't clearly see the people who were standing there. He heard a voice from the hedge call out, "Hey, you there—stop! An important person is coming, so you can't go that way now." Norimitsu thought, "Well, someone must be coming," but he saw no way of turning back, so he kept on walking quickly. Then someone came running toward him, calling out, "How dare you pass by?"

Norimitsu threw himself on the ground. He looked around and saw that the other person had no bow, though he noticed the glint of a sword. He felt relieved that his assailant had no bow, so he ran off, keeping his body low. The other person chased after him. Just at the moment when he thought, "Now for sure my head will be struck and broken," he suddenly stepped aside and his pursuer ran on, unable to stop quickly. Thereupon, Norimitsu drew his sword and struck his assailant, cleaving his head in two. The man collapsed and fell.

Thinking to himself, "Well done, indeed," another man came running along and demanded, "What's happened here?" Since Norimitsu had no time to put his sword back into its sheath, he ran off with the sword under his arm. His attacker kept running after him, muttering, "That's some bold fellow." As this attacker seemed to be faster than the first one, Norimitsu feared he might not be able to take care of him as he had done before. Thinking quickly, he suddenly crouched down and the assailant stumbled over him. Before the man could get up again, Norimitsu stood up, turned around, struck his head hard and broke it.

While he was thinking, "That should be the end of this," yet another man came running along. "What a bold fellow this is," he remarked. "I won't let him go free." While this man chased after him, Norimitsu prayed, "This time it looks like I won't be able to get away. May the gods and the Buddha save me!" He held out his sword as if wielding a halberd and confronted the man who came running. He pressed himself against the man. The man attempted to strike him with his sword, but being too close he couldn't even cut through his clothes. But since Norimitsu had held his sword out like a halberd, it pierced through his opponent's body. He pulled out his sword, struck him with it, and then the man fell on his back. The arm that had held a sword was severed from his body and it fell.

Norimitsu ran off and then listened, wondering if there were still any other men. Sensing that there was no one else around, he ran back inside the gate and hid himself behind a pillar. He waited for his boy servant, wondering what had happened to him. Then the boy came along, walking northward along Ohmiya Street in tears. Norimitsu called out to him and he came running. He sent the boy to the night watchmen's room, telling him to bring back a change of clothing. The robe and trousers he had been wearing were stained with blood. He firmly told the boy not to say anything about what had happened. He washed the blood from the hilt of his sword, changed his robe and trousers, and then returned to the night watchmen's room, and slept as if nothing had happened.

All night he worried, "They may find out what I have done." When day broke, he heard some people talking loudly. One said, "Around Ohino-mikado Gate on Ohmiya Street, three big men are lying there, cut down, not far from each other. The swordsmanship is excellent. First, we thought they might have fought among themselves, but when we looked carefully at the openings of their wounds, it appeared that the cuttings were all done by the same man. We wondered if it was the work of our enemies, but the man seems to have tried to make it look as if it was done by a bandit." On hearing this story, even court nobles wanted to go and take a look. So they went off saying, "Let's have a look." They asked Norimitsu to go along too. He didn't feel like going, but reluctantly he went with them, thinking, "If I don't go they may suspect me."

The wagons in which they rode were overcrowded. When they arrived at the scene, the bodies still lay there, unattended. Standing there was a bearded, scruffy looking man, around thirty years of age, wearing plain trousers and a worn-out, dark blue lined garment, covered by a yellow top with faded sleeves. He was equipped with a sword, the sheath of which was covered with boar skin, and he was wearing a pair of deerskin shoes. He was thumping his chest proudly, pointing at the bodies with his finger and talking to the people gathered around him, who wondered who he was. Some lower-class workers, who had arrived with the wagons, were saying, "This guy's saying they were his enemies and he killed them." Hearing this, Norimitsu was very happy.

Some court nobles on the wagon cried out, "Bring that man here. Let's question him about the incident," and so the man was summoned.

The man had prominent cheekbones, a wide lower jaw, a hooked nose, and reddish hair. His eyes were bloodshot, perhaps from rubbing them too much. He knelt down on one knee, holding the hilt of his sword. The court nobles asked him, "What really happened here?" The man replied, "When I was passing this place around midnight, three men ran up and called out, 'How dare you pass this place freely?' I realized they were bandits and so I got them all. When I looked at them carefully, I could see they had been looking for a chance to kill me. I thought I was lucky to have been able to get my enemies. I was just thinking of cutting their heads off." After saying this, he stood up. He talked on, sometimes pointing at the bodies with his finger and then looking up and looking down, by turns. The court nobles listened to him saying, "Well, is that so?" They continued asking him question and he talked on and on, seeming to become increasingly deranged.

While this was going on, Norimitsu found it very amusing. Happily, he thought, "It's good that this guy is proclaiming himself the killer of those men. Now the crime has been turned over to him." He raised his head in relief. It has been said that when he got older, Norimitsu told his children that he had secretly been worrying about what would happen if it were found out that he was the real killer, and that he was very relieved when this person had announced himself as the killer.

Norimitsu was the son of a man named Toshimasa and the father of Tachibana no Suemichi, the former administrative officer of Surugu Province. And this is the story as it has been passed on down.

Vol. 23, Tale 15

A Wrestler Named Amano Tsuneyo Meets a Snake and Tries His Strength

In olden times, in Tango Province, there was a sumo wrestler named Amano Tsuneyo. By the house where he lived, there was an old river. One summer day, Tsuneyo stopped to rest beneath a tree by the riverbank where the water ran deeply. He was wearing a summer kimono, an obi sash, a pair of wooden clogs, and holding a two-pronged stick. Accompanied by a page, he had been walking around the countryside trying to catch cool breezes and thus, he had come to the foot of the tree by the deep spot of the river.

The deep spot looked blue and slow moving, and its bottom could not be seen. Tsuneyo was standing there looking at the reeds, when he noticed, about ten yards away from the far side of the river, the surface of the water rising and moving toward him. He wondered what it could be. As the thing approached closer to his side of the river, Tsuneyo could see that it was a big snake, with its head sticking up and out of the water. Looking at it, Tsuneyo thought, "Judging from its head, it must be quite large. I wonder if it will come all the way over here." Then, raising its head, the snake stared at him for a while. "I wonder what that snake thinks of me," he thought. Standing several feet away from the edge of the water, Tsuneyo kept looking at it. The snake, too, looked at him for a while and then slipped its head back into the water.

Soon after, the surface of the water on the other side of the river seemed to rise, and then it seemed to move toward the near side, causing ripples to form on the surface. Then, sticking its tail up out of the water, the snake came closer. Tsuneyo thought, "The snake must be scheming to do something." As he watched, the snake extended its tail and coiled it twice around his legs. Tsuneyo kept standing there wondering, "What is it going to do?" When it had finished coiling its tail around his legs, the snake began to pull him tightly. The supports of his clogs were strained by the pressure. Tsuneyo thought, "It must be trying to pull me into the river." Then, as he braced his legs firmly on the ground, the snake pulled on him with great strength until the supports of his clogs broke off. Realizing that he could be pulled down, Tsuneyo planted himself firmly, but the snake pulled on him with even greater force, until he really feared he might be pulled down. So Tsuneyo planted himself there with all his might. His feet sunk about seven inches into the hard ground. While he wondered in amazement at its strength, the snake snapped like a rope. Blood seemed to spread out across the river, and so he pulled with his feet, and in time the snake was hauled up onto the shore. The tail of the snake that had been coiled around Tsuneyo's legs lay there uncoiled. Though he washed his legs, the marks from the snake's tail would not come off.

In the meantime, a large number of Tsuneyo's men came along. Someone said, "Let's wash off the marks with sake," and so, immediately, they got some sake and began washing Tsuneyo's legs. When they finally pulled up all of the snake's tail and looked, it was enormous indeed. In cross section it looked to be about one foot wide. When they sent someone to the other side of the river to get the upper part of the snake, they found it was coiled several times around a big tree on the riverbank. The snake had extended its tail and coiled itself around Tsuneyo's legs and pulled. Yet Tsuneyo's strength was still stronger than the snake's, so it broke in the middle. It's strange that the snake would pull its tail to the extent that its body broke.

After that, the people wanted to estimate how many men's strength was equal to that of the snake, so they coiled a big rope around Tsuneyo's legs, in the same way as the snake had wrapped its tail around him, and they had ten men pull. Tsuneyo said, "They're not as strong as the snake." So then they added three more men, and then again another five, but still Tsuneyo said, "They aren't as strong as the snake." Finally, when about sixty more men were there and pulling, he said, "That's about it." So judging from this, Tsuneyo must have been as strong as about one hundred men put together.

Such a feat is really quite astonishing. It has been said that there used to be a number of sumo wrestlers as strong as that in those days. Such then is the story as it has been handed down to us.

Vol. 23, Tale 22

46

Kudara no Kawanari the Painter Competes with the Craftsman of Hida

In olden times, there was a painter named Kudara no Kawanari. He was an artist beyond compare. It was he who designed the rock garden by the Waterfall Pavilion and painted the murals on its walls.

One day Kawanari's young attendant ran off. The painter searched everywhere for the boy, but it was to no avail, and so he said to a certain noble's servant, "The young attendant I have been using these past few years has run away. I would like you to find him for me." The servant replied, "That shouldn't be too difficult, but first I'll need to know what he looks like. How can I catch him unless I know that?" Kawanari replied, "That's true." And so he took out some paper he had in his pocket and drew a likeness of the boy. He handed it to the servant and said, "Find a boy who looks like this. A lot of people gather in the marketplaces in the east and west parts of Kyoto, so go and look there." The servant took the sketch and went to the marketplaces at once. There were many people, but he could find no one who looked like the boy in the picture. He waited for some time, thinking, "Someone who looks like this may show up," and then, after a while, a boy who looked like the one in the picture came along. When the servant took out the picture and compared it with the boy, they were exactly the same. "This is the one!" he exclaimed, and so he caught the boy and took him back to Kawanari. When Kawanari saw him, sure enough, it was the boy. Kawanari was very glad. Those who heard the story were very impressed, and it furthered his reputation for painting with such realism and skill.

At that time, there also lived a craftsman who was known as the Craftsman of Hida. This craftsman had played an important role when the capital was moved from Nara to Kyoto. He was a craftsman beyond compare. He built the exquisitely beautiful Burakuin Hall. As it happened, this craftsman was trying to compete with Kawanari. One day, the Craftsman of Hida mentioned to Kawanari, "At my house I have built a six-foot square shrine. Why don't you come over and take a look? I'd like to have you paint murals in it." Kawanari thought, "He may be saying this since we have been on friendly terms and competing with each other," and so he went to the house of the Craftsman of Hida. When he looked around, he saw an elaborately designed small shrine. On each of the four sides was an open door. The Craftsman of Hida said to him, "Go inside the shrine and take a look." Kawanari stepped onto the verandah and tried to enter through the door on the south side, but suddenly it closed with a bang. Surprised, he walked around and tried to enter by the door on the west, but like the other door, it too closed with a bang. Then the door on the south side opened again. Then, when he tried to enter by the door on the north side, it shut, and the door on the west opened. And when he tried to enter by the door on the east side, it too closed, and the door on the north side opened. In this manner, Kawanari went round and round several times. The doors kept opening and closing, and he was unable to get in. In frustration, he stepped down from the verandah. At that, the Craftsman of Hida burst out into laughter. Kawanari felt chagrined and went back home.

Several days later, Kawanari sent a messenger to the Craftsman of Hida with the message, "Please come over to my place. I have something to show you." The Craftsman of Hida thought, "He must be planning to play a trick on me," and so he didn't go. But since Kawanari kept asking him cordially to come over for a visit, in time, he did go. On announcing his arrival, a servant said, "Please come this way." When he had been shown in, he pulled open the sliding door by the corridor and there he saw a large human body, all black and swollen, lying near the entrance of the room. Its stench stung his nose. On encountering this most unexpected thing, he uttered a cry of fear and stepped back. When Kawanari heard the cry from inside the house, he laughed out loud. The Craftsman of Hida kept standing there in fright. Kawanari stuck his head out from the sliding door and said, "Well now, what's happened? Do come in." The Craftsman of Hida stepped closer, trembling with fear. He looked, and then saw that it was a picture of a dead man, drawn on the sliding paper door. This had been done to get even with him for what he had done at the small shrine.

Such was the skill of the two men. Their story was talked about everywhere, and everyone praised them both. And such then is the story as it has been handed down to us.

Vol. 24, Tale 5

47

A Woman Visits a Physician, Is Healed, and Runs Away

In olden times, there lived a prominent court physician. He was the finest court physician of the age and was highly respected by all.

One day, a gorgeously decorated carriage carrying a lady came to the court physician's house. Seeing the carriage, the court physician asked, "Whose carriage is this?" but no one answered, and it proceeded into the yard. Then several attendants detached the carriage from the ox, hung the yoke on a latticed wall, and the men sat by the gate.

The court physician went over to the carriage and asked, "Who has come? What is the purpose of your visit?" Someone inside the carriage spoke in a sweet and attractive voice without identifying herself, "Would you please prepare a room for me, and then I will get out." Since the old court physician was by nature a man of strong sexual passions and he lusted for women, he kept a room prepared in a corner of the house that was far away from the other rooms. He had it tidied up and had a folding screen brought in and tatami mats placed in it. Then he returned to the carriage and told the woman that the room was ready. The woman requested, "Would you please step out of my way," and so the court physician stepped back. Then the woman emerged from the carriage, hiding her face with a fan. He had thought there might be another woman accompanying her, but no one else was there. When the woman was out of the carriage, a girl of about fifteen or sixteen came over to it and took out a gold-lacquered comb box. Then the attendants came back and attached the ox to the carriage and dashed off, as if flying away.

The woman sat down in the room. The girl brought in the wrapped comb box and sat behind the folding screen. Then the court physician walked closer and asked, "Who, may I ask, are you, and why did you come here? Please let me know at once." The woman replied, "Please come in. I won't be bashful." And so the court physician entered the area beyond the reed screen. They sat there facing each other. The woman was about thirty, and from her hair on down, everything—her eyes, nose, and mouth—all looked extremely beautiful. Her hair was very long. She was wearing exquisite clothing that smelled of fragrant incense. She didn't appear to be bashful and she sat comfortably facing the man, as if she were his wife of many years.

Looking at her, the court physician thought, "This is odd," and he mused, "I'd like to make a conquest of this woman, by all means." Showing a determined grin on his toothless withered face, he came closer and talked with her. Moreover, as he had lost his wife of many years a few years back and was now a widower, he was particularly happy to see the woman. The woman said, "The human heart is such a foolish thing. I consider my life so precious that I will do anything to save it, no matter what embarrassment I may incur. That is why I came here. It is now up to you, whether you will let me live or die. I will entrust my life to you." And on saying this, she wept bitterly.

The court physician pitied her deeply and asked, "What is it that is troubling you?" The woman tucked up her skirt and showed him her thigh. Her thigh was white as snow, but it had a somewhat swollen area. Since the swelling looked suspicious, he asked her to loosen the cords of her skirt and then he examined the part above. As it was covered in hair, he couldn't see the affected part well. Then the court physician probed with his hand and found a red swelling near her private parts. He pushed aside the hair with both hands and took a careful look—it was a very dangerous tumor. Pitying her immensely, he thought, "As I am a physician with many years of experience, I will do my utmost to cure this swelling." From then on he allowed no others to come near. Day and night, with his sleeves rolled up, he did everything he could.

After he had treated the woman for about a week, she became quite well. The court physician was very pleased, but he thought, "I'll have her stay here for a while like this. After I find out who she is, then I'll let her go home." He stopped cooling the affected area. He ground up something in a cup and applied it to the spot with a feather, five or six times a day. "Now," he thought, "everything is all right." He was very pleased.

Then the woman said, "I have shown you my secret self. Now, quite honestly, I look on you as a parent. So when I go home, would you please send me back in a carriage? Then I will let you know my name. And I will come here to visit from time to time." The court physician thought eagerly, "She'll stay here for several more days." But toward evening, while he was a bit careless, the woman, wearing a nightgown of thin cotton, slipped away taking the girl with her. Unaware of this, the physician thought, "I'll serve her evening meal." So he placed some food on a tray and brought it to the woman's room. Seeing no one in the room, he thought, "She must be attending to her needs or something," and so he went back with the food.

The sun had set, so the physician thought he would light a candle. He placed the candle on a candle stand and went back into the room. There he saw her clothes, taken off and scattered around. The comb box was there too. He wondered, "What has she been doing, hiding behind the folding screen for such a long time?" After calling out, "What have you been doing in there for so long?" he looked behind the screen, but he saw neither the woman nor the girl. The clothes were heaped one on top of the other, and the skirt was left abandoned. Only the nightgown of thin cotton was missing. He wondered, "Has the woman gone off wearing just that?" Shocked and dumbfounded, he couldn't think what to do.

The gate was barred and many people carrying around lights searched all through the household. But what was there to find? In

169

his mind, the court physician envisioned the woman's features and his regret was immense. He thought, "I should have fulfilled my desire when she was ill. Why did I refrain from making a conquest of her, waiting for her to get well?" He felt chagrined at his squandered opportunity. Until then he had been thinking, "I have no wife. I should never have refrained from winning that woman. Even if she is someone else's wife, I could have visited her from time to time. That would have been wonderful, even if I couldn't make her my own wife." Now he had been completely fooled, and she had managed to get away. He was so terribly disappointed that he beat his hands and stamped furiously on the ground. As he wept bitterly, making his ugly face even uglier, his medical disciples laughed heartily when he wasn't looking. Hearing of the incident, people among the general public also laughed and asked the court physician about it. He grew very angry about this, but then, reluctantly, he explained the situation.

We can see how very smart the woman was. The identity of that woman, we are told, still remains unknown. And such then is the story as it has been handed down.

Vol. 24, Tale 8

48

The Monk Tojo Predicts
the Fall of Shujaku Gate

In olden times, there was a monk named Tojo. He could foretell people's longevity, their wealth or poverty, and their levels of official rank by looking at their figures, listening to their voices, and noting their behavior. His predictions were invariably correct, and therefore many men and women, as well as monks and laymen, from all over Kyoto made their way to his living quarters.

One day, when he was out on business, he passed by Shujaku Gate. Seeing many people—men, women, young, and old—resting under the gate, he could foresee that they might all die very soon. He stood there wondering, "What could this all mean?" Their physiognomies clearly indicated the circumstances of their deaths.

Thinking about this, he wondered, "How could all these people die all at once? Even if some evil person should come to kill them, he could only kill a few—but not all of them at once. This is so strange." Then he thought, "I wonder, might this gate be about to collapse? If so, all of these people could be crushed to death." So he cried out loudly to the people under the gate, "Look out! The gate is about to fall and crush you all to death. Quick! Get out!" On hearing this, people ran out in consternation.

Tojo, too, moved far away from the gate. No wind blew, no earthquake struck, and the gate had showed no signs of falling. But then, suddenly, the gate tilted more and more and finally it fell. Those who had run away quickly were saved, but those who were careless and moved away slowly were crushed to death. Later, when he told others about this, they were deeply impressed by his profound ability to read peoples' physiognomies.

Tojo's living quarters were near Ichijo Street. One night, when a spring rain was falling quietly, he heard someone passing along the street playing a flute. On hearing it, he called his disciple and said, "I don't know who is passing by playing the flute, but I can tell that there is very little time left in his life. I'd like to talk to him about it." But because it was raining hard and the flute-player soon passed on his way, Tojo didn't get to talk to him.

The next day, it stopped raining. Toward evening, the flute player of the previous night passed by again. Hearing it, Tojo said, "That man passing by playing the flute, he must be the one who passed by last night. It's very odd." His disciple replied, "That's right, but what have you got to do with him?" Tojo told his disciple, "Go and call that man playing the flute." So the disciple ran off and brought him back.

Looking at him, Tojo saw that it was a young man, and he seemed to be a samurai. Tojo had him come before him and said, "I called you because when you passed by playing the flute last night, I could foresee that your life would end that day or the next and I wanted to tell you about it. But it was raining so hard and you just passed by, so I couldn't talk to you about it. I was feeling so sorry for you, but since I just heard you playing the flute now, I can see that your life has been extended. What kind of religious service did you perform?" The samurai replied, "I didn't perform any particular service, but some people were holding a study meeting about Fugen Bodhisattva at Kawasaki, to the east of this place, and I accompanied the sutra-chanting with my flute, all through the night." When Tojo heard this, he thought, "This man was able to exonerate himself from a sin and extend his life, owing to the merit of his good work in playing the flute at the study meeting on Fugen Bodhisattva." He was deeply touched and, in tears, he bowed deeply to the man. The samurai, too, was happy and he went away with a glad heart.

This story took place quite recently. And so we have been told that there was such a profound teller of fortunes. And such is the story as it has been handed down to us.

Vol. 24, Tale 21

Minamoto no Hiromasa, a High-ranking Court Noble, Visits the Blind Man Living in Ausaka

In olden times, there lived a man named Minamoto no Hiromasa. He was a son of the Prince in Charge of Military Affairs, who was the son of Emperor Daigo. He was skilled in many fields and was especially accomplished at playing wind and string instruments. He played the *biwa* lute beautifully. He also played the flute exquisitely. He was a court noble during the reign of Emperor Murakami.

Around that time, in a hut by the border-checking station in Ausaka, there lived a blind man whose name was Semimaro. He had been a worker at the house of Prince Atsumi, the minister of ceremonies. Prince Atsumi was the son of the Emperor Uta and he excelled at playing wind and string instruments. Semimaro had listened to him play the *biwa* for many years, and thus, he himself came to play it excellently.

Hiromasa continued to enjoy devoting himself to playing the *biwa*. One day, he was told that the blind man at the checking station of Ausaka was an excellent *biwa* player and so he wished to hear this blind *biwa* player. The blind man's hut was so humble that he did not deign to make a visit there, himself, but he sent a messenger to the blind man and conveyed the message: "Why do you live in such an out-of-the-way place? You should come to live in Kyoto." When the blind man heard the message, he replied with a poem instead of giving a usual answer:

One can live
in any place of the world
one wishes,
since whether a palace or a hut,
both will fall into decay eventually.

The messenger returned to his master and reported this. Hearing of it, Hiromasa was greatly impressed and thought deeply, "As I am so devoted to this art, I am eager to meet the blind man. I don't know when this man may die. I don't know when I myself may die, either. I know there are pieces for the *biwa* called "Ryusen" and "Takuboku." These pieces may die out from the world some day. Only the blind man must know them. I must try to hear him play those pieces, by all means." And so, one night he went to the checking station of Ausaka. Semimaro, however, didn't play the pieces. So night after night, Hiromasa kept visiting the area around the blind man's hut. For three years he stood there secretly, expecting him to play those pieces. Still, he never played them. But after three years, on the night of August 15, the moon was veiled slightly in mist, and a faint wind was blowing. Hiromasa thought, "Ah, this is an especially charming night. I have a feeling the blind man of Ausaka may play "Ryusen" and "Takuboku." So he went to Ausaka and stood there, pricking up his ears to listen, and then the blind man began to strum the *biwa*, as if deep in thought.

While Hiromasa was listening, rapt with pleasure, the blind man spoke to himself with great emotion:

The storm
at the checking station of Ausaka
is so strong
that I remain sleepless,
sitting up to pass the night.

As the blind man played on the lute, Hiromasa listened to him, indescribably touched by the music, and shedding tears.

Again, the blind man spoke to himself, "Ah, this is such a beautiful night! Would that there were another man who realized the beauty of the world! How I wish a refined person would come along tonight. How I would like to talk with such a person." When Hiromasa heard these words, he spoke out loud, "I, a man named Hiromasa from Kyoto, am here." The blind man asked, "Who was it who just spoke?" Hiromasa answered, "I am Hiromasa, who has been so interested in the art of the *biwa* that I have come and stood by your hut for three years. Fortunately, tonight I've been able to meet you." The blind man was very happy to hear this. Hiromasa, too, was very happy, and they both entered the hut and talked. Hiromasa said, "I would like to hear you play 'Ryusen' and 'Takuboku.'" And so the blind man played the pieces, saying, "The late prince used to play like this." He showed him the way to play the pieces. As Hiromasa had not brought a *biwa* with him, he learned the art from the blind man's oral instruction. He was very pleased and returned home at daybreak.

As we can see from this story, one should study an art ardently, in such a way. But nowadays things are so different. Therefore, there are few masters in the arts in this degenerate age. It is lamentable indeed.

Although Semimaro was a humble person, he had listened to the prince play the *biwa* over the years and so he had learned to be such a skillful player. When he became blind, he went to live in Ausaka. It is said that blind people have come to play the *biwa* ever since. And this is the story that has been passed down to us.

Vol. 24, Tale 23

50

The Nun at Ohe no Asatsuna's Home Gives a Correct Reading of a Poem

In olden times, during the reign of Emperor Murakami, there was a literary scholar named Ohe no Asatsuna. He was an excellent scholar and he served for many years at the imperial court in the field of literature. He was always competent and finally he became Councilor of State and passed away at an age of over seventy.

Since his house was located at the corner of Nijo Street and Kyo-goku Avenue, it had a very good view over the riverbed to the east. From it, one could view the moon very beautifully. Many years after Asatsuna's death, on the night of August 15, the moon was magnifi-cently beautiful, and so a group of about a dozen lovers of literature got together and thought of holding a moon-viewing party. "Let's go to the house of the late Asatsuna," they said. And so they went.

When they saw the compound, it was old and desolate and it seemed to have no humans living in it. Its buildings were ram-shackle, and only the one for cooking remained standing. They sat on the broken verandah and viewed the moon, reciting poems. There was one poem that read:

> *I stand on the sand of the river's shore,*
> *a shawl on my shoulder in clear autumn air.*
> *The moon climbs the hundred-foot-high tower*
> *of Changan Castle.*

It was written by a Chinese poet of the Tang Dynasty on the night of August 15, while he was viewing the moon. The group recited this poem and was talking about the late Asatsuna's literary excellence when a nun appeared from the northeast direction and asked, "Who are you, reciting this poem?" They answered, "We have come to view the moon. And who, might we ask, are you?" The nun replied, "I served the late councilor, and now I am the only one left. There were many men and women who served at this house, but all are now gone now, and I am the only one left and I may be gone today or tomorrow." Those in the poetry group were deeply touched by the nun's words and some shed tears.

Then the nun said, "Just now you read, 'The moon climbs the hundred-foot-high tower of Changan Castle.' The late councilor, however, read it: 'I climb the hundred-foot-high tower by the light of the moon.' Your reading differs from that of the late councilor. How could the moon climb the tower? It is people who climb a tower to view the moon." Hearing this, all were impressed by the nun's remark and they shed tears.

They asked, "What kind of person were you in the past?" The nun replied, "I used to wash and stretch pieces of kimonos at the house of the late councilor. Because I used to hear the master reciting that poem all the time, I remembered it when I heard you reciting it." They went on to talk with the nun all through the night and gave her gifts, and finally they returned home at dawn.

We can see that Asatsuna's family tradition was refined. Even his lowly maidservant was like that. How much more refined then, must have been Asatsuna's literary talent? And such then is the story as it has been handed down to us.

Vol. 24, Tale 27

51
Arihara no Narihira Composes Tanka Poems on His Trip East

In olden times, there lived a man named Arihara no Narihira. He was well known as a womanizer.

Narihira, however, considered himself worthless—not worthy of living in this world—so he decided he should no longer live in Kyoto. He thought there might be a place for him to live in the eastern part of the country, so he took a couple of his trusted men and set off on a journey. None of them knew the way very well and so, as they traveled, they lost their way from time to time.

After some time, they arrived at a place called Eight Bridges in the province of Mikawa. It was called Eight Bridges because the river branched off in different directions and there were eight bridges over the forks. There was shade under the trees on the riverbank. There, Narihira dismounted his horse, sat down, and ate his meal of dried rice. Along the sides of the river, there were irises blooming beautifully, so the men accompanying him proposed that he compose a poem using the four letters, I, R, I, S, at the beginning of each line*, to express his feelings as a traveler. And so Narihira wrote a poem as follows:

> *I left my longtime wife*
> *Remaining at home.*

---

* In the original Japanese the men do not, of course, propose using the Roman alphabet letters I, R, I, S; rather, they suggest using the Japanese syllabic characters *ka, ki, tsu, ba,* and *ta*. Put together, *kakitsubata* means a kind of iris. By a fortunate coincidence, the meaning of the poem, translated into English, fits the format of using the alphabet letters I, R, I, and S at the beginning of each line. Thus, we have employed this surprising transformation, maintaining the connection with iris.

I now think on how it is
Such a long journey I have made.

The men who heard the poem were deeply impressed and shed tears. Their tears dropped onto their meal of dried rice, such that it became wet and soggy.

Leaving that place, they traveled for a long distance on their way and arrived in the province of Suruga. They were about to go up a mountain called Mt. Utsu. The road was dark and they felt terribly apprehensive. Ivy vines and maple trees grew rank, and the road looked dreary. While Narihira was thinking, "What a terrible road we have to take," quite unexpectedly, he met a monk. Looking at him carefully, it turned out that the monk was someone he had known in Kyoto. The monk looked at Narihira and thought it strange to find him so unexpectedly in such a place. "Why on earth are you traveling here?" he asked. Narihira dismounted his horse and wrote a poem and then asked the monk to take it to his wife in Kyoto. The poem read:

I've come as far as Mt. Utsu
of Suruga Province.
I've been longing to see you,
but I cannot see you,
either in reality or in dream.

From there, they continued on their way. They approached Mt. Fuji, white with snow piled high at the end of May. Looking at the mountain, Narihira composed a poem:

Mt. Fuji doesn't care
about seasons.
What season does the mountain think it is?
It is speckled like a fawn
with snow.

Mt. Fuji is as big as twenty Mt. Hieis piled one on top of another. Its shape is like a pile of salt.

Still they pushed on farther, and eventually they came to a large river between Musashi and Shimousa Provinces, called the Sumida River. They sat on the bank of the river and thought about the long journey they had taken. "How far we have come," they mused. While reminiscing about their long journey, the boatman called out to them, "Hurry up! Get on board, quick. The sun is setting." So they got on the boat, and while riding on it, they thought of the people they had left in Kyoto, and longed for them. Then they saw some white birds, as large as longbills, with red bills and legs, hovering and hunting for fish.

Narihira asked the boatman, "What do you call those birds?" The boatman replied, "Those are called capital birds." Hearing this, Narihira wrote a poem:

> *As you are called capital birds,*
> *let me ask you a question,*
> *"Is the person I love in Kyoto*
> *well,*
> *and getting along all right?"*

Hearing this, the people on the boat were deeply moved and brought to tears. It is said that Narihira was an excellent tanka poet. And such then is the story as it has been handed down to us.

Vol. 24, Tale 35

52

Fujiwara no Noritaka Composes Tanka Poems Even after His Death

In olden times, there lived a man named Fujiwara no Noritaka, who was the third-ranking officer of the Imperial Guards of the Right and the son of Regent Ichijo. He was handsome, and his personality and talents surpassed those of others. Moreover, he was deeply religious, but he passed away at a young age. His friends all grieved deeply, yet there was nothing that could be done about it.

About ten months after his passing, however, Noritaka appeared in the dream of a monk named Gaen. He seemed to be playing pleasantly on a flute, although actually he was whistling. In the dream, Gaen said to him, "While your mother is so deeply grieving, how can you look so happy?" Without answering directly, Noritaka, the third-ranking officer, recited a poem:

> *When you have rain*
> *in late autumn,*
> *here we have flowers blooming and falling abundantly.*
> *Why keep your sleeves wet with tears,*
> *still grieving over my death?*

Gaen awoke from the dream in astonishment and wept. In the autumn of the following year, Noritaka appeared in a dream of his sister and recited a poem:

> *While the sleeves*
> *of the mourning dress you've been wearing*
> *still haven't dried,*

*one year has passed
and another autumn has come around.*

His sister was surprised when she awoke from her dream and she cried bitterly. When Noritaka had been sick in bed, he had said to his sister, "If I should die before I finish reading the sutra, please don't bury me straight away. I will finish reading it first, even though I am dead." But he died soon thereafter, and his family buried him shortly after his death, completely forgetting his request. Then he appeared in a dream of his mother and spoke as follows:

*Although I beseeched you
so earnestly,
you forgot about it,
even before I looked back
from the bank of the River of Three Crossings.*

When his mother awoke from her dream, she was confused and she wept.

And thus, it is said that in those days, a tanka poet composed such wonderful poems, even after his death. And this is the story as it has been handed down to us.

Vol. 24, Tale 39

53

Fujiwara no Yasumasa Meets a Notorious Bandit Named Hakamadare

In olden times, there lived a notorious master bandit named Haka-madare. He was spunky, strong, fleet-footed, skillful, and clever. He had no match in all the world. It was his business to rob everyone of their belongings and he seized every opportunity to do so.

One day in October, this man found himself in need of some clothes and so he decided to obtain them. Under a hazy moon, around midnight when most people were asleep, he was roaming about looking for an opportunity in a suitable place, when a man happened along wearing many clothes. The man had on informal trousers with their lower edges tucked up and a soft informal gown and was sauntering along alone playing a flute.

Seeing him, Hakamadare thought, "Well now, there's a man who could provide me with some clothes." So, eagerly, he thought of running toward him and he was just about to pounce. But some-how, the man looked quite formidable, so he followed him for a few hundred yards. The man continued playing gently on a flute and seemed unaware that anyone was following him. Determined to leap on him, Hakamadare ran up to him with loud footsteps, but the man never showed any sense of alarm. Then he turned back, still playing the flute. Because of this, Hakamadare didn't feel like robbing him and he ran off.

Several times Hakamadare tried to pounce on the man like this, but the man never seemed disturbed at all, so Hakamadare thought, "This man must be someone special." He continued following him for about a thousand yards, thinking, "I can't just let him get away like this." And so he ran toward the man with his sword drawn. At this, the man stopped playing his flute, looked back, and called out, "Who goes there?" Although it shouldn't have been such a frightening thing for Hakamadare to attack a lone man like this—even if he should prove to be a demon or a god—somehow, he felt scared out of his wits. Scared to death, involuntarily, he knelt down on his knees. Again the man demanded, "Who goes there?" Realizing that he couldn't run away even if he tried, he answered, "I'm a robber. My name is Hakamadare." The man said, "Ah yes, I've heard there's such a one around here. Come on and follow me, you damned, lawless fellow!" And at that, he started to walk on, resuming his flute playing as before.

Judging from the man's demeanor, Hakamadare thought, "This can't be just any ordinary man," and he felt afraid, as if he had been caught by a demon. And so, dumbfounded, he followed the man. Presently, the man passed through the gate of a large house. Judging from how he stepped up onto the verandah with his shoes on, it seemed he was the master of the house. The man entered the house and soon came out again. He called out to Hakamadare and handed him a thick cotton kimono, saying, "If you need something like this from now on, just come here and ask. If you attack someone you don't know, you're bound to get yourself into big trouble." Having said this, he went back into the house.

After that, Hakamadare found out that the house was that of Fujiwara no Yasumasa, a former high-ranking official of Settsu Province. When Hakamadare realized that the man was Fujiwara no Yasumasa, he was petrified with fear. He was so terrified that he ran off quickly. Later, when Hakamadare was captured, he said, "That was an incredibly awesome person."

The high-ranking court noble Yasumasa was not descended from a military family; he was just an ordinary man. But because he was as strong, skillful, and thoughtful as any man from a military family, the imperial court used him in the field of military affairs, where he was perfectly reliable. People everywhere respected him deeply for his military skills. It has been said, however, that because he was not from a military family, his descendants did not become samurai. And such then is the story as it has been handed down to us.

Vol. 25, Tale 7

54

Fujiwara no Akihira Visits a Woman in His Youth

In olden times, there was a scholar named Fujiwara no Akihira, who was the headmaster of Scholar's Residence Hall. When he was a young man, he had an intimate relationship with a lady who was serving in the court and he often visited her in secret.

One night, he visited her living quarters, but felt it inappropriate to spend the night there, so he went to the home of a poor, lower class couple who lived nearby and asked, "Could you let my lady and me spend the night here?" The husband was out and the wife was there alone. She answered, "Yes, you may stay here tonight." Since it was a very small house, and there was no other room for sleeping besides the bedroom, she offered the bedroom to them. Akihira then had the woman bring over a reed mat from the ladies' quarters to sleep on.

As it happened, the master of the house had recently heard from someone, "Your wife has been having secret relations with another man." And another person had also told him, "Her secret partner is supposed to visit her tonight." So the husband thought, "I'll go and kill him." He had told his wife that he would be away on business for several days. He pretended to go away, but in fact he stayed and watched to see what was going on.

Unaware of all this, Akihira entered the house and went to sleep quite peacefully. When the night had advanced, secretly, the master of the house crept up to the house and tried to find out what was happening. He could tell that a man and a woman were talking together secretly inside, so he decided, "Sure enough, it's just as I've heard." Stealthily, he made his way into the house and watched carefully. He was quite certain that a man and woman were lying together in his bedroom. Because it was dark, he couldn't quite see things clearly. Quietly, he approached the man, who was now snoring. He held his dagger with a reverse grip. He searched for the man's belly and aimed to stab it. Just as he was raising his arm, a gleam of moonlight shone through a slit in the boards of the roof and he saw the long cords of a pair of formal trousers hanging from the wall. When he noticed them, suddenly he thought, "No man wearing such formal trousers would ever visit my wife. If I should harm the wrong person by mistake I'll be damned." Then a wonderful fragrance wafted past him. "Aha," he thought. He pulled his hand back and then gently he reached to touch the clothes, which felt very soft. At this, the lady awoke suddenly. Surprised, she said, "It seems someone is here. Who could it be?" The voice sounded stealthy and soft, and it wasn't that of his wife, so the husband concluded, "Aha, it's as I thought," and he drew back. Thereupon, Akihira awoke too and called out, "Who's there?"

The man's wife was sleeping in a corner of the house. Hearing the voices, she thought, "My husband's behavior earlier today was rather strange. He went off somewhere, but he must have come back and become confused by these people." In surprise she called out loudly, "Who's there—a robber?" Since it was his wife who spoke, the husband thought, "That wasn't my wife—some other persons must be in there sleeping." He left them there and went to the place where his wife was. He tugged on her hair and asked in a low voice, "What's all this about?" His wife thought to herself, "So, it's just as I imagined." Then she answered, "This high-class couple asked for a place to stay for the night so I told them they could, and I slept out here. You were about to make a grave mistake."

Akihira, too, was surprised and he asked, "What's going on here?" Hearing those words, the husband recognized the voice and replied, "I am in the service of the Lord of Kai and my name is Maro. I didn't know you were here and I was about to commit a terrible mistake. Owing to the circumstances, I was secretly watching and I realized that a man and a woman were in the bedroom.

I thought I'd figured out the situation, so I snuck up with my dagger drawn and was looking for the middle of your belly. I raised my arm, and then, with the moonlight shining through a slit in the roof, I saw the cords of your trousers on the wall. Suddenly I came to my senses and thought, 'No lover wearing such formal trousers would ever visit my wife.' It would have been terrible if I had harmed a person by mistake. So I pulled back my arm and gave up my plan. If I hadn't seen those formal trousers, I would have committed a grave mistake." When Akihira heard this he felt relieved, and astonished as well.

The Lord of Kai was the husband of Akihira's younger sister. His name was Fujiwara no Kiminari. Since Maro was one of his servants, he often came to Akihira's place on errands and was seen there all the time. Truly Akihira was saved, quite unexpectedly, by the cords of his trousers.

Those who heard the story remarked, "Even if one wishes to keep an affair secret, one shouldn't make use of a poor, lower-class person's house." But this, too, was a turn of destiny, connected to the events of a previous life. As it was destined that the poor man should not die, he changed his mind. If it had been meant that he should die, he would have stabbed Akihira to death, without changing his mind.

Thus, it has been said that everything in the world is brought about by the karmic Law of Cause and Effect. And such then is the story as it has been handed down to us.

Vol. 26, Tale 4

55

A Monk Visits a Person's Home, Holds a Purification Ceremony for a Woman, and Is Killed

In olden times, in a certain county of a certain province, there lived a man who kept dogs and made his living by going into the mountains and having his dogs kill the deer and wild boar that lived there. People called the place where he worked Dog Mountain.

When he went out hunting, taking a number of his dogs along, sometimes he would bring food with him into the mountains and stay there for a long time, and other times he would just stay away for a few days. During the times he was away, his young wife stayed at home alone. One such time, a monk made a visit to the house, chanted a sutra reverently, and then asked for some food. As the monk was very handsome, the young wife thought, "He may not be just a humble mendicant." But she thought highly of his sutra chanting and so she invited him to come into the house and served him some food. Then the monk told her, "To tell the truth, I am not a mendicant. I've been training myself in Buddhist practices and traveling around the country, but as I'm short on food now, I came here and asked you for something to eat."

Hearing this, the housewife respected him even more highly. The monk continued, "I'm well versed in the way of yin and yang and I can perform a miraculous ritual." The woman asked, "What blessings would come if you were to perform that ritual?" The monk answered, "If you lived a clean life and abstained from eating meat and performed the ritual, you'd be free from sickness, your wealth would increase, no gods would trouble you, you'd get

189

along well with your husband, and everything would go well." The woman asked, "What would you need to perform the ritual?" The monk replied, "Nothing special is necessary. All you need to offer is a little paper, a small amount of rice, some fruits of the season, and some oil." The woman said, "I could easily get those things ready. If I did so, would you please perform the ceremony for this house?" The monk replied, "I'd be glad to." And so he stayed, and soon he had the woman bathe to purify herself.

The monk got things ready for the purification ceremony and then, on the third day, he said, "The ritual should be performed in the deep, pure mountains and it should be carried out by ourselves alone." On the third day, the monk and the woman, carrying the things themselves, went deep into the mountains, stood the paper streamers in a row, and ceremoniously displayed the washed rice and the fruits of the season. The monk read the prayer for the ritual, and then the ceremony came to an end.

The woman thought, "While my husband is away, I have offered a wonderful prayer," and then she promptly started to leave for home. But in looking at the lovely young woman, the monk's carnal desires had been roused and he became entirely drawn to her. He took the woman by the hand and said, "I have never touched a woman before, but the moment I saw you, I wanted to satisfy my desire, although I know what the Buddha would think of this." The woman tried to shake off the monk's hand and get away, but the monk drew his dagger and exclaimed, "If you don't accept me, I'll stab you with this." With no one there in the mountains to help her, there was nothing the woman could do. The monk dragged her into the bushes, trying to satisfy his desire. The woman could not resist monk's force.

Just then the woman's husband was walking along on his way home from hunting, his dogs following after him. Perhaps it had all been predestined, but he happened to pass the very place where the two were and he noticed something rustling and moving in the bushes. He stopped and looked and thought, "There must be a deer there in the bushes." So he fixed an arrow to the bowstring, powerfully drew the bow, and then shot the arrow at the moving spot. Then he heard a human voice groan, "Ah!" Surprised and suspicious, he walked closer, pushed his way through the grass, and there he saw a monk on top of a woman. He found the arrow sticking into the monk. Surprised, he came still closer and pulled the monk away from the woman. The arrow had penetrated deep into the monk's body and he was dead. When he looked at the woman below, he realized that it was his wife. He couldn't believe his eyes, but he pulled her up. Unmistakably, the woman was his own wife. "What's been going on here?" he asked. Then his wife told him everything that had happened. When he looked by her side, he saw some sacramental strips of paper and other offerings set up ceremoniously. Then he dragged the monk's body away and pushed it into the gorge, and finally he took his wife home.

The Buddha must have thought the monk outrageous and abominable. We should realize that all of this happened because of his actions in a previous life.

As these events show, people in this world, both high and low, should realize that women must be careful not to be taken in by men's honeyed words. And such then is the story as it has been handed down to us.

Vol. 26, Tale 21

A Man is Eaten by the Demon at Agi Bridge in Ohmi Province

In olden times, when a certain governor ruled in Ohmi Province, there was a spirited group of young men living at his residence. They indulged in all sorts of pastimes, such as trading stories about the past and present, playing go and backgammon, and eating and drinking. One day, one of them said, "You know that old Agi Bridge in our province? They say that in the old days, lots of people used to cross over it, but now, for some reason, no one uses it anymore." Others joined in the discussion, until one, who was particularly outspoken as well as skeptical of the story, declared, "All right then, I'll cross over that bridge. No matter what sort of fearful demon may be there, I'll take the fastest horse from the stables and ride right over it."

At that, the others shouted out their approval. "Great!" they cried. "It should be only natural to cross straight over that bridge, but people have been going around it on account of that rumor. We should find out if it's true. And it'll be a good test of your guts." And so they all excitedly urged him on as he talked about his plan.

As they made so much of the coming venture, the governor heard about it and asked, "What's all this talk about?" When they told him of the plan, he replied, "It sounds like foolishness to me, but if you need a horse, then go ahead, you can have one of mine." The man replied, "Well, it was sort of a rash idea; sorry I brought it up." But the others urged him on, saying, "It would be shameful to give up. Look, you're turning into a coward!"

"I'm not afraid of crossing over the bridge," the man protested, "but I don't want you all thinking I'm just trying to get a horse out of the deal." The others clamored, "Come on, time's wasting. The sun's already high in the sky!" And so they saddled up the horse and got it ready. The man felt his heart sink, but since it was he who had brought up the idea, he rubbed some oil on the horse's rump, tightened the saddle ropes, mounted up with light equipage, and rode off brandishing his whip.

As he approached the foot of the bridge, he was seized with apprehension, yet there was nothing he could do but continue on. Already, the sun was nearing the edge of the mountains. His fear deepened. What was more, the place was so eerie—without a soul around. The village was far off, and only faint traces of smoke could be seen rising from the distant houses. Filled with fear as he went on, he could vaguely see a human figure in the middle of the bridge.

"That must be the demon," he thought, as he glanced uneasily. It was a woman wearing a light purple kimono with a darker colored covering and long crimson trousers. She covered her mouth with her hand and looked on, expressing a sense of grief, as if she had been brought there against her own will. She stood clutching the high railing of the bridge, and when he looked at her she gazed bashfully, but also with a sense of delight.

Seeing her, quite instinctively the man felt he should, out of compassion, dismount and ask her to ride on the horse. But then he thought, "This must be a demon. No human would be out in a place like this at this hour. I must pass her by." And so, with his eyes shut, he galloped off swiftly.

Though the woman had expected him to say something, the man passed by without a word. "Why, sir," she cried out, "how can you pass me by so indifferently? I've been abandoned in this forsaken place. Won't you at least take me to the village?" But he refused to listen to her words, right until the end. He felt so terrified that he forced his horse to gallop past her, as if it were flying. "What a cold-hearted man you are!" she wailed in a voice that shook the ground as she ran in pursuit.

"Just as I thought," he said to himself and he began repeating, "Dear Kannon, I pray of you, save me!" He whipped his horse to make it charge ahead faster, while the demon chased him and tried again and again to grab hold of the horse's rump and stop it. But since it had been smeared with oil, the horse kept slipping out of the demon's hands, and the man was able to get away.

When the man turned back to look, he saw that the demon's face was red, and as large as a round straw sitting mat, and it had just one eye. The demon stood about nine feet tall. Its hands had three fingers each, with fingernails like knives, about six inches long. Its body was bluish green, and its eye was amber. Its hair was all disheveled. Just looking at it filled one's heart with unspeakable terror. But because he continued praying to Kannon as he urged his horse along, at last he managed to make it to a village. At that the demon declared, "Well then, even if I didn't get you this time, I'll catch you yet!" and vanished instantly.

Panting and gasping and not feeling himself, finally he made it back to his master's residence by dusk. The others stood up and asked, "What happened to you?" But he felt so faint from his fear that he could not even speak. When his companions gathered around to encourage him, he calmed down a bit. The governor also questioned him about what had happened, and finally he related all that had taken place. "That was a rather foolish matter to get involved in; you're lucky you escaped with your life," chided the governor, but he handed over the horse. The man returned home with an air of triumph and related the events of his tale to his wife, children, and household, who all listened in fear.

From that time on, however, sinister things began to occur at his house. He consulted a yin-yang diviner about this and was advised, "On a certain day you should confine yourself to your house." And so, when that day arrived, he shut the gate to his house and confined himself inside. However, this man had a younger brother who had accompanied the governor of Michinoku Province when he took up his post there. The younger brother had taken their mother with him to Michinoku and now he happened to show up at his elder brother's house on the very day he went into seclusion. When the younger brother knocked at the gate, he was given the reply, "Today is an inauspicious day, and we have gone into seclusion, so would you please stay with someone else for now and come back after tomorrow."

The younger brother replied, "I can't do that. It's already late in the day. If I were alone, I might find a place somewhere else, but . . . And then, what about all the luggage? Today was a lucky day for me, and I was able to make it all the way here. However, I have to tell you, our mother has died in Michinoku and I need to talk about that too." When the elder brother thought of his mother, about whom he had been worrying all these years, he was sorely distressed. "This day of confinement must have been meant for me to hear this news. All right then, just open the door quickly," he conceded, and in tears he let his brother in.

They ate in the parlor, facing each other, and both broke into copious tears. The younger brother was wearing a black mourning kimono and weeping as he spoke. The elder brother was in tears, too. From the other side of the reed screen, the elder brother's wife was listening in, wondering what was going on. Then, for some reason, with a big commotion, the two brothers began to scuffle. "What's going on there?" the wife asked. The husband, shoving his brother down, cried out, "Quick, get me the sword by the bedside!" His wife replied, "What are you talking about? Have you gone mad? What on earth is this about?" When she refused to bring him the sword, he shouted, "Just give me the sword—or do you want me to die?"

Then the younger brother managed to reverse his position, get on top, and pin his brother down. He bit off his head and danced around with it. He glanced back at the wife and cried out, "Such a joy!" When she looked at him carefully, she realized that this was the face of the demon her husband had told her about—the one who had chased him on the bridge. Then, suddenly, it vanished.

At that, the wife and all the people in the house broke into tears, wondering what had happened, but there was nothing they could do about it.

And so we can see what happens when a woman interferes and tries to act too clever. What had looked like horses and various goods had just been animals' bones and skulls. Everyone who heard the story agreed, "It's stupid to argue about useless matters like that and lose your life over it," and they all blamed the man for what happened.

It is said that after that happened, the people offered various prayers and the demon has been banished and things are now safe at Agi Bridge. Such then is the story as it has been handed down to us.

Vol. 27, Tale 13

A Woman Sees Her Departed Husband Visit Her

In olden times, there lived a man in a certain county of Yamato Province. He had a daughter who was fair of figure and gentle of heart. He and his wife took great care in raising her.

There was also a man who lived in a certain county of Kawachi Province. He had a son who was very handsome. The son went to Kyoto to serve at the imperial court, and he was also very good at playing the flute. He was a good-hearted young man and his parents loved him dearly.

In time, the young man heard of the beauty of the daughter of the man in Yamato Province and so he sent her letters, trying to win her love. For some time, however, her parents would not permit his advances. But since he was exceedingly persistent in approaching her, finally, her parents allowed him to meet their daughter. From then on, the young couple became deeply in love and came to share their lives together. After about three years had passed, however, the husband fell sick unexpectedly. He suffered for some days and then he died.

The woman grieved terribly over her husband's death. Men from all over the province sent her love letters trying to win her affections, but she never accepted any of their advances. She just kept on longing for her departed husband and crying. For three years, she lived in this manner. Then in the autumn, when she was lamenting even more deeply than ever, she heard someone in the distance playing a flute, at about midnight. She thought it sounded exactly like her departed husband's flute. She felt intensely moved. It came nearer and nearer, and finally it came to the foot of the latticed shutters where she was sitting. "Open the door," someone said. The voice was unmistakably that of her deceased husband. She was indescribably happy, yet at the same time terribly apprehensive. So she got up softly, peered through the slit of the latticed shutters, and there she saw a man standing and saying, through his tears:

> *I have come over the mountain of death.*
> *Why am I so lonely?*
> *It is because I cannot see*
> *the one I love so deeply.*

The figure standing there looked just like her husband when he was alive, yet it was so frightening. The cords of his pleated trousers were untied and smoke was rising from his body. The woman was so afraid, she was speechless. Then the man said, "It is no wonder you are afraid. Since you were longing for me so bitterly, I asked for permission, which is so hard to obtain, and I came to see you. But as you are so afraid, I will go back. There, I receive scorching torments three times each day." And then, after saying this, he disappeared in an instant.

The woman wondered whether it had been a dream, but it had not. She could only regard it all as terribly strange.

This reminds us how a departed person may appear like this. And such then is the story as it has been handed down to us.

Vol. 27, Tale 26

58

A Fox Whose Ball Is Returned Repays a Man's Kindness

In olden times, there was a house that became haunted by an evil spirit when a person became sick. A sorceress who was able to contact spirits was called in, and the spirit had her speak for it; "I am a fox. I did not come to bring evil. I just thought there might be some food scattered around in this place, so I looked in, but then I got trapped inside." After saying this, the sorceress took a white ball, about the size of a tangerine, from the inside pocket of her kimono and tossed it in the air like a beanbag. When the people saw it, they thought with some suspicion, "That's quite a beautiful ball. The sorceress must have had it in her pocket all along to fool us." Sitting nearby was a brave young samurai, and while the sorceress was tossing the ball, he snatched it with his hands and placed it in his pocket.

At that, the fox who had entered the sorceress exclaimed, "What a terrible thing you're doing! Please return the ball to me," entreating him most earnestly. But the man would not listen. In tears, the fox pleaded, "You took the ball, but since you don't know how to use it, it's useless to you. But it will be a terrible loss for me if I should lose it. If you don't give it back to me, I will never forgive you. But if you return it, I will treat you like a god and protect you." Hearing this, the man decided it would be useless to keep the ball and so he asked, "Will you promise to protect me?" The fox replied, "Certainly I will protect you. Unlike humans, we never tell lies. And we never forget what we owe others." The man asked further, "May the guardian god of the Law, who has caught you, serve as a witness?" The fox replied, "Indeed, may the god who protects the Law hear my request! If you return the ball to me, he will certainly

199

protect you." And so the man took the ball from his inner pocket and handed it back to the sorceress. The fox was terribly happy to receive it. Then a monk chased the fox away.

At that, the people grabbed the sorceress and searched her pocket for the ball, but it could not be found. And so they realized that the fox had really taken it.

After that, the man who had taken the ball made a visit to Uzumaki Temple. When he left the temple, it had grown dark, so by the time he passed through Uchino, it was already night. When he passed by Ohtenmon Gate, he felt terribly afraid. He wondered why, and then he remembered the fox and thought, "That fox said, 'I will protect you.'" And so as he stood alone in the dark, he called out, "Come, Fox! Come, Fox!" At that, the fox came along, yelping. Certainly, it was the very same fox.

"Surely it has come," the man thought and so he spoke to the fox, "Fox, I see you don't tell lies. This is wonderful, just wonderful. When I was passing by here, I became terribly scared, so you must walk along with me." And so the fox walked along calmly ahead of the man and looking back from time to time, like a person who knows things well, while the man followed the fox. The fox took a different route, stopping from time to time, turning around, walking stealthily, and looking back. The man also walked stealthily, following the fox. Then they came to a place where there seemed to be some human beings. Looking about carefully, he saw many men armed with bows, arrows, and swords and discussing something. Listening from beyond the fence, he realized they were discussing a scheme to break into a house. He also realized, "Those robbers are standing on the street I usually take, so the fox must have taken me along a byway. The fox knew what was going on, so it didn't take the road where the robbers were." When they had passed beyond that place, the fox vanished. The man arrived home safely. This was not the only time that the fox helped the man. Many more times it came along and helped him. The fox had said, "I will protect you." And just as it had promised, unmistakably, it helped the man. The man was deeply impressed by the fox's help. If he hadn't returned the ball, he would not have obtained this good fortune. And so, he was very glad he had done so.

We can realize that even animals such as the fox don't forget what they owe to others and they don't tell lies. Therefore, we should help animals in such ways, whenever we can. Human beings, however, who can think and who should know better about the Law of Cause and Effect, are less grateful and less faithful than animals. Such then is the story as it has been handed down to us.

Vol. 27, Tale 40

A Fox from the Koya River Changes into a Woman and Rides on a Horse

In olden times, there was a river called the Koya River, to the east of Ninnaji Temple. At nightfall, a pretty young girl would stand by this river and when she saw a man riding a horse toward Kyoto, she would say, "Would you please let me sit behind you and ride to Kyoto?" The man on the horse would say, "All right, get on," and would let her ride with him on the horse. When she had ridden for several hundred yards, suddenly she would leap off the horse and run away. If the man ran and chased after her she would turn into a fox, yelping as she escaped.

When rumors spread that this had happened several times, the men at the Takiguchi guard station of the imperial court began talking about this girl by the Koya River who rode behind the riders on their horses. Then a spirited young guard proposed, "I'll go and catch that girl, no matter what. The others have all been so damned inept they couldn't do it." On hearing him boast like that, the other guards jeered, "Oh, come on, we'll bet you never catch her." The one who had claimed he could catch her replied, "All right then, tomorrow night I'll go, and surely I'll get her and bring her back." The other guards maintained that he could never do it, and they argued bitterly. So the next night, the man left alone and went to the river, riding an excellent horse. He crossed over the river, but no girl appeared.

So he turned back and rode toward Kyoto. Then he saw a girl standing there. Looking at the man passing by she said, "Would you let me ride behind you on your horse?" She smiled and looked friendly, so the guard said, "All right then, get on quickly. Where are you going?" The girl answered, "I'm going to Kyoto, but as the sun has set I'd like to ride with you." And so he let the girl ride with him. As soon as she got on the horse he tied the girl's hips to the saddle with the rope he had prepared. The girl protested, "Why are you doing such a thing?" The man replied, "Because I want to take you and sleep with you in my arms tonight and I don't want you to get away." As he rode along with her on the horse, the night grew dark.

As they were riding eastward along Ichijo Street and passing West Ohmiya Avenue, the man saw a procession of wagons approaching from the east, with many torches lit and people shouting and telling others to make way. So the man thought, "Someone important must be coming," and he turned back and went south along West Ohmiya Avenue as far as Second Street. At Second Street, he turned east and went from East Ohmiya Avenue to Tsuchimi Gate. He had told his men in advance to wait for him at Tsuchimi Gate, so he called out, "Are my men here?" At that, about ten of his men came out, saying, "Yes, here we are."

Then he untied the rope with which had bound the girl to the saddle, let her down from the horse, grabbed her elbow, and finally entered the gate, where he had ordered his men to light the way to the guards' station with torches. All the guards were waiting there. When they heard the man's voice, they asked, "How did it go?" He answered, "I've caught her and brought her here." Then the girl cried out, "Please let me go! There are so many people here!" She was in anguish, indeed, but he wouldn't release her and he led her along. Then other guards came out and surrounded them, illuminating them with their torches. "Set her free in the middle of this space here," they said. But the man said, "She may run away. I can't set her free." Then some guards fixed their arrows to the bowstrings and said, "Now, release her. It should be fun. We'll shoot at her rear. One man might miss hitting her, but we are many." When about ten men had fixed their arrows to their bowstrings and aimed at her, the man thought he could set her free and so he loosened his grip. At that, the girl turned into a fox and ran off yelping. All the guards vanished instantly as well, and all the lights went out too, and it was pitch dark.

Totally astonished, the guard called to his men, but none of them were there. He looked around and found that he was in the middle of an unfamiliar field. He was troubled and his fear was indescribable. Indeed, he was scared out of his wits, but he endured his fears and looked around, and from seeing the shapes of the mountains and the setting, he figured that he must be somewhere in the area around Torinobe. He thought he had dismounted his horse at Tsuchimi Gate, but now he couldn't even see his horse. He pondered; "I thought I went along West Ohmiya Avenue, but how is it that I'm here now? That procession of people carrying the lights I saw at Ichijo Street— they must have been foxes." As he couldn't linger around the place, he walked home and got back around midnight.

He was so emotionally distressed that he lay in bed like a dead man. The other guards had been waiting for him all night long, but since he hadn't come back, they said, "That guy was boasting he would catch the Koya River fox, but what's happened to him?" They laughed and sent for him and then, on the evening of the third day, he reported to the guards' station, looking like a very sick man. They asked, "What happened to the fox that night?" The man replied, "I was very sick that evening and couldn't go, but I'll go there tonight."

They chided him and said, "This time, you should catch two foxes." So the man went out, not talking much with them. He thought to himself, "I outsmarted the fox that night, so it probably won't come out tonight. But if it does show up tonight, I'll tie it up and keep it bound all night. If I release it, surely it will run away. If it doesn't come out I'll no longer go to the guards' station and I'll confine myself in my house." And so, having made up his mind, he mounted the horse and, accompanied by several of his best men, he left for the Koya River. Secretly, he thought, "I may lose my own life by insisting on my pretentious gallantry." But because of his boasting, he had to act.

When he crossed the Koya River, no girl appeared. When he turned back, however, he saw a girl standing by the river. The girl looked different from the one he had seen before, but she asked him to let her ride on his horse, and so he let her. And then, just as before, he tied her tightly to the saddle and rode along Ichijo Street toward Kyoto. As it grew dark, he had his followers light torches. He had some of them walk alongside his horse. As he proceeded, some cried out, "Make way! Make way!" But this time, he met no one. He dismounted his horse at Tsuchimi Gate and grabbed the girl's hair and tried to take her to the guards' station. The girl resisted and cried, but he dragged her to the guards' station.

The guards asked, "What now? What now?" The man answered, "Here she is." This time, he tied her tightly and pushed her down by force. For a while, she was still a human being, but as he kept torturing her, at length she turned into a fox. He burned its hair with a torch, shot it repeatedly with arrows, and then said, "From now on you must never try to bewitch us." At last, he released the fox without killing it. The fox couldn't walk, but somehow it managed to get away. Then the man talked in detail about what had happened the time before, when he was bewitched and ended up in Torinobe.

About ten days after that, the man thought he would try the same thing again, so he went back to the Koya River on a horse. There he saw the same girl, standing by the river and looking very sick. He called to her, "Why don't you ride on my horse, dear." The girl answered, "I'd like to, but I don't wish to get caught and burned." After saying that she disappeared.

It was the fox who tried to bewitch humans and who came on a terrible time as a result. It even seems as if this happened rather recently. It's a strange story and it has been passed on from person to person.

We should realize that, since ancient times, foxes have often turned into human beings. But the fox in this story was so good at bewitching humans that it even took the man as far as Torinobe. Why then didn't any wagons appear the second time, and why didn't the fox change its course ? Perhaps the fox changed its strategy according to the human being's state of mind. Such then is the story as it has been handed down to us.

Vol. 27, Tale 41

60

Taira no Suetake, a Retainer of Yorimitsu, Comes across a Woman with a Baby

In olden times, Minamoto no Yorimitsu was the governor of Mino Province. One time, he went off to a certain county in the province. One night, a number of samurai were gathered in their quarters, engaging in idle talk. Someone said, "I hear a certain woman has been showing up with a newborn baby at a place called Watari in this province. When someone goes across the river, the woman appears with a crying baby and requests of him, 'Hold this baby. Won't you hold this baby, please?'" Hearing this, one of the men said, "Is there anyone here brave enough to go across that river to Watari right now?" A man named Taira no Suetake replied, "I could go there even at this very moment." Some other men said, "No, you might be able to fight a thousand enemies, but you won't be able to go across that river now." But the man insisted, "It'll be nothing for me to cross that river." The others chided, "No matter how brave you may be, you'll never be able to get across that river."

Since Suetake had spoken so boldly, he insisted on going. About ten men argued with him and then proposed, "It's no use just arguing. Let's each of us bet something, like some armor, helmets, arrows, quivers, a saddled horse, or a sword." And so they made bets. Suetake, too, wagered, "If I can't go across that river, I'll give those things to you. Will you all swear on your bets too?" The others replied, "Of course we will! So now get going, immediately." Suetake prepared himself with armor, a helmet, and arrows in a quiver. The men asked, "How will you prove that you've made it across the

206

river?" He replied, "I'll pull out one of the arrows from my quiver and stick it in the dirt on the other side of the river. You may go there tomorrow morning and see for yourself." And on saying this, he left. Soon after, three feisty young men from among those who had opposed Suetake suggested, "We should go and make sure he really crosses the river." So secretly, they ran out, following after Suetake's horse. Suetake was already there.

It was a moonless night, near the end of September. They could hear Suetake wading through the river with a loud splashing. Presently, he reached the other side. The three men listened, hiding in the pampas grass on the near side. Then Suetake must have quickly pulled out an arrow and stuck it into the ground, for soon he seemed to be wading his way back. Straining their ears, they could hear a woman's voice calling out to him from the middle of the river. "Hold this baby," it said, "Won't you hold this baby, please?" And then they also heard the squealing voice of a baby. At that time, an awful, fishy smell drifted over the river to their side. Although the three men were together, they were terribly frightened. Just imagining the fear of the man wading across the river gave them the chills.

Then Suetake said, "All right then, let me hold it." The woman said, "Here it is," and she handed it over to him. Suetake cradled the baby in the sleeves of his robe. Then the woman came running after him, demanding, "Give me back the baby." Suetake said, "No, I'll never give it back," and he walked back up the riverbank on the near side. Then he returned to the governor's residence, with the three men running after him. He dismounted his horse, entered the house, and said to the men who had doubted him, "You said I couldn't do it, but I went to Watari and waded across the river and I've even brought the baby here." And on saying this, he opened the folds of his right sleeve. But, lo and behold, there was nothing there but a few tree leaves.

After that, the three men who had secretly followed Suetake told everyone about what they had seen at the river. Those who hadn't gone were all terribly frightened by it. Then they brought out all the things they had bet, but Suetake didn't take any of them. "I only said I would do it. Who wouldn't have been able do such a simple thing?" And then, after saying this, he returned all the wagers.

Those who heard the story were deeply impressed and praised him. Some said that the woman with the newborn baby was a fox trying to bewitch humans, while others said that she was the ghost of a woman who had died in childbirth. Such then is the story as it has been handed down to us.

Vol. 27. Tale 43

Three Men Spend a Night at an Unfamiliar Temple in Suzuka

In olden times, three young men were passing over the mountains from Ise Province to Ohmi Province one summer. They were men from the lower class, but all were thoughtful and bold. When they were crossing Mt. Suzuka, they came to an old temple that, for some reason, was said to be haunted by a demon. Fearing this, people never stayed there. The temple was situated on a difficult mountain path, and people avoided it because of the rumor.

While the three men were passing over the mountain, suddenly it grew overcast, and a shower burst on them. Hoping it would clear up soon, they took refuge under a tree with luxuriant foliage and waited for the rain to stop. But it didn't stop, and the sun was beginning to set. One of them suggested, "Why don't we spend the night at that temple?" The other two replied, "No one stays at that temple because it's said to be haunted by a demon." The first man—the one who had suggested they stay there—said, "Why don't we just see if a demon really appears. If we're eaten by a demon that will be OK, since we're all going to die sooner or later anyway. Or maybe people just started a rumor after seeing a fox or a wild boar trying to trick human beings." And so the other two agreed, though somewhat reluctantly, saying, "Well, let's stay there and see what happens." When the sun had set and it had grown dark, they entered the temple and stayed there.

Since the temple was in such an ominous place, they kept talking without sleeping. Then one of them said, "While we were walking in the daytime, we saw a dead man back there in the mountains, didn't we? Who'll go and bring that body here now?" The one who had suggested they stay at the temple said, "All right, why don't I go and bring it back?" The other two replied, "No one could go out and bring it here now." But the man continued, "Well, I'll just go and get it." And in so saying, he took off his clothes and ran out into the night, stark naked.

The rain kept falling, and it was pitch dark. One of the other men also took off his clothes and ran after the first man. But this man ran secretly, passing the first man quickly, and ran ahead of him. He arrived at the spot where the dead man was, picked up the body, and threw it down into the gorge. Then he lay on the spot where the man had been.

Shortly after, the first man arrived and began to shoulder the man who lay in place of the dead man. The man who was being carried bit hard on the shoulder of the man carrying him. "Hey there old corpse, don't bite like that!" shouted the man who was carrying the body and he ran back to the temple, with the man on his shoulders. He placed him at the doorway of the temple and said, "All right, now I've brought back the dead man," and then he entered the temple. While he was inside, the man who had been carried ran off. When the first man came back out of the temple, he saw that the "dead man" he had brought back had disappeared. "What's this?" he exclaimed, "The dead man has run off." He just kept standing there. Then the man who had been carried back came out from the side of the temple and, in laughter, told him what he had done. The first man said, "How could you dare do such a thing to me!" and they both entered the temple.

Those two men were both so bold, it was hard to tell who was bolder. But the man who carried the other must have been the bolder of the two. There might be others who could act like a dead man, but a man bold enough to go out and bring back a dead man would surely be hard to find.

In the meantime, while the two men were out, various faces had appeared from each frame of the latticework in the ceiling. Then, when the third man—the one who had remained in the temple—drew his sword and brandished it, all the faces laughed and then they vanished as one. The man didn't feel troubled at all. And so, this man was equally bold. The three men were all undauntedly bold. When day broke, they crossed over the mountain and passed into Ohmi Province.

It seems the faces that appeared in the ceiling must have been the doings of foxes. The people who had seen them must have taken them to be demons. After these three men left the temple without trouble, nothing dreadful happened there again. If there really had been a demon still in the temple, how could things have remained peaceful from then on? Such then is the story as it has been handed down to us.

Vol. 27, Tale 44

62

Fujiwara no Nobutada, the Governor of Shinano, Falls into a Gorge

In olden times there was a man named Fujiwara no Nobutada, who served as governor of Shinano Province. He had gone to the province and carried out his work as governor, and then, when his term of office was completed, he was traveling back to Kyoto. He and his men were crossing over the Misaka Pass with horses carrying the loads of his belongings, and with riders too numerous to count. Among the riders was the governor. While his horse was crossing over a log bridge, the horse's rear leg broke one of the logs at the edge, and both rider and horse were pitched headlong into the depths of the gorge.

The gorge appeared fathomless, and it seemed impossible that the governor could have survived. The tops of the cypresses and cedars rose a hundred twenty feet or more, and it was unimagineable how far below the bottom might lie. Having fallen into such a place, there seemed to be no hope for the governor.

The governor's men dismounted their horses and stood along the edge of the bridge and peered down into the gorge, but the situation seemed beyond all hope. "There's nothing we can do," they concurred. "If there were any way to get down there, we might go and check on what happened. Or if this had happened one day farther along the road, in a place where it's not so deep, we'd be able to go and look for him. But here, there's no way we can get to the bottom of this gorge. What shall we do?" But then, as they were debating the situation, from the depths of the gorge they heard the faint voice of someone calling out.

"The governor, he's alive!" they exclaimed. They shouted down into the gorge, and from the far distance below they could just hear their master calling something back in reply.

"Listen! He's saying something. Quiet! Let's hear what it is!" Then they heard their master call out, "Send me a basket tied to the end of a long rope." So they imagined that the governor must have caught on something and still be alive. They tied together the reins of some of their horses to make a rope and attached a basket to it and then they lowered it down into the gorge. Just when they had let out the reins as far as they could, they felt the basket come to a stop.

"It must have reached the bottom," they thought. Then they heard a voice call out from below, "Now pull it up." So they said, "Let's pull it up." But as they pulled it up, the weight seemed very light. "The basket's so light," they remarked. "If our master were in it, it should be heavier." Another person suggested, "Our master must be pulling himself up using tree branches. That's why the basket is so light." When they had pulled the basket all the way to the top and they looked inside, they found it was filled with oyster mushrooms. Puzzled at the sight, they stared at each other. "What could this mean?" they asked. And then, once again, they heard a voice calling out from the bottom, "Send the basket down again."

Hearing this, they replied, "All right, we'll send it," and so they lowered it down. Then they heard the voice call back, "Now pull it up." And so, following the instructions of the voice, they pulled the basket up once again, and this time it was very heavy. With the efforts of several men pulling, they were able to haul it up. When they looked in, they saw the governor holding onto the rope with one hand, and clutching three bunches of oyster mushrooms in the other. When they had lifted him out, they set him on the wooden roadway and all were happy to see him safely back. Then they asked the governor, "What's the meaning of all these mushrooms?"

"When I fell," the governor replied, "my horse dropped to the bottom faster than I did. I went down after the horse and slipped through a lot of thick branches that broke my fall. I grabbed onto the branches and finally I came to the branch of a big tree that held me. So I clung to it and then, right in a fork of the big tree, I saw lots of oyster mushrooms growing there. I couldn't keep my eyes off them, so I picked as many as I could and put them in the basket and had you pull them up. There must be lots more left—more than you can imagine. I feel it's a terrible loss." His men replied, "Indeed, it is a terrible loss!" and they burst out into laughter.

"That's nothing to laugh about!" the governor retorted. "I feel like a man who's gone to a mountain of treasures and returned empty handed. You know the old saying, 'A governor should snatch the dirt where he falls,' don't you?" One of the governor's senior assistants—though in truth appalled by his master's attitude—replied, "Indeed, sir, you are so right. Why should one hesitate to take things that are near at hand? No one in such a situation would have done otherwise. But only a man who is sagacious by nature, like yourself, could have kept his mind undisturbed at such a perilous moment and carried on just as in normal times. And so, calm as ever, you were able to pick those oyster mushrooms. And likewise, sir, you were able to rule the province calmly, getting the people to pay their taxes just as you wished, and now you are returning to the capital. And the people in the province miss you, as if you were a parent. And so, may you ever continue as such, through a thousand autumns, through ten thousand years." And as he spoke, the comrades in the back all snickered together.

And so we can see that the governor was calm and undisturbed enough to pick oyster mushrooms at such a critical moment, and then to send them up. Such a greedy heart was his! We can only imagine how he must have squeezed the people for as much as he could during his term as governor.

This story shows how the people detested the governor and laughed when they heard of his doings. And such then is the story as it has been handed down to us.

Vol. 28, Tale 38

63

A Man Pretending to Be Brave Is Frightened by His Own Shadow

In olden times, there was a man who wanted to look brave in others' eyes and so he behaved as if he were indeed a brave man. This man was employed in the service of the governor of a province.

One day he was planning to go out somewhere early in the morning. While he was still in bed, his wife was up and getting his breakfast ready. The moon at dawn was shining into the house through a space between the boards of the wall. Happening to see her own shadow on the wall, she thought, "A big robber with disheveled hair is breaking into the house to steal our things!" She was so afraid, that she ran to her husband and whispered to him that a big robber with dishevelled hair was breaking into the house to rob them. Her husband replied, "That's terrible. What should we do now?" He reached for his sword at his bedside and exclaimed, "I'll cut his head off." He got up, still naked, and with his topknot sticking out he grasped his sword. Seeing his own shadow, he thought, "That's not a man with disheveled hair, it's a man with a drawn sword! He might chop my head off." He cried out, "Oh!" but not loudly and then ran to his wife and said, "I thought you were a brave samurai's wife, but you don't see things well. How could you have seen a man with disheveled hair? It's a man with his topknot sticking out and he's carrying a drawn sword. But that guy's a miserable coward. When he saw me come out, he was trembling and he almost dropped his sword." This, the husband had said from seeing his own trembling shadow.

Then he said to his wife, "Go chase him away. He was trembling just from looking at me because he was so afraid. Since I'm going out today, it wouldn't do if I got injured in a fight now. But since you're a woman, he wouldn't strike you." And after saying this, he crept back into bed and covered himself with a kimono. At this, his wife said, "What a spineless coward you are! You go out moon-viewing equipped with a bow and arrows, don't you?" Then she got up, intending to go and take a look. Suddenly, the sliding paper door next to the husband fell on top of him, and he let out a scream of fear, assuming that the robber had pounced on him. Angry and disgusted, the wife said, "Look, the robber's already gone. What fell on you just now was nothing but a sliding paper door." At this, the husband got up and looked around and realized that there had in fact been no robber at all, and that it was a sliding paper door that had fallen on him. Then he stood up, folded his arms bravely on his chest, spit gallantly into his hands, and said, "That bastard couldn't break into my house, rob me, and get away. All he could do was make the sliding paper door fall. If he'd stayed a while longer, I'd have caught him for sure. Because of your ineptitude, that robber got away." At this, the wife laughed out loud.

There are such foolish people in this world. As the wife said, "How could such a cowardly man ever fulfill his duties as a guard carrying a sword and a bow and arrows?" When people heard about this they all laughed at the husband.

It is said that this is the tale that the wife told to other people. And so this is how the story came to be handed down to us.

Vol. 28, Tale 42

64

A Group of Ex-convicts Tries to Rob a House and Gets Caught

In olden times, there was a certain man who lived in the northern part of Kyoto. Ever since his youth, he had worked for a governor and accompanied him to the seats of the provincial governments. Gradually, he grew wealthy and he kept a house of good means where he employed many servants. He also obtained a sizeable amount of land.

As it happened, his house was located near the Prison of the East, and one day a group of ex-convicts got together and made plans to break into his house and rob it. Because they didn't know much about the house, they thought they might try to persuade one of the servants to become their collaborator. There was one servant who came from Settsu Province and was working as a night watchman. "Since that guy is from the countryside," they reasoned, "we should easily be able to talk him into joining us. If we give him something, he'll listen to us." And so the ex-convicts invited the night watchman to their house. They gave him food and drink and then they said to him, "We understand you're from the countryside. You might sometimes find yourself in need of something in Kyoto. Or you might want something to do. We feel sorry for you—terribly sorry for you. Since you're young, there may be certain things you don't understand. While you're here in Kyoto, come visit us any time you like. We'll be happy to treat you to a meal. If there's anything you want, just let us know." Although the man felt happy, at the same time he felt suspicious and he went home thinking, "There may be some motive hidden behind their offer."

After this sort of meeting had taken place several times, the ex-convicts thought, "Now we've talked him into joining our side." After urging him to the point where it seemed he wouldn't be able to refuse their proposal, they confided, "To tell the truth, we'd like to ask you to tell us how we can break into the house where you work as a night watchman. We'll pay you well for your work. We'll give you enough to live on for all your life. No one else knows about this. Everyone in the world, whether high or low, works for their own profit." And thus, they tried to talk him into accepting their proposal.

Although he was of humble origins, the man was wise and thoughtful. He thought to himself, "This is such a wicked thing. I shouldn't get involved in it." But on second thought, he reasoned, "It might be unwise if I refused them just now." So he accepted the proposal, saying, "All right, that should be no problem."

The ex-convicts were very pleased and they offered him some silk cloth as an expression of thanks. "You don't have to rush to thank me now," the man said. "You can repay me after everything has been done." Then the ex-convicts said, "We're planning to rob the house tomorrow night. When we come to the gate at midnight and push on it, open the gate." The man replied, "All right, I've got it," and after saying this, he went back to the master's house. As the house was not a samurai's, the robbers thought it should be easy enough to break into. They made plans to have the ten of their members who were most familiar with carrying out robberies get together on the following night, and then they dispersed.

When the man got back to the master's house, he thought, "I have to tell my master about this." He waited for a chance, and then his master went out onto the verandah. The man knelt on the ground and appeared anxious to talk with his master when nobody else was around. The master asked him, "What do you wish to tell me? Do you want permission to go back to your home province?" The man answered, "No, sir. I have something to tell you in secret." His master wondered what it could be that he wanted to tell him, so he took him to a secret place where there was no one else around and asked him about it. The man said, "It is something I hesitate to tell you, but I think I must. A group of ex-convicts is planning to break into your house tomorrow night." The master said, "Well, I'm certainly glad you've told me of this. A poor man can become easy prey to a gift. It's wise of you to tell me about this in advance." He continued, "All right then, tomorrow night open the gate and let them in." The master thought to himself, "If we chase them out, we won't be able to catch them or even tell who they are. That would be no good." So at first, he was at a loss for what to do. But soon after, he dashed off to see a samurai, a longtime friend, and told him about the ex-convicts' plan. The friend was surprised and said, "Tomorrow evening, secretly, I'll send to your house some fifty men who are good fighters—irrespective of whether they're vassals or servants." And so the master returned home, feeling relieved.

By the following evening, the samurai had bows and arrows wrapped up and placed in chests, and they sent them ahead, without attracting any notice. When night came, each of the warriors, pretending to be just an ordinary person, went to the house, one by one, and hid himself. As the prearranged time approached, the men took out the bows and arrows, put on suits of armor, and waited eagerly for the robbers. A few of them were posted at the corners outside, expecting that some of the robbers might try to run away.

Utterly unaware of all this, the ex-convicts came to the gate of the house at midnight, completely trusting the night watchman they had talked into joining their plans. They pushed on the gate. Ready to do what was expected of him, the man went to the gate and opened it. As soon as he did this, he ran back and crept deep under the verandah. Then the ex-convicts rushed in. After letting them all in, the warriors caught them one by one, just as planned. The robbers numbered about a dozen in all, but the excellent fighters numbered forty or fifty, and had been prepared and waiting for them. They caught them all and tied them to the posts of the cart house. They left the robbers there through the night, and when day broke, the robbers remained there, tied up and blinking their eyes.

The master and fighters decided that such men were beyond being reformed. Even if they were thrown in jail again, when they got out again, they would just go back to their evil ways. And so, when night came, they led the robbers away secretly and shot them all.

The ex-convicts had intended to rob the house, but ended up getting killed. They lost their lives on account of their greed. It is said that the master was saved by the virtue of the wise man. And such then is the story as it has been handed down to us.

Vol. 29, Tale 6

Robbers Come to a Temple
and Steal Its Bell

In olden times, in a certain county in Settsu Province, there was a temple known as the Little Temple.

One day, a monk who appeared to be about eighty years of age came to the temple and said to its head priest, "I am from a western province and on my way to Kyoto, but my aged body is exhausted. I don't think I can walk any longer. I would like to stay at this temple for a few days. Could you please allow me to stay here in some suitable place?" The head priest replied, "I can't think of any good place for you right now. If you stayed in the open corridor of the temple, you'd be exposed to cold winds." The old monk suggested, "Then perhaps I could stay under the bell tower. It's sheltered all around. I wonder if you could let me stay there." The head priest replied, "Well, yes, that might be a suitable place. You may stay there. And if you would kindly strike the bell, that would be appreciated." The aged monk was very happy.

Then the head priest of the temple took the aged monk to the foot of the bell tower and said, "There are some straw mats that are used by our bell ringer. You may use them as you please during your stay." Later, he explained to the bell ringer, "An old wandering monk came along and asked to stay under the bell tower. I'm going to let him stay there. He says he'll strike the bell for us, and I asked him to do that as long as he stays. During that time you may take a rest." The bell ringer replied, "I would be glad to do so," and then he left.

After that, the old monk struck the bell for a couple of nights. The following day the bell ringer came by at about ten in the morning, planning to see what kind of monk was now striking the bell. He went to the foot of the bell tower and called out, "Are you there, venerable monk?" He opened the door and entered the tower, only to find the tall aged monk lying there—his hips wrapped in rough, shabby cloth and his hands and legs stretched out—dead. After looking at the scene, the bell ringer rushed back to the head priest and cried out in panic, "The old monk is dead! What should we do with him?" The head priest of the temple was shocked and he rushed to the bell tower with the bell ringer. Opening the door just slightly, he looked in. The old monk was lying there dead.

The head priest closed the door and then informed all the monks about what had happened. The monks said to themselves, "Our great head priest let that strange old monk stay at our temple, and now the old monk has defiled it with his dying." Although upset, they continued, "But it's no use saying anything like that now. Let's get the villagers together and have them take him away." But when they had gathered the villagers and told them about the monk's death, the people objected, "The festival of our village shrine is coming up. How could we defile the festival by doing that now?" So there was no one who would touch the dead monk. They continued arguing, "But we can't just leave the body as it is." As they continued arguing, it got to be about one in the afternoon.

In the meantime, two men who were about thirty years old came along. They wore informal gray silk clothing and dark purple trousers with the cuffs tucked up high. They carried large ostentatious swords and had rush hats hanging from their necks. Though they were from the lower class, they didn't look shabby and they walked along with light steps. They went to the resident monks' quarters and asked, "Did you happen to see an old monk around this temple?" The monks replied, "We heard that the other day a tall old monk, about eighty years old, came here and stayed under the bell tower, but when someone went to see him this morning, he was lying there dead." The two men exclaimed, "Oh no!" and they began to cry, on and on. The monks inquired, "Who are you, and why is it that are you crying?" The men replied, "That old monk is our father. As he grew older, he sometimes got stubborn and when he didn't get his own way, he would run away from home and travel around. We live in Akashi County of Harima Province, and he ran away from home the other day, so we've been looking for him in many places. We aren't poor. We have about twenty-five acres of rice fields to our names. We have lots of men working for us in the neighboring county, too. By the way, we'd like to make sure if it's really our father who died. And if that's the case, we would like to bury him." And so, they went to the foot of the bell tower.

The temple's head priest went along with them, too, and he stood outside. The men went into the bell tower and as soon as they saw the old monk's face, they exclaimed, "That's our father!" They threw themselves on the floor and began to cry loudly. The head priest felt so sorry for them that he too wept. The men went on to say, "You got stubborn as you grew older. And you sometimes ran away from home. And now you've passed away in such an unfamiliar place. How sad it is we couldn't be present at your deathbed." They continued crying, on and on. Then, a while later, they said to the monks, "Now we would like to make some preparations for the funeral." They closed the door and left. The head priest of the temple told the monks about the men's crying, showing his utmost sympathy. Listening to this talk, some of the monks even cried as well.

In the meantime, about forty or fifty men came along at around eight at night and carried away the old monk's body, talking noisily. There were some who were armed with bows and arrows. As the monks' quarters were far away from the bell tower, none of them went out to watch the men carry away the old monk. They were all afraid, so they barred the doors and listened. The men took the body into the pine woods at the foot of a mountain in the back, about a thousand yards away. There they chanted prayers all night long, rang handbells, and performed a service until dawn, and then they left.

After that, none of the monks went near the bell tower where the old monk had died. And for the period of thirty days after the old monk's death, even the bell ringer did not go near the bell tower. When at last the thirty days had passed, the bell ringer went to the bell tower to sweep up around it. When he looked in, he saw that the large bell was gone. "What on earth has happened?" he wondered and then he went and told the monks about it. They all gathered together and went to see the bell. But when they got there they saw that the bell had disappeared. And since it had indeed been stolen, how could they have seen it there? They reasoned, "Those guys must have been plotting to steal the bell and so they pretended to perform a funeral service for the old monk." They pondered, "What do you suppose the place where they buried the monk looks like?" And so the monks, along with many villagers, got together and went to the pine woods. There they found broken pieces of copper scattered all around. They saw that a large pine tree had been cut down and burned in order to melt down the bell. "We were completely taken in by them!" They cursed among themselves, stamping their feet with mortification, but they had no idea just who it was that had done it, and there was nothing they could do. Ever since that time, there has been no bell at the temple.

We know there are people who try to steal things in a carefully planned manner, but who could ever pretend to be dead and remain still like that for such a long period of time? And how could those men ever have shed tears like that at will? On seeing the sight, even people who had no particular connection to the matter felt terribly sad. All those who saw and heard of the incident agreed emphatically, "Those robbers really knew what they were doing!" And so, even things that may look entirely reasonable should be watched over carefully when an unfamiliar person is involved. And such then is the story as it has been handed down to us.

Vol. 29, Tale 17

A Robber Climbs to the Upper Structure of Rashomon Gate and Sees a Corpse

In olden times, a man came to Kyoto from Settsu Province for the purpose of stealing. As it was still daylight when he arrived, he stood under Rashomon Gate, waiting for night to fall. Since there were many people walking down Shujaku Street, he thought he would wait under the gate until things quieted down. But then he heard a lot of people approaching from the direction of Yamashiro and decided it would be better to keep out of sight, so he quietly climbed up into the upper structure of the gate. Looking in, he saw a light burning faintly.

Thinking this strange, the robber looked carefully through a latticed window and there he saw the corpse of a young woman. Seated by the head of the dead woman, near the burning light, was a very old woman with white hair. She was roughly pulling out the dead woman's hair.

The robber had trouble comprehending what he was seeing. "Could that be a demon?" he wondered in fear. "Or perhaps it's just the ghost of a dead person. Why don't I give it a scare and find out." So he opened the door carefully, drew his sword, and rushed toward her, shouting, "You there, who are you?" The old woman was flustered and she rubbed her hands together. "Old woman, who are you and what are you doing here?" he demanded. The old woman answered, "The truth is, the mistress I've been serving passed away and there was no one who could give her a proper burial, so I brought her up here. Since she has such nice long hair, I'm pulling it out to make a wig from it—please understand." Hearing this, the robber stripped off the clothing from both the dead woman and the old woman, snatched the hair that had been pulled out, and then rushed down from the upper story of the gate and ran off.

In the upper structure of that gate, there were many skeletons. When people were unable to give someone a proper burial, they would bring the body to the upper story of the gate and leave it there.

The robber told other people about this, and so it became widely known. And thus, this story came to be handed down to us.

Vol. 29, Tale 18

A Man Traveling with His Wife to Tamba Province Gets Tied Up by a Young Man at Mt. Ohe

In olden times, there was a man from Kyoto whose wife was from Tamba Province. Together they set off on a journey to Tamba. The wife rode their horse, while the husband walked behind with a bamboo quiver holding a dozen or so arrows strapped to his back and a bow in his hand. When they reached Mt. Ohe, they met a strong-looking young man carrying a sword and they began traveling together.

As they walked along, they fell into conversation, trading questions like, "Where are you headed?" and such. After a time, the young man with the sword said, "This sword is from Michinoku Province. It's really quite a fine piece. Here, why don't you have a look." And at that, he drew the sword and showed it. The man could see that it was indeed an excellent sword and he was seized with a desire to possess it. Noting his interest, the young man went on, "If you'd like this sword, I'll exchange it for your bow." The man from Kyoto had no particular attachment to his bow and he realized the young man's sword was certainly a superb one. Coveting the sword and imagining how wonderful it would be if it were his, he readily agreed to trade his bow for the sword.

After walking along for a while, the young man said, "Carrying only a bow like this, somehow it doesn't look right. While we're in the mountains, could I borrow a couple of your arrows? It'll be good for you too, since we're traveling together." The man thought, "Well, that's quite true." And so, feeling happy about the exchange of his humble bow for the excellent sword, he let the other man have a couple of his arrows, as requested. From there, the young man carrying the bow and arrows followed along behind, while the man from Kyoto with the sword and quiver walked in front.

When it was time for lunch, they stopped by a grove of trees. "Let's go a little farther back into the grove so we won't have any passersby watching us," the young man suggested. And so, they walked back into the grove somewhat farther. But suddenly, as the man was helping his wife dismount the horse, the young man fixed an arrow to the bow, aimed directly at the man and ordered, "Don't move, or I'll shoot!" The man was dumbfounded by this unexpected turn of events and just stood there staring. The young man called to him threateningly, "Go on, deeper into the mountains. Now go!" Fearing for his life, the man walked on with his wife a half a mile or so deeper into the mountains. Then the young man commanded, "Throw down the sword and your knife!" And so the man threw them both down. The young man grabbed them and then overpowered the man, hurled him to the ground, and bound him tightly to a tree with the reins of the horse.

Then the young man walked over to the woman and looked at her more closely. She was a little over twenty years old and of humble birth, but very beautiful and appealing. The young man was seized with desire and, forgetting all else, he began to tear off her clothes. Having no alternative, she removed her clothing, according to his demand. He then took off his own clothes and forced her to submit to his desire. The woman could not help but yield. Tied to the tree and seeing what was going on, how do you suppose the husband must have felt?

After that, the young man got up and dressed as before. He picked up the quiver and bow, fixed the sword to his waist, and mounted the horse. To the woman, he said, "I'm sorry about this, but it can't be helped. I have to be off. But for your sake, I didn't kill that man. I have to take the horse now, so I can get away quickly." And on saying this, he galloped off—to no one knows where.

At that point, the woman went over to her husband and untied him from the tree. He looked dazed. "What a worthless lout," she said "How can I ever depend on you from now on?" The husband could say nothing in return, and they proceeded on to Tamba Province together.

The young man showed at least some sense of decency. He didn't rob the woman of her clothes. But the husband's behavior was pitifully stupid. How could he just hand over his bow and arrows to a complete stranger in the mountains? What a fool he was. As for the young man, there's no telling what became of him. Such then is the story as it has been handed down.

Vol. 29, Tale 23

A Bandit Living to the South of Kiyomizu Temple Uses a Woman to Lure Men and Kill Them

In olden times, there lived a handsome young nobleman of high birth. It seems he served as assistant director of the Imperial Guards, or in some such position.

One day, he made a secret visit to Kiyomizu Temple and, on his way, he met a very beautiful woman, dressed most attractively, on her way to the temple. When he saw her, the assistant director thought, "This doesn't look like a person of humble origins. She's come on foot to visit the temple in secret." From catching her glancing up nonchalantly, it appeared that she was about twenty. Finding her so incredibly beautiful and attractive, he thought, "What kind of person could this be? I must speak to her, by all means." Obsessed by her charm, when he saw her emerging from the temple, he called to his young footman and told him, "Go follow that woman and find out where her home is."

Soon after, when the assistant director of the Imperial Guards arrived at his home, his young footman returned and reported to him, "Indeed, I followed her and I found out where she went. She doesn't live in Kyoto. She went to a house that's to the south of Kiyomizu Temple and north of Amida Peak. Her house looks quite impressive. When the older lady accompanying her saw me following them, she said, 'That's strange. Why do you act as if you are in her company?' I told her, 'When my master saw the lady at the main hall of Kiyomizu Temple, he instructed me to follow her and find out where she lives. That's why I've been following.' Then the younger lady herself said, 'Well, if you ever come by here again in the future, do let me know.'" Hearing of this, with great pleasure, the assistant director of the Imperial Guards wrote a letter and sent it. In turn, the woman replied, with exquisite handwriting.

And so they began exchanging letters, and in one of them the woman wrote, "Since I'm from a mountain village, I don't have many opportunities to get to Kyoto. So won't you please come and visit me here. We could talk, even if we have to be separated by a screen." Reading this, the man was terribly eager to see the woman and so, accompanied by two samurai, his young footman, and a groom for the horses, he rode off secretly and proceeded with great anticipation through the dark of Kyoto to her place.

When they arrived at the place, he sent the young footman to announce his arrival. The older lady came out and said, "Please do come in." So the man followed her. Looking around, he found the area was surrounded by strong earthen walls with a high gate. There was also a deep moat around the yard and a bridge that crossed the moat. The man started to cross the bridge, together with his assistants, but he was told that his men and horses should remain outside the moat. When the assistant director went in alone, he saw there were many buildings inside. Among them was one that seemed to be for guests. When he entered the building through its swinging double doors, he found it was carefully arranged, with a folding screen and curtains placed around a clean mat floor. Reed screens had also been hung around the main house.

The assistant director was quite impressed by the house, which looked quite elegant considering that it was in a remote mountain village. Then, when the night had advanced considerably, the lady of the house appeared. They entered the screened area within and there they lay down together. On embracing each other, the woman appeared even more attractive to the man.

The man talked on of his love for her, and of his pledge to love her through the years to come; yet the woman looked terribly pensive and sobbed to herself. Wondering what was the matter, the man asked, "Why do you look so sad?" The woman replied, "I just feel sad." Becoming even more worried, the man continued, "As we are now so intimate, you must not hide anything from me. Tell me what is troubling you." In tears, the woman said, "I don't wish to hide anything, but it is so hard for me to tell you." The man said, "Just tell me—even if it should mean that I must die." The woman replied, "It is not something I should hide from you. I was born the daughter of a couple in Kyoto. But both my parents passed away, and I was left an orphan. The master of this house was originally a beggar, but he became very well off. He has been living here for many years now. He kidnapped me in Kyoto. He raised me and now he dresses me in fine clothing and makes me go off to visit Kiyomizu Temple. When a man visits the temple and looks at me, he takes a fancy to me and approaches me, and then we lure him back to this house—just as we did in getting you to come here. While the man is sleeping, a spear is lowered from the ceiling and after I guide its point to the man's chest, the spear is powerfully thrust. Then the dead man is stripped of his clothes. His retainers are all put into a house outside the moat, where they too are killed and stripped of their clothes. And their carts are taken too. This kind of thing has already been carried out twice. It will be done again from now on. Therefore, this time, I ask to be stabbed and killed in place of you. Please run away at once. All your retainers will be killed. When I think I'll never see you again, I can't help but weep." And on saying this, she broke down in bitter tears.

When the man heard this, he was dumbfounded. But he took heart and said, "What an abominable situation this is! I am grateful to you for offering to sacrifice yourself for me, but I cannot just run away and abandon you. Let us escape together, you and me." The woman replied, "I too thought of that several times, but if my master does not feel the spear stabbing you, he will surely come down to look, and if he finds both of us gone, he will tell his men to chase after us. Then both of us will be caught and killed. So please save your life, and then perform meritorious deeds to save my soul. How could I ever continue to do this kind of deed?" The man replied, "If you were to sacrifice yourself for me, how could I ever not accumulate the virtuous deeds to repay you for your goodwill? But then, how could I ever escape from here?" The woman said, "They must have pulled the bridge away from the moat after you crossed it. So go out through that sliding door there and then pass along the narrow embankment. You'll see a narrow floodgate by the mud wall. Creep out from there. Now it's time. When the spear comes down, I'll guide its point into my breast to be stabbed and die." Even as she was speaking, footsteps were heard in the inner part of the house. How terrifying it was!

In tears, the man got up, put on his kimono, tucked it in at the bottom, and escaped secretly through the sliding door, just as he was told. He went along the embankment and crept out through the floodgate. So far he was safe, but he didn't know where to go from there. So he started to run wherever his feet led him, until he noticed someone running along behind him. Thinking someone was chasing after him, unconsciously he looked back. It was his young footman. In joy and relief, he asked, "What's going on?" His young footman explained, "When I saw them pull away the bridge as soon as you entered the premises I thought it was very strange. So I managed to climb over the mud wall and I heard the rest of our men being killed. I worried about what had become of you and I dared not leave. I hid in the bushes, intending to find out about you, and then I saw someone running. I thought it might be you, so I started running, and then I saw it was, in fact, you." The man said, "What a horrible thing! I never knew anything about their plot." The two men ran off together in the direction of Kyoto. When they came to the riverbed near Gojo Street, they looked back, only to see a great fire raging about the site where the house had been.

When the bandit lowered the spear from the ceiling and stabbed at the person below, he didn't hear the woman's usual report of the plot's success. So he went down, wondering what had happened, only to find that the man was gone and the woman had been stabbed to death. "If that man has escaped," the bandit thought, "the police will come and catch me soon." And so first, he set fire to the house and then he ran away.

When the assistant director of the Imperial Guards got back home, he told his young footman not to say anything about what had happened. And never did they say a word about the incident to anyone else. Every year, the man held a splendid religious ceremony and accumulated meritorious deeds, without ever telling others whom it was for. All this must have been done in honor of the woman. But somehow, the public came to hear of this, and someone built a temple at the site of that house. It still exists, even today, and it has a certain name.

We can realize that the woman's heart was most praiseworthy. So too, was the young footman's heart wise. People came to say, "When we hear this story, we realize we should never allow ourselves to be taken to a strange place and lured by a lovely woman." And such is the story as it has been handed down to us.

Vol. 29, Tale 28

A Hunter's Dog in the North Country Kills a Serpent

In olden times, in a certain county of Michinoku Province, there lived a man of humble birth. He kept many dogs in his house and he would take them out into the deep mountains where he hunted wild boars and deer by having the dogs bite them. This he did day and night, morning and evening. In this way, the dogs grew accustomed to biting wild boars and deer. When their master took them off into the mountains, they were in joy and bliss; now walking ahead of him, now walking behind him. People called this work the "dogs' mountain hiking."

When the man went off into the mountains with his dogs, he would take food and stay for a few days. One night, he slept in the hollow of a very large tree. By his side, he placed his humble bow, a quiver of arrows, and his sword. In front of him, he built a fire. As the night advanced, all the dogs were lying around him. Among them was an especially wise dog. While all the other dogs were asleep, suddenly this particular dog leapt to its feet and began to bark furiously, looking toward its master in the hollow of the tree. "What's he barking at?" the master wondered. He looked about, but he saw nothing.

But the dog kept on barking and then it jumped at its master. The man was astonished. He thought, "Though I see nothing the dog should bark at, he keeps leaping at me and barking. As this animal can't understand its master, it must be trying to eat me here in the mountains, where there are no humans. I'll have to kill this dog." So he drew his sword and threatened him, but the dog didn't stop leaping toward him and it kept on barking. So the master thought, "It's no good to stay here in the hollow of this tree and get bitten by the dog," and he leapt out from the hollow. Then the dog jumped up into the air, right above the spot where the master was standing, and bit into something.

At that, the master realized, "The dog didn't mean to bark and bite at me. But what then was it biting at?" He looked up, and there he saw something huge and horrible hanging down from above and descending. When he saw what his dog had been biting at, he realized it was a huge snake, some eight inches thick and twenty feet long. The snake's head was being bitten by the dog, so it could not help but hang down. Looking at it, the man was terribly frightened and was deeply moved by the dog's spirit. He struck the snake with his sword and killed it. Only then did the dog let go of it and retreat.

The man had been sleeping in the hollow of a tall tree whose top was far above, without knowing that a huge snake was dwelling in it. When the snake came down to swallow the man, the dog had seen its head and began to jump at it and bark. The dog's master hadn't realized what was going on and he didn't look up. First he thought, "The dog must be trying to bite me," and so he drew his sword and wanted to kill it. "If I had killed the dog, how greatly would I have regretted it," he realized. And with such thoughts in mind, he stayed awake all night and waited for day to break. When he saw the size of the snake, it almost took his breath away. "If this snake had come down and wrapped itself around me while I was sleeping," he thought, "what could I have done? How wonderful this dog is. He is my most valued treasure in the world." And then the man returned home with his dog.

We can realize that if the man had killed the dog, not only would the dog have died, but also the man would have been swallowed by the snake. And so, under such circumstances, we should keep our hearts calm and act accordingly.

This story tells us how wonderful things such as this happened in ancient times. And so in this way has this tale been handed down to us.

Vol. 29, Tale 32

An Eagle in Higo Province Bites and Kills a Snake

In olden times, there lived a man in a certain county in Higo Province. In front of his house, there stood a big hackberry tree, with lush overhanging branches. The man built a cage and placed it under the tree and, in it, he kept an eagle.

One day, when many people were gathered around there and were watching, a big snake, about seven or eight feet long, crawled down along a lower branch of the tree to the eagle's cage. The people looked on with great interest, wondering what the snake might do. The snake slipped down along the lower branch and stopped on top of the eagle's cage. Stretching its neck, it peered inside. At that time the eagle happened to be sleeping soundly. Watching the eagle, the snake slipped along the branch that was holding the eagle's cage and crept inside. The snake pressed its head against the belly of the eagle, for the eagle was asleep. Then, opening its mouth wide, the snake swallowed the eagle's beak, right up to its base, and wound its long body around the eagle five or six times beginning with the eagle's neck. It coiled the remaining part of its tail around one of the eagle's legs, about three times. When the snake tightened its coils, the eagle's feathers rose up and the snake sank its body in amidst the feathers. When the snake further tightened its coils, the eagle looked thinner. Then the eagle opened its eyes. But since its beak had been swallowed, it just closed its eyes and appeared to go back to sleep.

Some of the people watching said, "That eagle must have been hypnotized by the snake. Surely it will die. Let's hit the snake and set the eagle free." But others said, "No matter what happens, that eagle won't be choked by the snake. Let's see what happens." And then, while the people were just watching and not doing anything, the eagle opened its eyes again and shook its head back and forth. When the snake tried to further take in the eagle's beak, which had already been swallowed to its base, the eagle lifted its free leg and with its claws it clutched the snake that had wound itself around its shoulders. It braced its legs and then proceeded to pull off the head of the snake that had swallowed its beak. Then it lifted up the leg that had been trapped by the snake, clutched the body that was wound around its wings, and pulled it off. Then the eagle grabbed the same part it was holding, lifted it up, and bit it off completely. In doing so, the snake's head was reduced to a piece about one foot long. Then, again lifting the leg that was clutching the snake, the eagle bit the head off. The eagle proceeded to bite off the remaining part of the snake that was wound around its leg. Having thus severed the snake into three parts, the eagle picked up the remaining pieces with its beak and tossed them away. It shook itself, groomed its feathers and flicked its tail, as if nothing had happened.

Seeing this, the people who had said, "No matter what happens, the eagle won't be choked by the snake," exclaimed, "Did you see that? The eagle couldn't be choked by the snake, no matter what happened. Since the eagle is the king of the animals, its spirit is different from that of others." They praised the eagle heartily.

We can realize that the snake acted with presumptuous spirit. Although the snake could swallow something that was larger than itself, it was foolish to think of attacking an eagle.

And so, human beings, too, should learn from this. We should never think of destroying superior beings. Doing so could lead to our own death. Such then is the story as it has been handed down.

Vol. 29, Tale 33

A Monkey in Chinzei Kills Eagles to Repay a Woman for Her Kindness

In olden times, there lived a man of humble origins in a certain county of a certain province in Chinzei. The man lived by the seaside, and his wife always went there to get shellfish. One day, she went there with a woman who was her neighbor. One of the women was carrying a child of about two years old on her back, and when they got to the seaside, she put the child on a flat rock and let it play with another child who was there, while she went off to gather shellfish. The seashore was at the foot of the mountains, and there, the women saw a monkey by the water's edge. One of the women exclaimed, "Look, there's a monkey. It must be looking for fish. Let's go take a look." The two women walked toward it together. The monkey appeared anxious to run away and it looked afraid, as if enduring great pain, but it seemed unable to escape and was crying. The women wondered, "What's going on?" and so they went over to look. They found that the monkey's paw was caught in the shell of a big jackknife clam, and he couldn't pull it out. The clam must have opened its shell and caught the monkey's paw while the monkey was trying to get at it and eat it. When the clam closed its shell the monkey's paw must have been trapped. The tide was rising and the clam was sinking deeper to the bottom in the sand.

In a short time, the tide would be high and the monkey would be covered by the sea. The women laughed at the sight. One of them picked up a big rock and wanted to strike the monkey and kill it. But the other woman, the one who had been carrying the child on her back, said, "What a horrible thing to do! Look how pitiful he is," and she took the rock from the woman. The woman who wanted to kill the monkey said, "This is a good chance to kill that guy and take him home, broil him, and eat him." The other woman pleaded with her to spare the monkey. She stuck a stick into the clam's mouth and poked with it. The clam opened its mouth a bit, and the monkey was able to pull its paw out. The woman said, "I wanted to save the monkey. I also don't want to kill this clam." Although the women had come to get shellfish, this woman picked up the clam softly and then buried it in the sand.

In this way the monkey freed its paw and ran off. Looking at the woman, the monkey showed an expression of happiness on its face. The woman said, "Monkey, when the other woman said she wanted to kill you, I asked her to spare your life. My heart gave you special kindness. Even if you are a beast, you must not forget this kindness." The monkey looked as if he understood. He ran toward the mountains and then toward the rock on which the woman's child was playing. The woman thought this somewhat strange. Then the monkey picked up her child and ran off into the mountains. When the other child who had been with him saw this, he felt afraid and burst out crying. Hearing the crying voice, the mother looked and saw the monkey running off into the mountains, holding her child. She cried, "That monkey is taking my child. How heartless he is!" At that, the woman who had wanted to kill the monkey said, "Now look, see what I told you? How could a beast with fur on its face know kindness? If we'd killed him, I'd have made some profit and your child wouldn't have been taken away. What a vile beast that monkey is!" At that, the two women ran after the monkey. The monkey didn't go far into the mountains. When the women ran quickly after the monkey, it ran quickly, and when the women walked slowly, the monkey walked slowly, too. Keeping a distance of about a hundred yards between them, they proceeded deep into the mountains. Then the woman stopped and called to the monkey, "What a heartless monkey you are! When you were about to lose your life, I saved you. You need not feel indebted to me, but what is the purpose of taking my child? Even if you wish to eat my child, you must give it back to me since I have saved your life." As she spoke, the monkey went deeper into the mountains and climbed high up into a big tree, holding the child.

Standing at the foot of the tree and looking up, the mother thought, "What a horrible thing!" The monkey sat on a big branch, holding the child. The other woman said, "I'll run back to your home and tell your husband about this," and then she ran off.

The mother remained at the foot of the tree and sobbed as she looked up. Then the monkey pulled on a branch of the tree and bent it back, while rocking the child under his arm. The child cried out loudly. When the child stopped crying, the monkey made it cry again. Then, hearing the child crying, an eagle came swooping down, intending to snatch the child. Watching this, the mother said tearfully, "Either way, my child will be eaten. Even if the monkey doesn't eat my child, certainly the eagle will." While she was crying like this, the monkey pulled and bent the branch back a little more, and when the eagle came close, the monkey let go of the branch at just the right moment, so that it hit the eagle's head, and the bird plunged downward, head first.

After that, once again the monkey pulled on the branch and made the child cry, and then another eagle came flying down, and then the monkey hit this eagle in the same manner. Seeing this, the mother realized, "Now I understand. The monkey doesn't mean to take my child. He's been trying to kill the eagles for me, in return for my kindness." Through her tears, she called out, "Oh monkey, now I see your true intentions. But now won't you please give me back my child." Using the same technique, the monkey had killed five eagles. After that, he moved to another tree, came down, and gently laid the child at the foot of the tree. Then he climbed back up the tree and sat there, rubbing and scratching his own body. The mother rejoiced and cried while holding her child and nursing it at her breast. Then, when the child's father came along running and gasping, the monkey moved through the trees and vanished. Five eagles lay dead at the foot of the tree. His wife told her husband what had happened. Just imagine how astonished he must have been to hear all of this.

The husband cut off the feathers and tails of the five eagles. The mother held her child and took him home. Later, they sold the tails and feathers and earned some money. The monkey did all this to repay the woman for her kindness—though she must have been in great anguish all the while.

Thinking of this story, we can see that even the beast understood the kindness it had received. How much more then should we humans keep in mind the kindness that we receive. And so people have continued to tell this story about the monkey's clever trick. And in this way, the tale has been handed down to us.

Vol. 29, Tale 35

Wasps Sting and Kill the Robbers at Mt. Suzuka

In olden times, there lived a man who sold mercury in Kyoto. He had been engaged in the mercury business for many years, and by this trade he obtained a great profit, and his house became very wealthy.

In conducting his business, he had been going back and forth between Kyoto and Ise Province all those many years, carrying such goods as silk, cloth, thread, cotton, and rice, all piled on more than one hundred horses. He just had some young boys lead the horses. Continuing his business in this manner, he grew old, but not once had he ever been robbed of even a single sheet of paper. And so his wealth ever increased, and he never lost any property. Nor did he suffer any misfortune from fire or flood.

Ise Province, at that time, was particularly known as a place where people would rob even their parents of their belongings. They took things from the weak without compunction, irrespective of relationship, rank, or social status, ever looking for a chance to cheat others and to increase their own wealth. They wouldn't, however, rob the mercury merchant of anything, even though he traveled both day and night.

During this time, however, a certain group of more than eighty robbers formed a band around Mt. Suzuka and robbed travelers from various provinces of their possessions—no matter whether the properties were public or private. They even killed the travelers. Although they continued this for many years, neither the emperor nor the provincial governor was able to catch them. One day, the mercury merchant was traveling as usual from Ise Province to Kyoto, carrying various goods mounted on more than a hundred horses, led by the young boys and accompanied by women who were in charge of cooking. Seeing this, the eighty-or-more robbers thought, "That's certainly a bunch of incredible fools. Let's take all they've got."

And so, in the depths of Mt. Suzuka, they surrounded the travelers from both the front and the rear and threatened them. The young boys quickly ran away. Then they chased after the horses loaded with goods and took them all. They stripped the women of their clothes and chased them off. The mercury merchant was wearing a light yellow gown, dark blue hunting trousers, and three thick layers of yellowish cotton clothing, topped off by a sedge hat, and was riding on a mare. He managed to escape and he ascended a high hill. The robbers saw him, but they just said, "That guy won't be able to do much now." So they ignored him and went back down into the valley.

And so the eighty-or-more robbers took everything, wrangling over what they wanted for themselves. As there was no one there to censure or seize them, they were free and at their ease. Then the mercury merchant stood on top of the high hill, looked up into the sky quite nonchalantly and called out, "How come you're late? You're late!" About an hour later, a terrible-looking wasp, about four inches long, flew down from the sky, buzzing, and it alighted on a tall tree nearby. Looking at it, the mercury merchant repeated even more insistently, "You're late! You're late!" Then, far off in the distance, a red cloud, about twenty feet long, appeared.

On seeing the cloud, the people who passed along the road wondered, "What kind of cloud could that be?" While the robbers were busy packing up the goods they had robbed, the cloud descended lower and lower and then it entered the valley where the robbers were. Then the wasp that had been on the tree also flew off to that place. It became apparent that the cloud was in fact an enormous swarm of wasps.

Then the countless wasps swarmed around each of the robbers and proceeded to sting them all to death. And how could it have turned out otherwise when several hundred wasps attacked each person? Some of the wasps got swatted, but all of the robbers were stung to death. Then all the wasps flew away, and once again, the sky appeared free of clouds.

Then the mercury merchant went back down into the valley and collected everything the robbers had hoarded through the long years—things such as bows, quivers, horses, saddles, and clothes, and he brought them all back to Kyoto. And thus, his wealth increased even more.

The fact is, this mercury merchant had been brewing sake at his house and he had been keeping it just for the wasps to drink, offering his deep thanks to them. No other robbers had ever stolen from him, but these ones, who didn't know that the merchant kept wasps at his home for protection and who had tried to rob him, got stung by the wasps, and all were killed.

And thus, we can see that even wasps know how to repay kindness. Sensible people must likewise repay the kindness they owe to others. And so, if you should happen to see a big wasp, you must not kill it. Surely it will bring lots of other wasps and revenge itself.

We are not certain just when these events took place, but such is the story as it has been handed down to us.

Vol. 29, Tale 36

73

Wasps Attack a Spider in Revenge

In olden times, a spider spun a web beneath the eaves of the Amida Hall of Hojoji Temple. Its long thread extended to a lotus leaf in the pond to the east. While a person was looking at it and exclaiming, "What a long spider thread that is!" a large wasp flew by, and while it was hovering around the thread, it got caught in the web.

Then the spider appeared, creeping out along the thread from somewhere and quickly it wound its threads around the wasp—round and round. The wasp had no way to escape. Seeing this, the head priest of the temple felt sorry for the wasp that was about to die and so he shook it off with a stick. The wasp fell to the ground, but, since its wings were still securely bound by the thread, it couldn't fly away. So the priest held the wasp with a stick and released it from the threads, and then the wasp flew away.

A day or two after, a large wasp came flying in and it hovered about under the eaves of the hall, buzzing away. Following it, a swarm of two or three hundred wasps of the same kind came flying in from somewhere. They flew around the spider's web, searching the chinks of the rafters for the spider, but they could not find it. A while later, the wasps examined the thread that stretched to the lotus leaf in the pond to the east. They hovered around it, but they couldn't find the spider there, either. So after about an hour, they flew away.

Watching this with interest, the head priest of the temple thought, "Surely the wasp that was caught by the spider's web and got bound up in its threads the other day must have brought many of its friends to find it and get revenge on the spider. So the spider must have hidden itself, knowing their intention." When the wasps had flown away, the priest went to the spider's web under the eaves, but he could not find the spider there. Then he went to the pond to look at the lotus leaf to which the thread was attached. The lotus leaf had been stung all over, with no space left unscathed. But the spider had hidden itself under the lotus leaf, without touching the back side of the leaf, hanging on a thread that dangled down toward the surface of the pond and just out of range of the wasps' stings. The lotus leaf was hanging down, turned over, mixed in among the profusion of various water grasses. The spider was hiding there, where it couldn't be found by the wasps. The head priest saw this and, when he returned to the temple, he told others about it.

We can realize that even a smart human being might not think of such a thing. It was very likely that a wasp would bring many other wasps to get revenge on its enemy. Beasts naturally seek revenge on their enemies. But the spider thought, "That wasp is going to come back to revenge itself on me, so hiding myself will be the only way to save my life." And so the spider managed to save itself by hiding, using such extraordinary means. For this reason, the spider was far wiser than the wasp.

We are told that this is the story that was faithfully told by the head priest of the temple. And so it is that the story came to be handed down to us.

Vol. 29, Tale 37

74

A Mother Cow Gores
a Wolf to Death

In olden times, there was a humble man who lived in the western part of Nara, where he kept a cow that he used on his farm. His cow had a calf, and in the autumn he let them out into the fields. Normally, a boy would go to the field in the evenings and bring them back. But one day the man and the boy forgot to bring the animals back, and so the cow and calf remained out grazing in the field. In the evening, a large wolf came along. It paced about, stalking the calf, and intending to eat it. As the mother cow loved her calf, she followed the wolf and vowed, "I'll not let you eat my child." She walked about, facing the wolf and guarding her calf. When the wolf was pacing along an earthen embankment, suddenly the cow dashed at the wolf and pierced it with her horns. The wolf was gored right through its belly and pinned against the earth embankment, with its body motionless. The cow must have thought, "If I release him, I'll be bitten to death." So the cow held her hind legs firm, using all her might, steadfastly piercing the wolf. The wolf could not endure this, and so it died.

The cow, however, didn't realize what had happened. She must have thought, "The wolf may be still alive," and so, throughout the long autumn night, she kept bracing her legs with her horns stuck into the wolf, while her calf stood beside her and mooed. In fact, on the previous evening, the boy from the house next to the cow's owner had seen a wolf walk around the cow and calf when he was out bringing his own cow back from the field, but he just led his cow home as the sun was going down without saying anything about his neighbor's cow and calf. When the next day broke, the owner of the cow and calf said, "Ah, I forgot to bring in my cow and calf last night. They may have gotten lost while grazing." Then the boy from the neighboring house said, "Last night I saw a wolf walking around your cow and calf." Hearing this, the owner of the cow and calf got worried and quickly ran off to the field. There he saw the cow standing motionless, with a large wolf gored and pinned against the embankment. The calf was lying beside its mother, crying. Only when the cow saw its owner did it release the wolf. The wolf had already died.

When the owner saw this scene he was very surprised. He thought, "When the wolf came to attack the calf last night, the cow gored it like this, but she must have thought that if she let it go they would be killed, so she stayed there all night long, goring the wolf. What a smart cow she is!" And so he praised his cow and then led her back home.

We can see then, that even an animal can act like this if it is wise and smart. It is said that the people in the area who heard this story passed it on, and this is how it came to be handed down to us today.

Vol. 29, Tale 38

The Daughter of the Governor of Ohmi Province Becomes Intimate with Priest Jozo

In olden times, there was a certain governor of Ohmi Province. He was wealthy and he had many children. Among them was a daughter.

This daughter was young and beautiful, with long hair and graceful manners. Her parents loved her exceedingly and raised her with all their love, paying her constant attention. Many were the princes and court nobles who sought her hand, but her father believed presumptuously that he would offer her to the emperor. He would not allow her to marry and he raised her most carefully. During this time, however, the daughter became possessed by an evil spirit and was sick for many days. Her parents were terribly worried about her, and had prayers offered for healing her, but they were all in vain. At this time, while they were worrying so, there was an eminent priest named Jozo the Virtuous. He could work wonders; indeed, he was as effective as the Buddha, and the entire world respected him completely.

And so the governor of Ohmi Province thought, "I would like to ask Priest Jozo to offer prayers to heal my daughter." And thus, with due respect, he requested him to come. The Priest Jozo complied with his request and paid a visit. The governor was happy to have the priest offer prayers to heal his daughter, and soon the evil spirit left her, and her illness was cured. But the parents strongly urged the priest to stay on a little longer and continue offering prayers. And so, accepting their request, Priest Jozo remained there for a while longer. But when the priest gazed at the daughter, his carnal desires were roused, and his heart was completely taken in by the young woman. He could think of nothing else. At the same time, the young woman, too, must have sensed this passion, and in a few days, aided by some opportune moments, she came to have an intimate relationship with the priest.

From that time on, the two tried to keep their relationship secret, but eventually it came to be known by others, and word spread among the general public. When people gossiped about it, Priest Jozo felt terribly embarrassed and he stopped visiting the home. "Now that I have such a bad reputation," he rued, "I dare not face the world." And so, he hid himself and went away somewhere. How ashamed of himself he must have felt.

After that, Priest Jozo confined himself deep in Mt. Kurama, devoting himself to religious practices. Yet, perhaps owing to some deep connection from a previous life, he constantly thought of that sick girl and he could not help longing for her. He just could not concentrate on his religious practices. One day, when he got up after taking a nap, he found a letter beside him. As one of his disciples was nearby, he asked him, "What sort of letter is that?" The disciple replied that he didn't know. Then Jozo picked it up, opened it, and read it. Lo and behold, it was in the handwriting of the person for whom he had been so longing! Wondering what it might contain, he read it:

> *You, wearing a dark robe*
> *deep in Mt. Kurama,*
> *may you come back*
> *to me,*
> *finding a path, searching for me.*

Seeing this, Priest Jozo wondered greatly and thought, "Who was the messenger who brought this here? I can't imagine how it got here. This is so strange." Then he thought again, "I must stop thinking of that woman. I will just devote myself to my religious practices." And yet, Jozo just could not ignore his desire. And so that night, secretly, he stole off and went to Kyoto. He went to the woman's home and asked a person there to tell her that he had come to visit. Secretly, the young woman called him in and they met. Then Jozo returned to Mt. Kurama that very night. Priest Jozo still longed for her and he sent her a poem:

> *I had been trying*
> *to forget my longing*
> *for you,*
> *but the bush warbler's song*
> *rouses my longing anew.*

In reply, the woman wrote:

> *You must have forgotten me,*
> *mustn't you?*
> *Only when you hear the bush warbler's song*
> *do you remember*
> *me again.*

Priest Jozo wrote in return:

> *You make me languish*
> *for you.*
> *How unfair of you*
> *to blame me,*
> *saying I've forgotten you.*

Since they kept on writing back and forth to each other, many people came to know about it. The governor of Ohmi Province had loved his daughter very much and had ignored all the princes and court nobles who had been seeking his daughter's hand, as he had been expecting to offer her to the emperor. But now that her bad reputation had spread all over, finally he decided to stop looking after her.

This all happened because of the woman's foolishness. No matter how eagerly Priest Jozo may have tried to approach her, she should have ignored him and not accepted him. Amidst all the people's gossip, the conclusion that was reached was, "She wasted her life because of her own thoughtlessness." And such then is the story that has been handed down to us.

Vol. 30, Tale 3

A Man from Shimotsuke Province Leaves His Wife and Then Returns to Her

In olden times, there lived a man in a certain county of Shimotsuke Province. He had been living with his wife for many years, but one day, for some reason, he left her and found another woman. His mind had changed completely. He took everything from the house of his former wife and brought it all to the house of his new wife. His former wife thought it loathsome, but she just watched what the man was doing as he took everything away. The only thing he left behind was the trough for feeding his horse.

The man had a boy servant named Makaji Maro ("True Rudder"), who took care of the horse. He sent the boy to bring back the horse's feeding trough. When the boy was about to leave the former wife's house, she said, "You won't be coming back to this house again, will you?" The boy replied, "Why wouldn't I come back? Why do you say so casually that I won't come back?" Just when the boy was about to take away the trough, which was shaped like a boat, the woman said, "I have something to tell your master. Would you give him my message?" The boy replied, "Certainly I'll convey your message." The woman said, "If I send him a letter he won't read it, so would you just tell him this message?"

> *The boat won't come back.*
> *And Makaji Maro won't*
> *come back either.*
> *How shall I sail on through the world*
> *from now on?*

The boy listened to her words and, on returning to his master's house, he said to him, "The lady asked me to convey this message to you." When the man heard the words, he was deeply moved. Thereupon, he gathered up everything he had taken and brought it back to his former wife's house. Then he returned to the house and resumed living with her and he paid attention to the other woman no more.

It has been said that a man of refined taste could behave like that. And such then is the story as it has been handed down to us.

Vol. 30, Tale 10

A Man of Refined Taste Leaves His Wife and Then Returns to Her

In olden times, there lived a young nobleman who was an official of considerable status, although I will not mention his name here. He was a man of refined taste and good character, yet he left his wife of many years and moved in with another woman who seemed more modern. Thereupon, he gave up all thoughts of his former wife's home. The former wife thought his living at the other woman's house was despicable and she felt terribly lonely.

As the man had some property in Settsu Province, he went there for a visit. On his way, while passing by Naniwa, he enjoyed the beautiful scenery and there he found a small clam with a tuft of sea staghorn growing on it. Thinking this very interesting, it occurred to him to send it to his beloved to make her happy. He called to the pageboy he had chosen on account of his fine taste and said to him, "Take this clam to the lady and tell her it's something very interesting and that I would like her to see it." And so he sent the boy, but by mistake the boy took it not to the present wife, but to the former wife and he told her to take a look at it. The former wife was surprised, for she hadn't expected a messenger from her former husband—much less one bringing her such an interesting object and, with it, the message, "Please enjoy looking at this until I return to Kyoto." Then she asked, "Where is the master?" The boy replied, "He is in Settsu Province. This is what he found in Naniwa and asked me to take to you." Hearing this, the former wife felt something was strange and thought, "The page must have brought this to me by mistake," but she accepted it anyway and asked the boy to tell his master that she certainly appreciated it. The page ran back to Settsu Province and reported to his master, "I have given it to the lady, just as you told me to." So the master thought the boy had taken it to his present wife. The former wife enjoyed looking at the gift because it was such an interesting thing. She put some water in a basin and placed it within.

About ten days later, the man returned to Kyoto from Settsu Province. With a smile, he asked his present wife, "Do you still have what I sent you?" The new wife replied, "Did you send me something? What was it?" The man said, "What? I found a small clam with a tuft of sea staghorn growing on it on the beach of Naniwa, and since it was so interesting I sent it to you right away." The wife said, "I haven't seen any such thing. Who did you have bring it? If I'd gotten it, I'd have broiled the clam and eaten it, and as for the sea staghorn, I'd have put it in vinegar and eaten it, too." Hearing her say this, the man felt disappointed and he lost some of his interest in her.

Then the man went out of his house and called the boy and asked him, "Where did you take that thing?" The boy said that he had taken it to his former wife, by mistake. The man grew furious and rebuked him, saying, "Go quickly and bring it back to me, right now!" The boy realized the gravity of his mistake and was shocked. So he ran to the house of his master's former wife and explained the situation. The man's former wife thought, "Just as I suspected, the boy made a mistake." And so she picked up the clam she had placed in the basin and enjoyed watching. She wrapped it in some paper and gave it back to the boy. On the paper she wrote the following words:

> As the gift
> from the sea was not intended for me,
> I am not supposed
> to keep it, by any means,
> and so I return it to you.

The boy took it back to his master and announced that he had returned with it. The man stepped out of the house and looked at it. He noticed that the clam was just as it had been before and he was very happy to know that she had kept it safe. Then he took it into the house and looked at it and read the poem. When he read it, he felt very sorry. Comparing its words with what his present wife had said—"If it had been brought to me, I'd have broiled the clam and eaten it, and as for the sea staghorn I'd have put it in vinegar and eaten it, too,"—he immediately changed his mind and decided he would go back to his former wife. So he picked up the clam and went to her home. He must have told her what his present wife had said. And thus, he abandoned the new wife and went back to living with his former wife.

Such is the heart of a person of refined taste. What the new wife said must have been repugnant to him. The grace of his former wife's heart made him want to return to her. And such then is the story as it has been handed down to us.

Vol. 30, Tale 11

A Man from Tamba Province Reads His Wife's Poem

In olden times, there was a man who lived in a certain county of Tamba Province. Although he was a man from the countryside, he had refined tastes. This man had two wives and he had them live in houses right next to each other. His first wife was from the countryside. Having been dissatisfied with his first wife, he had taken the new wife from Kyoto. As he loved the new wife more than the first one, the first wife found the situation miserable.

One day in autumn, a deer called out very plaintively from the mountain behind the village to the north. The man happened to be in the house of his present wife and he asked her, "What did you think of the call of that deer?" The present wife answered, "Deer meat tastes good, either cooked in an earthen pot or broiled on a fire." The man felt dissatisfied with her answer and he reflected, "I thought the woman from Kyoto would be interested in such a thing, but I'm rather disappointed by her response." So then he went to his first wife and asked her, "What did you think of the deer's call?" The first wife replied:

> *Like the deer was I.*
> *You raised your call,*
> *longing for me.*
> *But now I hear your call*
> *as something not intended for me.*

Hearing these words, the man felt immensely touched. Comparing them with what his present wife had just said, he lost his love for her, and so he sent her back to Kyoto. He went back to his first wife and resumed living with her again.

We realize that although his first wife was a woman from the countryside, nonetheless, she touched her husband with her graceful heart. It is said that because she was a woman of refined taste she was able to write a tanka poem like that. And such then is the story that has been handed down to us.

Vol. 30, Tale 12

Tsunezumi no Yasunaga's Dream at the Fuwa Barrier Station

In olden times, there lived a man named Tsunezumi no Yasunaga, who was a low-ranking official employed by Prince Koretaka. One day he went off on business to Kamutsuke Province to collect taxes from the prince's vassals. After several months away, he was on his way back to Kyoto and he stayed at the checking station by the Fuwa barrier of Mino Province.

He had left a young wife in Kyoto, and ever since his departure several months earlier, he had been thinking about her. Somehow, he couldn't help worrying deeply about her. "What makes me think of her so much?" he wondered. "I must make haste, as soon as day breaks." And so, filled with such thoughts, he fell into sleep at the house of the checking station guard. He dreamed a dream in which someone was coming from the direction of Kyoto, carrying a torch. Looking carefully, he saw the torch was being carried by a young man, accompanied by a woman. "Who could they be?" he wondered. When he saw them approaching the house where he was staying, he realized that the woman was his wife, whom he had left in Kyoto. As he wondered what this was all about, they entered the room on the opposite side of the wall from him. Peeping through a hole in the wall, he could see the young man sitting beside his wife. She took out a pot, cooked some rice, and then ate it with the young man. "Now I see," thought Yasunaga. "My wife has become that young fellow's wife while I've been away." Though terribly worried and disturbed, he decided to find out more about the situation and so he kept on watching. Then, after they had eaten, his wife and the young man lay together and embraced each other. Before long they began making love. As Yasunaga watched them, suddenly he became enraged and filled with jealousy and he charged into the room. But, to his surprise, there was no lamp, nor even were there any human beings. Then he awoke.

Realizing that it had been a dream, as he lay in bed he kept wondering what had happened in Kyoto. At daybreak, he left for Kyoto in haste, traveling even through the dark. When he arrived at his home in Kyoto, he found that his wife was safe and sound. He felt relieved and happy. Looking at him and laughing, his wife said, "Last night I dreamed a strange dream in which a young man I didn't know came and induced me to go along with him. He took me to an unfamiliar place, lit a torch, and took me to a vacant house. We entered it, cooked rice, ate, and then lay together. Then, suddenly, you broke into the room and both the young man and I were shocked. And then I awoke from the dream. And while I was still wondering about the dream, you just appeared now, like this." Hearing this, her husband exclaimed, "I, too, dreamed such a dream. So I rushed home, wondering what it meant. I even traveled at night." Hearing this, his wife, too, thought it very strange.

It seems astonishing that a wife and husband should dream the same dream at the same time. They must have had the same dream because of their worries about each other. But then, can we really assume that what they saw was each other's spirit?

And so we should remember not to worry too much about our spouse when traveling somewhere. If we dream such dreams, they can make us worried and disturbed. And such then is the story as it has been handed down to us.

Vol. 31, Tale 9

Magari no Tsunekata of Owari Province Sees His Wife in a Dream

In olden times, in Owari Province, there lived a man named Magari no Tsunekata, who was commonly called Magari no Kanju. He had everything he needed in life.

In addition to his wife, with whom he had lived for many years, Tsunekata had a lover in the province. His wife, as is natural with women, was terribly jealous. But Tsunekata visited the other woman secretly, making plausible excuses of various kinds, for it was difficult for him to leave her. His wife kept her eye on him desperately, and when she heard he had gone to the other woman's home, her face changed color, her temper raged, and she became madly jealous.

One day, some business matters came up to attend to in Kyoto, and so Tsunetaka had to make a trip. For several days, he made his preparations. The night before his departure, he thought eagerly of visiting the woman, but he worried about his wife's jealousy so he couldn't visit her openly. He devised a scheme and said, "I've been called to the governor's office," and then he went to the other woman's home.

He talked with the woman and they lay together and then they went to sleep. Tsunekata dreamed a dream in which his wife rushed in and screamed, "You two have been lying together like this for years, haven't you. How dare you tell me you're innocent?" She continued heaping all manner of abuse on them and then she broke in between them and separated them. Then he awoke from the dream.

After that, Tsunetaka felt terribly frightened and he hurried home. When the day broke, he readied himself for his departure for Kyoto. "I had a meeting at the governor's office last night," he said, "and I was kept so busy I couldn't get much sleep, so now I'm really tired." After saying this, he sat by down by his wife. "Hurry up and eat your breakfast," she said. When he looked at his wife, suddenly her hair bristled up, and then, immediately, it lay back down again. Tsunekata took this as an ominous sign. His wife continued, "How shameless you are! You went to that woman's place last night. What a shameless face you had when you two were lying together!" Tsunekata asked, "Who told you that?" His wife replied, "How abominable this is! Certainly, I saw it in my dream." Tsunekata felt suspicious and asked, "How could you ever have dreamed about that?" His wife answered, "When you went out last night, I was certain you'd go to her place. Then I dreamed a dream in which I went to her place and saw you two lying there together and talking. I listened to you very carefully and I told you, 'You said you wouldn't go to her place, but here you are lying with her like this.' I separated you, and then both you and the woman got up and made a big fuss." On hearing this, Tsunekata was very surprised and he said to his wife, "Then tell me what I said." His wife clearly recounted everything he had said, without missing a word. It seemed precisely what he had dreamed. Not only was he scared, but dumbfounded as well. However, he didn't speak to his wife about his dream. Later, he told others about it, saying, "Once I had such a very strange experience."

Thus, we can see that what we strongly feel in our hearts inevitably appears in our dreams. We can realize what a sinful woman the wife was. Jealousy is a grave sin. People agreed that in the next world the wife must have been reborn as a snake. And such then is the story as it has been handed down to us.

Vol. 31, Tale 10

A Monk Passing Through Ohmine Strays into a Country of Sake

In olden times, there was a monk who lived according to the Buddha's teachings. Once, while traveling through a place called Ohmine, he got lost and when he passed through an unfamiliar valley he came to a large village.

The monk felt relieved and thought, "I'll stop at one of those houses and ask what village this is." Continuing along, he came to a spring in the village. Stones were attractively placed on the bottom, and it was sheltered with a roof. The monk looked at it and thought he would take a drink from the spring. The color of the water seemed yellowish. He wondered why the water should be so yellowish. When he looked at it more carefully, he realized that it wasn't water, but sake that was gushing out.

The monk thought this very strange and he stood there looking at it. Then some people from the village appeared and asked him who he was. The monk answered, "As I was traveling through Ohmine I got lost and I happened to come this way, quite unexpectedly." One of the villagers said to him, "Would you please come along with me," and he led him along. The monk thought, "I wonder where he's going to take me. He may be leading me off to kill me." But he decided he couldn't resist, and so he just followed the man. After a while, they came to a house that seemed to belong to someone of great wealth. Then, a man who appeared to be the master of the house came out and asked the monk how he had happened to come this way. The monk answered as before.

Thereupon, the man called him in and gave him some food. After this, he called to a young man and said, "Take this man to that place." The monk guessed the older man must have been the leader of the village and he wondered where the man was ordering him to be taken to. He felt afraid. The young man said, "Please come along," and he led him off. The monk was frightened, but as there was no way to escape, he just followed the young man. He took him to a mountain far from the village and there he said, "To tell the truth, I've taken you to this place for the purpose of killing you. In the past we have killed those who have come to our village, so that no one would know there is such a village as ours."

When the monk heard this, he was stunned. In tears, he pleaded, "I've always followed the Buddha's Way and I was just passing through Ohmine intending to work for others and I was thinking of nothing but the Buddha's Way, completely devoting myself to it. However, I got lost and happened to come this way. Now I'm about to lose my life. No human being can escape death, and therefore, I'm not afraid of dying. But it would be a deadly crime for you to kill an innocent monk who is practicing the Buddha's Way. Won't you spare my life?"

In reply, the young man said, "What you say is true. I would like to save your life, but I'm afraid you might talk about this village after you return home." The monk said, "I will never tell anyone about this village after I go home. Since there is nothing more important than life, I will never forget your kindness, if only I may remain alive." The young man continued, "You are a monk and you are following the Buddha's Way all the time. I'd like to save you. So, if you will promise not to tell others about our village, I will save you and pretend that I've killed you." The monk was terribly happy to hear this and he earnestly promised not to tell anyone anything about the village. Over and over again, the young man said, "You must never tell anyone anything about our village," and then he showed him the way back. The monk bowed to the young man and promised that he would never forget his kindness, even on going to the next world. In tears, the monk parted from the young man and, after he had traveled along the way that had been shown to him, he got back to the road he knew.

As it so happened, when the monk returned to his own village, he spoke about the village to everyone he met, in spite of the fact that he had promised not to tell anyone about it, for he was a talkative man. Those who heard his story pestered the monk with questions: "Then what happened? Then what happened next?" And so the monk glibly told them in detail about the village and the spring of flowing sake. Then, several particularly hot-blooded young men said, "Since we've heard this much of the story, why don't we go and see for ourselves? We should watch out for demons and gods, but the villagers are just human beings. No matter how strong they may be, they can't be all that dreadful. Let's go and see."

And so, several bold young men—confident of their strength and armed with bows, arrows, and swords—were willing to go along with the monk. Some older men of discretion warned, "That's a foolish thing to do. They know their land very well and they must be well prepared. It's dangerous for you to go to such an unfamiliar place." They urged them not to go, but as the young men were all charged up with fervor, they wouldn't listen. And the monk, too, went along with the young men, for he had told them about the village.

The parents and relatives of those young men who had gone were all anxious about them and they worried immensely. As feared, the men did not return the first day, nor did they return the next day, nor in succeeding days. The parents and relatives grew ever more worried and they grieved, but it was in vain. The young men did not return for a long time, but no one proposed to go looking for them. They just grieved and lamented. Since none of the men ever returned, all of them must have been killed. There was no knowing how they were killed, for no one survived to tell the story.

The monk told others things he should never have spoken of. If he hadn't told them of what he had experienced, he would not have had to die, and many others, too, would not have had to die. How much better things would have been.

Thus, we can see that it is not good to have a loose mouth and to break promises made to others. And even if the monk talked glibly, those young men should not have gone off to the village so foolishly. Nothing has been heard of that country of sake, ever since.

This story was handed down by those who heard it told directly by the monk. And this is how the story has come down to us.

Vol. 31, Tale 13

82

Monks Passing through Remote Areas of Shikoku Stray into an Unknown House and Are Transformed into Horses

In olden times, three ascetic monks who were training themselves in the Way of the Buddha were passing through some remote districts of Shikoku, along the coasts of Iyo, Sanuki, Awa, and Tosa. While traveling through this region, they happened to stray. Finding themselves lost in deep mountains, they tried to get back out to the coast. When they entered a deep valley that seemed untrodden by humans, they grew even more worried than before. As they made their way along, pushing through the briars and thorns of orange shrubs, at length, they came to a flat area surrounded by a fence. "This must be someone's residence," they thought. They could see there were some houses and they entered the area with glad hearts. Even if the houses belonged to demons, what else could they have done but go and find out? Since they had got lost and didn't know which way to go, they went up to one house and called out, "Hello. May we ask you a favor?" Someone in the house called back, "Who is it?" They replied, "We are monks who are training ourselves in the Way of the Buddha and we have gotten lost. Could you please tell us the right way to go?" The man inside replied, "Wait a moment." Soon, a man came out. He was a monk, about sixty years of age, and he looked extremely fearsome.

When he called them in, they thought, "Even if he turns out to be a demon or a god, we might as well go in and see." And so, the three ascetics went up onto the verandah and sat there. The master of the house said, "You must be tired," and before long he brought them some food that looked very good. They thought to themselves, "It looks like he's just an ordinary human being," and they felt happy. When they had finished eating, the expression on the face of the master of the house grew fearsome, and he called to another man. The three ascetics found this terribly frightening. When the man appeared, they saw that he was a very suspicious-looking monk. The head monk said, "Bring in the customary items." Then, the assistant monk brought in a bit and the reins for a horse and a whip.

"Now do the customary thing," the head monk ordered. At that, the assistant monk pulled one of the ascetics from the verandah down to the ground. The other two wondered, "What will they do to him?" Then the man dragged the ascetic to the garden and lashed him with the whip. He must have lashed him about fifty times. The ascetic cried out, "Help!" But what could the other two do to help him? Then, stripping off the ascetic's coat, the monk lashed into his bare skin fifty more times. When he had been struck one hundred times, the ascetic dropped to the ground. The head monk commanded, "Pull him up." When the monk pulled him up, suddenly, the ascetic turned into a horse. He shook his body and reared up. Then the monk shoved a bit into the horse's mouth and led it off.

Seeing this, the other two ascetic monks wondered, "What is happening? This can't be the world of human beings. They may well do the same thing to us, too." They were so terribly afraid, that they could not even think. Then the man pulled a second ascetic from the verandah and lashed him with the whip, just as he had done to the first one. When the monk had finished striking him, he, too, was turned into a horse and he reared up. The monk placed a bit into the horse's mouth and led it away. The last remaining ascetic thought, "I, too, will be dragged down and struck, just like them." He was so miserable, that he prayed ardently to the Buddha saying, "Please save me, dear Buddha!" Then the head monk said, "Keep him here for a while." And while the ascetic sat there, as ordered, at last the sun set.

The ascetic monk thought, "I would hate to become a horse, so I must run away, at any cost. Even if I'm caught and killed, either way it will amount to losing my life." But since he was now in unfamiliar mountains, he had no idea which way to go. He thought of throwing himself into water and drowning. Immensely worried, he thought of various things. When the head monk called to the ascetic, he answered, "Yes, sir, I am here." Then the monk said, "There's a rice field out back. Go and see if it's filled with water." Terrified, the ascetic went out to the rice field and saw that it was filled with water. When he returned, he said, "It is filled with water, sir." The ascetic suspected the monk's words must have had some connection to what he was intending to do to him. He was so scared he couldn't even tell whether he was alive or not.

While the others were sleeping, the ascetic decided to escape, no matter what should happen. And so, without even taking his wicker pack, he ran off to wherever his legs might carry him. When he had gone about six hundred yards, he came to another house. He wondered what kind of house it might be. Feeling afraid, he was about to pass it by when a woman who was standing right in front of the house called out to him, "May I ask who you are?" He replied, "I'm an ascetic monk and I'm running away from a place where two of my fellow monks were turned into horses. I've just escaped and I'm thinking of throwing myself into a river or lake to die. Please help me!" The woman exclaimed, "Oh how pitiful! I'm so sorry to hear this. But first, won't you come in here." And so, he stepped into her house.

The woman continued, "I've seen them doing that kind of abominable thing for many years, but I haven't been able to stop them. I'd like to help you, if at all possible. I'm the lawful wife of the head of that house you just came from. My younger sister lives a little way down the road. Only she can help you. Tell her I told you about her. I'll write her a letter." She wrote the letter and then she said, "They've already changed two monks into horses and they want to kill you and bury you in the field. That's why the head monk told you to go and see if the rice field was filled with water."

When the ascetic heard this, he thought, "I've been very fortunate to escape. It's because of the Buddha's grace that I'm still alive, at least for the time being." As soon as he received the letter, he looked at the woman, placed his hands together respectfully, and, in tears, he bowed to her. Then, he dashed out to run in the direction she had instructed him to go. When he had run about two thousand yards, he came to a house on a remote mountainside. "This must be the house," he thought, and so, he approached it. When a servant came out of the house, the ascetic said, "I've brought a letter." The servant took the letter and went into the house and then came back out and told him, "Please come this way." So, he stepped into the house. Inside was a woman who said, "For many years I've suspected they've been doing such abominable things. Since my elder sister has written to me in this way, I'd like to help you. But this is a strange place, where terrible things could happen, so please, hide here for a while." She hid him in a small room in the back, about six feet square in area. Then she said, "The time has come. Don't make any noise whatsoever." The ascetic was terribly afraid of what would happen. He made no noise, nor did he make any movement.

A short time later, someone came in, creating a most fearsome atmosphere. He smelled of blood. The ascetic was scared to death. While he wondered what sort of person this could be, the man talked with the lady of the house and it seemed they lay together. As he listened, it seemed they had sex, and then the man left. The monk thought, "This woman must be the wife of a demon. The demon must visit her to have sex with her and then leave." It all seemed terribly fearful.

After that, the woman showed him the way to travel and said, "Your life, which had been destined to be lost, has been spared. Please consider yourself fortunate." The ascetic deeply bowed to the woman, as before, and left in tears. He went on his way as directed by the woman and then, finally, the day began to break. After walking for what seemed about a thousand yards or so, the sky began to grow light. Then, he found himself on the right way. He felt terribly relieved. He felt more than happy. From there, he continued along looking for a village and, eventually, he came to a house and told the people there about what he had experienced. The people in the house exclaimed, "That's a most extraordinary thing, indeed." Other villagers who heard of the story came in to hear more about it. The place he had wandered into was a in certain village, in a certain county, in a certain province.

What the two women had told the ascetic firmly and repeatedly was, "Your life, which had been in danger, has been saved. You must never tell anyone about this place." But the monk thought, "Why should I keep silent about such an extraordinary thing?" and so he told everyone he met about it. After a while, some brave young men from the province, who were good at martial arts, said, "Why don't we get up an armed group and go check this out." But since they didn't know the way, in time, they stopped thinking of their plans. Also, the head monk of the house had thought the ascetic would never be able to run away because he didn't know the way to escape, so he never attempted to chase after him.

After roaming through various provinces, the ascetic eventually made his way to Kyoto, and nothing more was ever heard of that place. It's hard to believe that someone could have turned human beings into horses by lashing them with a whip. The place where this occurred must have been in a kingdom of beasts.

The ascetic monk carried out meritorious deeds for the sake of his two fellow monks who had been changed into horses.

And so, we should realize that people should not go off carelessly to unfamiliar places, no matter how ardently they might wish to train in the Way of the Buddha.

It is said that this is the story that was related directly by the ascetic monk. And so it is that this tale came to be handed down to us.

Vol. 31, Tale 14

83

The Presiding Monk of Ryoganji Temple Breaks Apart a Rock

In olden times, there was a temple called Ryoganji in the mountains to the north of Kyoto. It was a place where the Myoken Bodhisattva sometimes made appearances. About three hundred yards in front of the temple there was a very large rock. In it, there was a hole through which a person could only pass by crouching down. People of all kinds visited the temple. As it possessed miraculous virtues that helped people, many monks' quarters were built there, and it was a very busy place.

One time, the emperor developed some trouble with his eyes, and the question of whether he should make a visit to Ryoganji Temple was discussed. Eventually, it was decided that he should not visit the temple because his wagon would not be able to pass through the rock. Hearing this, the monk in charge of the general affairs of the temple thought, "If this temple is graced by a visit from the emperor, I'll be made a bishop. If not, I'll never be able to become a bishop."

And so, in order to make such a visit possible, the monk thought about how to get rid of the rock. Consequently, he ordered laborers to cut lots of firewood and pile it all around the rock, and he was just about to set fire to it. Some of the older monks, however, protested that "The reason this temple has its miraculous powers is because it has that rock. If the rock is no longer here, the miraculous virtue of the temple will be lost and our temple will decline." Thus, they argued and complained, but the monk had already pushed the scheme along forcibly to realize his own ambitions and he wouldn't listen to them. And so, ignoring the protests, he set fire to the piles of firewood all around the rock.

When the rock heated up, the workers broke it apart with large hammers, and the shattered rock was scattered in all four directions. Then, from the broken pieces of the rock, the laughing voices of a hundred or more people could be heard. The monks all thought, "What a bizarre thing! This temple will be ruined. This act has been carried out through a plot of the devil." They cursed and accused the monk in charge of general affairs. The rock was gotten ridden of, but there was no visit from the emperor—nor was there a promotion of the monk.

After that, the monk in charge of general affairs was detested by the other monks of the temple and he could no longer go to the temple. More and more, the temple fell into ruin. The main hall and the monks' quarters were all lost, and monks no longer lived there. In time, the place turned into a mere woodcutters' trail.

We can realize that the monk did a foolish thing. If, because of his deeds in a previous existence, he had no destiny to become a bishop, how could he possibly have become one, even if he broke down the rock? He was a monk without wisdom. He didn't realize his own foolishness. Not only was he not made a bishop, but he also destroyed a place where miraculous events had occurred. It was such a sad thing.

Nonetheless, in some places, miraculous virtue does, in fact, work wonders. Such then is the story as it has been handed down.

Vol. 31, Tale 20

84

The Governor of Sanuki Province Destroys Manono Pond

In olden times, in a certain county of Sanuki Province, there was a large pond called Manono Pond. It was a reservoir that the Great Teacher of Mt. Koya had built, using many laborers, for the benefit of all the people of the province. As the circumference of this pond was so great and its banks were so high, it looked like a sea, not just a pond. Its size was so vast that the banks on its yonder side appeared to be very far away.

This reservoir remained undisturbed for a long time, and the farmers of the province who raised rice benefited greatly from its water, especially in times of drought, and all were very happy about it. Many streams flowed into the pond from above, and so it remained filled with plenty of water and never went dry. In the pond, there were also many fish, both large and small, and though the people of the province caught some of them, still the pond remained plentiful with fish.

In time, a man came to the province to take his post as the governor. While the people of the province and the officials of the governor's residence were talking, they mentioned, "The fish in Manono Pond are limitless. Some of the carp there are three feet long." When the governor heard this, he set his mind on getting those fish, by any means. The pond, however, was so deep that when they set out the nets they didn't reach the bottom. So then, the governor had them bore a large hole through the bank of the pond. They drained out the water through this hole and placed a net to catch the fish where the water poured out. As the water flowed out a great many fish came with it, and they were caught.

Then they tried to stop up the hole, but the force of the gushing water was so powerful that they could not do it. The reservoir had been maintained with a floodgate and a drainpipe, but now the hole they had bored through its bank grew bigger and bigger. When heavy rains fell, great amounts of water flowed into the reservoir, and the bank finally broke because of the hole. Then the water rushed out of the pond and flooded the houses and rice paddies, destroying them all. Many fish flowed out as well, and they all were caught. After that, just a little water remained in the center of the reservoir, but then it too dried up and not a trace of the pond was left.

We can realize that the reservoir was lost because of the greed of the governor. How immeasurably grave was his greed. He destroyed the pond which the Great Teacher had built for the benefit of the people. The bad effects were immensely reprehensible. Many people's houses, fields, and rice paddies were lost when the pond was destroyed; and for all of this, the governor was responsible. And who was responsible for trying to catch all the fish? The governor acted most foolishly.

Thus, we can see that all people should beware of greed. And the people of the province are still blaming that governor.

It is said that the shape of that pond still remains. And such then is the story as it has been handed down.

Vol. 31, Tale 22

85

One Brother Plants Daylilies, while the Other Plants Asters

In olden times, there lived a man in a certain county of a certain province. He had two sons and then he passed away. As the years passed, the two brothers grieved over their father's death ever more.

They buried their father in a grave, according to custom, and whenever they thought of their father, they visited his grave together. They shed tears and spoke to the grave about their worries and troubles in life, as if to a living father.

Years passed, and the two brothers took up posts at the imperial court. They became so busy that it was hard even to think of their own affairs. The elder brother thought, "If I go on like this, I won't feel at peace. I've heard that daylilies help those who look at them to forget their troubles. I'll plant some around our father's grave." And so, he planted daylilies there.

After that, the younger brother went to his elder brother's home and said, "Let's go visit father's grave as usual." But the elder brother did not go with him, owing to problems of one sort or the other. The younger brother considered his elder brother cold hearted and thought, "We two have passed each day thinking of our father. Now my elder brother seems to have forgotten Father, but I'll never forget to think of him." And after this, he planted some asters around his father's grave, so that he might never forget. He continued to visit the grave, as before, looking at the asters and never forgetting his father.

After some years had passed, a voice was heard from within the grave, saying, "I am the demon who protects your father's body. Don't be afraid of me. I wish to protect you, too." When the younger brother heard this voice, he was terribly afraid, but he remained there and listened to the demon without answering him. Then the demon said, "You have been thinking of your father, as always, though years have passed. Your elder brother had seemed to be grieving as much as you, but then he planted flowers that helped him forget things and, by looking at them, he has obtained what he wished for. You planted asters and you have obtained what you wished for by looking at them. I am deeply impressed by your love for your father. Although I have taken the form of a demon, I have mercy and compassion for things and I can clearly foretell what good or bad will occur each day. Therefore, I will let you see what I can see. I will show this to you in your dreams." Then the voice ceased. The younger brother was so filled with joy that he wept.

After that, he saw in his dreams what would happen each day, and what he saw in the dreams turned out to be exactly true. He could clearly see everything good and bad in his life. This was because of his deep love for his father.

And so it is said that those who find happy things in life should plant asters, while those who have troubles should plant daylilies to help them forget and they should look at them all the time. Such then is the story as it has been handed down.

Vol. 31, Tale 27

86

Fujiwara no Nobunori Dies in Etchu Province

In olden times, there was a man named Nobunori, who was the son of Fujiwara no Tameyoshi, a scholar and governor of Etchu Province. When Tameyoshi was appointed governor of Etchu and went to take up his post, his son was unable to go with him because he was employed at the imperial court, where he took charge of the emperor's wardrobe and provisions. After he was promoted to the grade of fifth-ranking court noble, Nobunori was finally able to make a visit to see his father in Etchu. On his way, however, he fell very ill, but since he could not tarry, he forced himself to go on. When he arrived in Etchu, his condition became grave.

When Tameyoshi heard of his son's coming, he was delighted and he looked forward to their reunion eagerly. But as his son was so terribly ill when he arrived, he grew extremely disturbed and worried. He did everything he could to save his son, but his condition looked hopeless. In time, he exclaimed, "It is useless to think of this world; we should think of the next world." So he called an important high priest to the bedside and asked him to recite prayers. When the priest arrived, he brought his mouth close to Nobunori's ear and said, "The pains of Hell are now pressing on you. The pains will be indescribable. Although it has not yet been decided what form you will be born into in the next world, you will have to travel all the way there, by yourself, through a wide field called the Intermediate Field, where there is not even a bird or an animal. Just imagine the loneliness there and the unbearable longing you will feel for the people of this world." Hearing this, Nobunori asked, breathing with difficulty, "In the sky of that Intermediate Field, are there not any red leaves that fall in storms or any bell crickets that sing beneath the pampas grass flowers as they sway in the wind?" Much displeased, the priest replied angrily, "Why on earth are you asking such a question at this time?" Nobunori answered painfully, in disconnected phrases, "If there . . . should be, I might put . . . myself . . . at ease . . . by looking . . . at them." Hearing this, the priest declared, "He's completely mad!" and departed in haste.

Nobunori's father decided he would look after his son as long as he was alive and he stayed by the bedside. Nobunori raised both his hands and moved them as if he were trying to write something. Unable to make out his meaning, those who were present just watched him. One person thought he was trying to write something and so he asked him, "Do you wish to write?" and then he gave him a brush moistened with ink, and some paper. Nobunori wrote:

As there are many people
dear to me in Kyoto,
I would like to live
and return to Kyo

Just before scribbling the character "to," he breathed his last breath. His father said, "He must have meant to write "to," and so he added the character "to" at the end. He said he would keep it as a memento. Sobbing, he gazed at it, on and on, and so, in time, it became moistened with tears and, finally, it disintegrated in tatters.

When his father returned to Kyoto and told the story to others, those who heard it were deeply moved.

How grave were Nobunori's sins. Even those who think faithfully on the Three Treasures—the Buddha, the Dharma, and the Sangha—while they are living cannot easily escape the pains of Hell. How sad it was then, that Nobunori didn't think on the Three Treasures while he was still alive. Such then is the story as it has been handed down.

Vol. 31, Tale 28

87

The Woman Fish Peddler at the Guardhouse

In olden times, when Emperor Sanjo was still a prince, there was a woman who came to the guardhouse at the palace to peddle fish. The guardsmen tried it and found that it tasted good, so they often enjoyed it with their meals. It was a dried fish that had been cut into small pieces.

One day in August, when the guardsmen were out hawking at Kitano, they happened to see the woman in the field. Since they recognized her, they wondered what she might be doing there, so they went over to her to find out. She had a large bamboo basket and, in one hand, she was holding a whip. When she saw the men, the woman became flustered. She muttered something or other and looked as if she wanted to run off. The guardsmen came up to her and tried to look into the bamboo basket to see what was inside, but the woman attempted to hide it from them. So they took it from her by force, looked inside, and there they saw snakes, cut up into pieces about five inches long. Surprised, they asked, "What the devil is this about?" The woman said nothing, but just kept standing there. Hard as it may be to believe, this woman had been chasing through the bushes with a whip, killing snakes when they came out, taking them home, salting and drying them, and then selling them. The guardsmen had been buying them without knowing they were actually snakes. It is said that snakes give us food poisoning, but why didn't those guardsmen get poisoned?

Those who heard this story have remarked that we should not carelessly buy fish and eat it without knowing just what it is. And such then is the story as it has been handed down to us.

Vol. 31, Tale 31

88

An Old Bamboo Cutter Finds
a Girl and Raises Her

In olden times, during the reign of a certain emperor, there was an old man who made his living by cutting bamboo and making baskets for others with it. One day, he went into the bamboo grove and was cutting the materials to make his baskets. While he was working, he came upon a bamboo tree that was shining with light. When he cut it down, between the joints of the bamboo, he found a human being, about four inches tall.

The old man thought, "I've been cutting bamboo for many years now, but this is the first time I've ever found such a thing." He was very happy. He held the tiny person in one hand and carried the bamboo in the other and returned to his home. He said to his old wife, "Look! In the bamboo grove, I found this little girl!" His old wife was also very happy to see the girl and she placed her in a basket. After they had raised the girl for about three months, she became a human baby of ordinary size. As she grew up, she became so beautiful that there was no other woman as fair as she, anywhere. The old couple loved her dearly and raised her with all their affection, and, in time, she became well known throughout the land.

Some time later, when the old man was off in the grove cutting bamboo, he found some gold in one of the bamboo stalks. He brought the gold back to his home. With it, he immediately became very rich. So, he built a palace with towers and great halls and there he lived. In his storehouses, he kept various treasures. He had many servants who worked for him. Ever since he found the girl, everything had gone well and according to his wishes. He continued to take care of her with all his love and affection.

During this time, many court nobles and courtiers began sending her letters, trying to woo her, but she would not respond. Nevertheless, they continued to court her, with all their hearts and minds. So then, she assigned them difficult tasks as tests. First, she told them, "Bring me the thunder that rumbles in the sky. Then I will see you." Next she said, "There is a flower called udonge. Bring it to me, and then I will see you." Then, later on, she said, "There is a drum that makes a sound when it is not beaten. If you can bring it to me, then I will do as you ask." And then, after saying this, she refused to meet anyone who could not meet her demands. All those who courted her became so crazed by her beauty that they tried to meet her requests, by any means. They searched for wise old men and asked them for help. Some left their homes and went to the seashore or to the mountains seeking the answer. In doing this, some wasted their lives, and others never returned home.

In the meantime, the emperor heard about the beauty of this woman. He thought to himself, "They say there is no one as beautiful as this woman. I'd like to go and see her and find out if she really is so beautiful. If it's true, I'll make her my empress." And so, the emperor took his ministers and one hundred officials and made a visit to the old man's house. When they arrived, they saw that the estate was no less gorgeous than the emperor's palace. When the emperor asked for the woman's presence, she appeared promptly. When the emperor saw her, he thought there was no other woman as beautiful as she. He also thought she had not accepted the other men's proposals because she wished to be his empress. He was so happy. He said, "I would like to take you to my palace now and make you my empress." However, she replied, "I would be most happy to be your empress, but in truth I am not really a human being."

The emperor asked, "What then are you? Are you a demon? Or a goddess?" The woman replied, "I am neither a demon nor a goddess. However, many people are expected to come down from Heaven to take me away, and so, I must request that Your Imperial Majesty please return to your palace immediately." When the emperor heard this, he wondered, "What could this possibly mean?

People can't come down from Heaven now. She's just saying this because she wants to refuse my request." However, a short while later, many people did descend from Heaven, bringing a palanquin, and they took the woman away, up into the sky. The people who came down from Heaven did not look like the people here on earth.

Thereupon, the emperor thought, "Truly, that woman was not an ordinary human being," and so he returned to his palace. After that, he believed that she truly had been a woman from beyond this world. He kept thinking of her longingly, but, after all, there was nothing he could do about it.

We do not know what kind of person the woman really was. Nor do we know how she had come to be the old man's child. All the people agreed that it had been a most mysterious thing. And such then is the story as it has been handed down to us.

Vol. 31, Tale 33

89

The Grave of Chopsticks

In olden times, there was a daughter of a certain emperor. She was very beautiful, and both the emperor and empress loved her very much and raised her with all their love and care.

When she was still single, a certain nobleman came to visit her secretly and said, "I would like to marry you." The girl replied, "I have never known a man. How could I possibly accept your proposal so readily? I would have to talk to my parents before I could accept your request." The man said, "Even if your parents find out about me, they will not be displeased." He continued to visit the princess every night, but she would not give herself to him.

One day the princess said to the emperor, "A certain man has been coming to my place every night and talking to me." The emperor said, "That could not be a human being. It must be a god." Then, before long, the princess came to sleep with the man. They loved each other deeply, but as she didn't know who the man was, she asked him, "Since I don't know who you are, I am very curious to know where you come from. If you really love me, do let me know who you are, and where you live." The man replied, "I live in this neighborhood. If you wish to see my real figure, please look into the vial of oil in your comb box, tomorrow. When you see it, do not be afraid. If you feel afraid of it, I will be in great trouble." The woman promised and said, "I won't be afraid of it," and at daybreak, the man left.

Soon after, the woman opened her comb box and looked into the vial of oil. In it, she saw something moving. She wondered what it was, so she lifted it up to take a good look. She saw that it was a tiny snake, coiled up. As it was in a vial of oil, you can imagine how small the snake must have been. Although the princess had promised not to be afraid, she could not help raising a cry of fear. Then she threw it down and ran away.

That night, the man came. He looked sullen and unlike his usual appearance. He didn't speak to her. Wondering about this, the princess came closer to him, and then the man said, "I asked you earnestly not to be afraid, and yet you were so scared by it. This is so very sad. I cannot see you any more." After saying this, the man was about to leave her abruptly. The woman thought it so lamentable that he should refuse to visit her just because of such a trifling thing. She attempted to stop him by grabbing his hand. At that, the man stuck a chopstick into her private parts. Immediately, the woman died. The emperor and empress grieved bitterly, but there was nothing they could do.

Afterwards, they made a grave for her in Shikinoshimo County of Yamato Province. It is said that the grave still exists today and that it is known as the "Grave of Chopsticks." And such then is the story as it has been handed down to us.

Vol. 31, Tale 34

90

The Great Oak Tree in Kurimoto County of Ohmi Province

In olden times, there was a great oak tree in Kurimoto County of Ohmi Province. Its trunk was three thousand feet in circumference, so you can well imagine how tall it must have been and how wide must have been the spread of its branches. It cast its shadow as far as Tamba Province in the morning, and as far as Ise Province in the evening. It remained ever calm, even when the thunder rolled. It never trembled, even in big storms.

In time, the farmers in the three counties of Shiga, Kurimoto, and Koga became unable to raise their crops because of the lack of sunlight caused by the tree's shadow. Therefore, the farmers in these three counties made a direct petition to the emperor about the situation. As a result, the emperor immediately sent his retainer Kanimori no Sukune and other officials and had the tree cut down, as requested by the farmers. After this great tree was cut down, the farmers were able to raise abundant crops.

The descendants of those farmers who made the petition to the emperor are still living in those counties. In olden times, there were such great trees. It is said that it was most remarkable. And such then is the story as it has been handed down.

Vol. 31, Tale 37